Tri Quarterly 103

Fall 1998

Editor
Susan Firestone Hahn

Publisher

Associate Editor
Ian Morris

T0164110

Production Manager
Bruce Frausto

Design
Gini Kondz.

TriQuarterly Fellow
Ben Pauley

Assistant Editors
Francine Arenson, Rachel Webster

Editorial Assistants
**Russell Geary, Jacob Harrell
Dylan Rice, Karen Sheets**

Contributing Editors
**John Barth, Rita Dove, Richard Ford, Sandra M. Gilbert, Robert Hass,
Edward Hirsch, Lee Huebner, Li-Young Lee, Lorrie Moore, Alicia Ostriker,
Carl Phillips, Robert Pinsky, Mark Strand, Alan Williamson**

TRIQUARTERLY IS AN INTERNATIONAL JOURNAL OF WRITING, ART AND CULTURAL INQUIRY PUBLISHED AT **NORTHWESTERN UNIVERSITY.**

Subscription rates (three issues a year) — Individuals: one year $24; two years $44; life $600. Institutions: one year $36; two years $68. Foreign subscriptions $5 per year additional. Price of back issues varies. Sample copies $5. Correspondence and subscriptions should be addressed to *TriQuarterly*, **Northwestern University**, 2020 Ridge Avenue, Evanston, IL 60208-4302. Phone: (847) 491-7614.

The editors invite submissions of fiction, poetry and literary essays, which must be postmarked between October 1 and March 31; manuscripts postmarked between April 1 and September 30 will not be read. No manuscripts will be returned unless accompanied by a stamped, self-addressed envelope. All manuscripts accepted for publication become the property of *TriQuarterly*, unless otherwise indicated.

Copyright © 1998 by *TriQuarterly*. No part of this volume may be reproduced in any manner without written permission. The views expressed in this magazine are to be attributed to the writers, not the editors or sponsors. Printed in the United States of America by A to Z Printing; typeset by *TriQuarterly*. ISSN: 0041-3097.

National distributors to retail trade: Ingram Periodicals (La Vergne, TN); B. DeBoer (Nutley, NJ); Ubiquity (Brooklyn, NY); Armadillo (Los Angeles, CA).

Reprints of issues #1–15 of *TriQuarterly* are available in full format from Kraus Reprint Company, Route 100, Millwood, NY 10546, and all issues in microfilm from University Microfilms International, 300 North Zeeb Road, Ann Arbor, MI 48106. *TriQuarterly* is indexed in the *Humanities Index* (H.W. Wilson Co.), the *American Humanities Index* (Whitson Publishing Co.), Historical Abstracts, MLA, EBSCO Publishing (Peabody, MA) and Information Access Co. (Foster City, CA).

TriQuarterly Magazine is pleased to announce that, as of *TQ* 102, Edward Hirsch is a Contributing Editor to the magazine. We welcome him and thank him for his past invaluable contributions to our pages.

Awards and honors have been given to the following authors for work that has appeared recently in the magazine:

★ *Michael Collins* received the Daniel Curley Award from the Illinois Arts Council for his short story, "The Rain in Kilrush" (*TQ* 98), as well as an Illinois Arts Council Literary Award.

★ *Stephen Dixon's* short story "The Poet" (*TQ* 98) has been selected to appear in *New Stories from the South: The Year's Best, 1998,* published by Algonquin Books and edited by Shannon Ravenel.

★ *Kimiko Hahn* was awarded a Pushcart Prize for her piece "Sewing Without Mother: A Zuihitsu" (*TQ* 100).

★ *Brigit Pegeen Kelly* received a Literary Award from the Illinois Arts Council for her poem "Elegy" (*TQ* 100).

★ *Carl Philips* was awarded a Pushcart Prize for his poem "Abundance" (*TQ* 98).

Contents

Cover: color photograph by Ray Hartl of a bas-relief sculpture located in the barrio of La Boca, Buenas Aires, Argentina

Cover design by Gini Kondziolka

Four Poems

Stuart Dybek

Inspiration

Finally, down an askew side street
of gingerbread houses held up by paint,
where bony kids crowded around the body
of a cripple who'd been trampled
when the shots rang out,
I spotted a taxi with a raised hood.
The driver was adding motor oil
which was leaking into the gutter
nearly as fast as he was pouring.
I threw in my suitcase and we started
down the mobbed streets,
him laying on the horn, yelling in Creole,
driving, by necessity, with his head
craned out the window. Cracks
ran the length of the windshield
from where a bullet left a crater
that had vaguely resembled the shape
of a pineapple, and since a cabbie
could never afford to replace the glass,
he'd painted the crater instead—
pineapple yellow with the bullet hole
gleaming at its center like a worm hole
emitting another dimension.
And once he'd painted the pineapple,
wasn't it not only logical, but inspired
to see the cracks that ran from it
as vines, and so he'd painted them
a tangled green that turned driving

through the streets of Port-au-Prince
into racing blindly through a jungle.
But he wasn't finished yet—
the vines grew flowers: rose red, orchid,
morning-glory blue, and to the flowers
came all manner of butterflies
and newly invented species of small,
colorful birds, twining serpents,
and deep in the shadows,
the mascaraed, black-slit golden eyes
of what may have been a jaguar.

Poinciana

Eternity temporarily
partitioned into days of revelatory blue
bordered by a profusion
of oleander,
       divided and redivided
into the lifespans of lizards,
and dragonflies the red of dried pepper pods,
into the generations
of fruit flies orbiting
a rotten guanabana,

a guanabana attracting travelers
like an oasis—
guinea fowl come
raking grubs from the shoulder's dirt,
and a caravan of goats
clopping along the concrete road
like a girl in her first high heels
down the center aisle of a church,

returning from the Communion rail
with her eyes closed
and her white skirt sashaying
to the beat of her strapless red shoes—
she kneels in the pew, in the heat,
and buries her burning face
in her palms, still able to feel
the wafer thin imprint where God
nearly dissolved in her mouth
before she swallowed him whole.

But before they can eat, the goats
are scattered by a loping blond dog
with fangs exposed and foam
on his lolling pink tongue,

who pauses only momentarily
to sniff the fallen fruit
before getting on with his day,
and who now, for reasons of his own,
has chosen the grease-stained shadow
of a gas pump in which to pant,
rather than the shade
of a red flowering tree.

In the Brightness That Makes Thought

In the brightness that makes thought
impossible, they have waded into perfect clarity
and from this distance—both of them young—
their gleaming bodies might be dissolving
into the water at their waists,

into the facets of aquamarine where light
and water are indistinguishable, a brightness
that obliterates horizons and other shadows,
a perspective from which the past seems less
than elementary—particle rather than wave—

in such dazzle, identity is juxtaposed
with the reflection of the heron shimmering in;
from this distance, where their faces
reflect the sparkle of water,
it's needless to wonder who they were

or will be, there's only a mirrored
shoreline—palms like heat waves where the future
has evaporated and memory become
as inconsequential as shadow (although
perhaps, their bodies do trail shadows

invisible along the rippled sand bottom
where schools of barbelled goatfish follow,
feeding off their footsteps, as they descend
a wavering slope of turtle grass.)
It's calm—so calm and bright—

vaporous palms streaking from shore,
an insubstantial glitter of minnows,
the marker of the irreducible white heron
they've waded beyond, out deeper
to where the slightest undulations rock

her breasts, even their irreducible nakedness
dissolving, until immersed in
the light that they've become—
shading their eyes, touching hands, laughing—
they disappear into the glare.

Tropical Autumn

for David

The shell of a cicada
clinging to the screen
is all that's left
of last night's shrill
insistent song.

And this morning, a woodpecker,
that might have migrated
from the stand of hardwoods
surrounding that loon-haunted lake
where at first light we'd cast
for pike to the thump of mallets
muffled in mist, woke me
by tapping at a phonepole as if typing
the Great American Novel.
I don't know what he was after,
not termites—
the phonepoles here are concrete.

Along the potholed, windward
highway overlooking Stumpy Point
the abandoned armor of land crabs
rusts like junked cars in the sun.
Vulnerable though it makes them

to the mongoose, nonetheless
it's time for tree snakes
to wrinkle out of their old skins.
By now, along the backroads
up in Michigan, the maples
must be shedding more light
than flamboyants.

Your letter, stamped with home's
foreign postmark waits in care
of General Delivery: news of friends
(a miscarriage, a drug bust, a divorce)
overlayed with a description
of the first frost on the panes
of the abandoned factory
that you inhabit, of painted leaves
whirlpooling in the dreary park
called Bug House Square
where you cruise for the boys in leather
that you turn to portraits.
Familiar lives and weather,
both, you write, *flying apart . . .*

Here, I'm not sure what to call it;
a season passes but without a name.
The tomato plants droop
about the time the restaurants
stop serving water. Weeds writhe
with lizards. It drives the stray
kitten I've acquired crazy.

I'm thinking of calling him either
Pogo or Nijinsky—Jinn, for short.
Pouncing has become his ordinary way
to get from place to place.

It's Saturday. I'm sitting beneath
a flapping awning, sipping
a Kaluha-laced iced coffee,
overlooking the choppy bay
where just last week a seaplane
loaded with sightseers capsized
before it could go anywhere.
Life vests over tourist shirts,
the passengers crawled out
along the wings. No one was hurt,
in fact, they were laughing.
One couple—honeymooners,
I later learned—waved off
the rescue boat, intent instead
on floating in . . .

Even in shadow, this paper
has a freshly whitewashed glare.
I'm writing another of those letters
that you claim I never finish
as an excuse not to send,
and yet, Dear Friend, I still view
the world as if reporting back to you,
seeing through your eyes
whenever there's something strange
or beautiful.

Perhaps, amidst its molting skins,
autumn can't help seeming emblematic
of the journeys
of the self through selves.
But I've moved here, where change
is measured in minute degrees;
it will take the cycle of a year
to tell when summer ends.

Kurt Vonnegut on Stage at the Steppenwolf Theater, Chicago

Interviewed by Lee Roloff

On the afternoon of September 29, 1996, and just hours before the premiere of a stage adaptation of his Slaughterhouse Five, *Kurt Vonnegut spoke of his life and work in a far ranging interview and conversation with Lee Roloff, Steppenwolf lecturer for the play discussion series, the PLAY talks. The conversation, which has been edited to place emphasis upon Mr. Vonnegut's remarks, began with exploring the various creative forms* Slaughterhouse Five *has taken: an American motion picture, a German opera, a Russian musical, and a stage adaptation. Mr. Vonnegut was asked to comment upon his experiences with these transformations of his novel.*

Well, what I want first to say about the play being performed here at Steppenwolf, and I have read the script, is that it is a separate work of art. And this is true of anybody who adapts anything of mine. As I said to Stephen Keller who did the motion picture script of the book, "Think of my book as a friendly ghost around the house." And the same thing is true of the play: it is an utterly separate work of art. And it would not be worth a damn if it were anything else. The adapter essentially starts from scratch, as Goethe did with the Faust plays. And so, I come to see the show, and the movie, and the opera, and the musical, and to have a good time. But I have nothing to do with it. I did the book!

Slaughterhouse Five when it was published in its novel form was a terrific hit in the Soviet Union and the Warsaw Pact countries because it was the only popular American novel that admitted that Russians or Soviet citizens were also in the war. Every other American war novel had had the United States and the British winning it single-handedly. And so they liked that. Another thing they liked about it was that I had an Alcoholics Anonymous prayer in there. And that meant a whole lot of things, too, because it doesn't simply apply to booze. It applies to life, and they found it extremely useful.

And I was very well thought of in the Soviet Union, particularly in Russia. I had a terrific translator, a woman named Rita Wright, a daughter of a Scotsman who had spent some time in Russia. She's dead now, but God, she did a terrific translation, and because in large part of her translation, the book was very popular. I was always welcome when I went over there and was treated very well. The *most* popular American book was *Catcher in the Rye*, and she translated that, and I know how it happened to get published. Rita Wright recognized this as a masterpiece almost as soon as it was published in the United States. And so she went to her cultural commissar, and said, "Please I want to publish this book. It is a very important book." The cultural commissar gave it to his wife to read and she said that it was a very dirty book because a kid walks into a subway station and sees the words "fuck you" written on the way. And this would never do for a very puritanical society as the Soviet Union or Russia was anyway. And every year Rita Wright would go to her commissar and say, "Please, this is a wonderful book. Don't you know how wonderful it is? I want to publish it." And finally there was an ecumenical meeting of the American cultural types and the Russians. Now it just so happened that Norman Cousins, no longer with us but he was a great pro-peace operative, was there and he turned to Rita's cultural commissar and said, "Tell me, so what American novels are you going to publish this year?" The commissar knew the name of only one American novel, and that American novel got published. So that is how *Catcher in the Rye* got published in the Soviet Union.

I have not been able to see either the Munich opera or the Moscow musical of *Slaughterhouse Five*. But I understand that the Moscow musical was apparently very good. I could not go, but a friend of mine went and represented me and he reported that it was quite wonderful. It was staged in the Red Army Theater, a venue about the size of the Michigan State University football stadium. As far as I know, it is the only pacifistic show that was ever put on there.

I want to compliment Steppenwolf Theater and its designers on the astonishing veracity of the setting. It is very close in appearance to where I lived—and I should say "we"—in Dresden and in Slaughterhouse Five, a cement block barn that was built in a slaughterhouse to house pigs awaiting death. Germany must have been out of pigs, as it was out of everything else, and this place became our bunk house.

The German opera experience has been mystifying to me, and

annoying. The composer some ten years ago asked my lawyer if he could write an opera based upon *Slaughterhouse Five*. My lawyer and I said, "Sure, go ahead." And that was the last we heard from the composer. And then about two weeks before the production was to open, I got a letter inviting me to come. And, to be frank, I was annoyed because the composer had never treated me as a colleague or having anything to do with it. It was the public relations person who wrote me a letter and asked me whether I would like to come. So I said that I had a previous engagement, and that was the end of it. I thought that the guy would say, "Well, look. We're sorry you can't come. We'll send you a tape; we'll send you a video." Not a word. I thought that the composer would call me up and said, "Hey, please, won't you come?" Nothing. Utter silence. I think what the Germans figured was that my contribution was minuscule compare to theirs. They had given us the city of Dresden and they had given us the war. But I had been there.

Writing *Slaughterhouse Five* was opportunism, among other things, because after the war, I was trying to make a living as a writer and was looking for "subjects" all the time. I had a family to support. May I say people hate to hear about writing as a business, but it is that. So I am asking myself, "What am I going to do next to make money?" And I thought: Dresden. My gosh, I *saw* this thing. *Heard* it. You couldn't *see* it without being killed. But I could hear it overhead—the firebombing of Dresden. And, also, I thought it was probably a pretty ordinary experience I had been through. I came back from the war to Indianapolis and looked in the February 14th edition of the *Indianapolis News* about the bombing and all it said was that our planes had been over Dresden that night. And *that* was all it said! And so I said, "God, that isn't much of a war story!" And then more and more information came out on the scale of this disaster, which I certainly couldn't judge from the ground. And this information came most from the British because in the House of Commons they had debated strategic bombing: was it a good idea or not? It might not be, you know, just on military grounds. To hell with ethics.

And so, ten or more years after I got home, I realized that the Dresden bombing was a pretty fancy event, including the fact that it is a *Guinness Book of Records* event. Near as anybody knows, it was the largest massacre in human history. I mean Auschwitz was a slow killing process. In order to qualify as a massacre there has to be the killing of a whole lot of people in a very short amount of time. And this was what Dresden was all about: killing about 135,000 people in the course of a night—let's say about eight hours, something like that. So I decided that if I were going to support my family, I should write about it. I was there. I am entitled. And so I started.

I wanted Frank Sinatra and Dean Martin and some of our other war heroes to be in this movie of mine. Duke Wayne, of course. So I tried this and I tried that and it wasn't working and it wasn't working. So I got in touch with some of my war buddies, people who had been there with me. And they wouldn't remember it. They didn't want to talk about it. So I had a particular war buddy who just died about two years ago, by the name of Bernard V. O'Hare. He had become a criminal lawyer. So I went and saw him and on a basis of friendship said to him, "Come on! Let's between us remember as much as we can because I want to write a book!" And his wife suddenly came into the room and was disgusted with the whole enterprise, in fact, was disgusted with the whole human race, and said, "You were just babies then." And indeed we were! And that's where I got the subtitle: "The Children's Crusade." In the anniversary edition of *Slaughterhouse Five* there's an additional subtitle, "A Duty Dance with Death." Well, I had seen a hell of a lot of it. I was teaching at City College in New York recently, and one of my students said she'd never seen a dead person. I said, "Be patient."

Yes, I saw a hell of a lot of death, and I saw a hell of a lot of it during the Battle of the Bulge when my division was wiped out. But then in Dresden I saw a mountain of dead people. And that makes you thoughtful. We were put to work. There were no air raid shelters in Dresden, and we got through it because we were in a slaughterhouse, and in that slaughterhouse there was a huge and very old meat locker dug out of the clay beneath the slaughterhouse. It was probably dug a hundred years ago where they could keep meat cool because they had no refrigeration. But we survived, ironically. And when we came up above ground, everybody else for miles around was dead. Day after day, we were sent into town to take corpses out of cellars because that's where the people went. The Germans did not expect a raid on Dresden. They thought it was an open city, although there is no such city under international law. It was just a dream. Of course, the corpses became a health hazard and we were forced to dig our way down into the cellars because the rubble had closed the staircases. We went down into these cellars and brought out the corpses on stretchers and put them on a big pyre. Believe me, it was a mountain a corpses. And then, when the kerosene was thrown on that pile and touched off—WOOOOOAHHH! It . . . made . . . you think about . . . death. I have said, too, that I would not have missed it for the world. It was a hell of an adventure. You know, as long as you going to see something, see something really thought provoking.

Vonnegut reflects upon Billy Pilgrim, the central character of Slaughterhouse Five.

I based Billy in part upon an experience I had with a very gawky guy with very narrow shoulders who should never have been in the army. His name was Edward Crone. He should never have been a soldier. He didn't look like a soldier, in fact he looked like a filthy flamingo. Yes, he really did look this way. He was a sophomore engineering student at Hobart when he was drafted. He should have been put in limited service, or he should have been classified 4F, or whatever. He wound up, as everybody eventually wound up, in the infantry. All the army needed at that time were riflemen. And . . . he died in Dresden. He died of what is called the "thousand mile stare." People did this same thing in prison camps, dying of the thousand mile stare. When one chooses the thousand mile stare, this is what happens: the person sits down on the floor with his back to the wall, will not talk, will not eat, and just stares into the space in front of him. We could not get the Germans to do anything about Edward Crone, and he finally died. And he was buried in Dresden. And the Germans buried him in a white paper suit. Why? Because I guess that is what the burial garments were. After the war, his parents—who were, by the way from Rochester, New York—went over to Germany and returned his body to the United States. He is buried in Rochester now. I paid a visit to his grave about a year ago when I was lecturing in Rochester. And that visit to his grave finally closed out the war for me. I talked to him a little. I know that he gave up to the "thousand mile stare" because life made absolutely no sense to him. And he was right. It wasn't making any sense at all. So he didn't want to pretend he understood it anymore, which is more than the rest of us did. We pretended we understood it.

It seemed important for Vonnegut to explain why the bombing of Dresden was neither a moral nor an immoral act, whereas the killing of a person by another person is a moral act. Could he explain this distinction?

The issue for me is *free will*. And these opportunities are very rare

21

really. After the bombing of Dresden, and after we came out of our shelter there, we had to walk out of town. It was hot, too, and the stones were hot. Suddenly two American fighter planes peeled off their machine guns as we were moving across the rubble. Now that was immoral I think. It was immoral because the pilots thought we were Germans and it appeared that they didn't have anything else to do and so they thought it would be a kind of fun. I guess they even talked about it on the radio before they peeled off after they saw this thin line of survivors walking across ruins.

The United States, of course, had Chicago. The University of Chicago is famous for performing the first man-made, man-controlled nuclear reaction under the bleachers at Stagg Field. At a memorial service there on the occasion of the fiftieth anniversary of the Bombing of Hiroshima, I came to speak. There was a physicist who had taken part in that tremendous moment in American history, that moment when scientists found out they could make matter behave in this manner. And one physicist who had taken part in the experiment apologized. I found that extremely interesting. Then the question came up as to whether or not we should have bombed Hiroshima. And I said that I had to honor the opinion of my friend, William Starling, who was a Marine in the Pacific. I was in Japan with him when he made his comment, "Thank God for the atom bomb on Hiroshima or I'd be dead now." (You don't want to go anywhere with him overseas because he's liable to say anything.) And I responded by saying that proof that my government can be racist, can behave in a ya-hoo, utterly uncivilized, cruel, nutty manner is . . . Nagasaki. Nagasaki had to be just for the fun of it, just for the hell of it because certainly the *military* point had been made with Hiroshima. For me it was exactly like being strafed by our own pilots in Dresden. And so it goes.

The issue of Vonnegut's German heritage came up in the conversation and the experience he had in his grandparent's home so rich in German sensibility. Then World War I and then silence. He was asked to explore the effect of this "silence" upon him, of the excising of the Old World, and the "something" that was lost in his soul.

It was as though I had been born incomplete—with only one car! Or something like that. Everybody else had a past, a family past. You know, a racial past. As I was growing up in Indianapolis, and it has a huge German population, it was as if they just lost interest in being German. It was when I was captured and made a prisoner of war that the German soldiers looked at my name and said, "Why are you fighting your brothers?" They might as well have asked General Eisenhower the same question. Everything we like about Germany is the music, the sentimentality about Christmas, and other German attitudes and forms of behavior that come from the twelve or fifteen Germanies. And everything we hate about Germany has come from *one*. And so, I hated when the Berlin Wall came down. So did Günther Grass. He thought it was a terrible idea. Why? Because these people are going to go crazy again. Heinrich Böll was a friend of mine, a Nobel prize winner, and a great novelist. I asked him what the flaw was in German character. And he said, "Obedience." Germany has so disgraced the idea of civilization *twice*. I just do not like to think about them anymore. I don't feel close to them anymore. Never did. I don't feel German.

I was an interpreter for our prison group. There were a hundred of us and we were a labor detail and we were all privates first class. Under the Geneva Convention, privates first class have to work for their keep when captured, non-coms and commissioned officers do not. It is better to work for your keep because you get out into the world and you get to talk to people. The non-coms and commissioned officers who were captured during World War II were all out in the countryside behind barbed wire. They did not get to see anything. We privates first class got to see a hell of a lot. We got to talk to people. When I go to Germany now and begin to speak German with the people, it is just another form of rollerblading. And as I am going to bed that night my brain says, "Look, if you think we are going to keep this up, you're crazy." And that's right. It shuts down.

But once again, the conversation veered back to his own German family and background, about his wealthy mother and his architect father.

Yes, my mother was one of the richest in town, and, yes, she married an architect. But you know, my mother, among other things, wanted to be a writer. I have a theory that if a woman wants to become something and is kept from becoming that, and if she has a son, he will make that dream come true. And my mother very much wanted to be a writer. Well, she lost all her money in the stock market, and because she was used to being one of the richest people in Indianapolis, she took her losses very hard. It was silly on her part. We weren't as rich as we used to be, that was all. But for my brother, my sister, and me, it didn't make any difference that we were not rich anymore. And it didn't appear to make a difference to our father. That "we weren't rich anymore" was a terrible blow to my mother. But, seeking a new identity other than being one of the richest women in town, she took some courses at the "Y" in short story writing and studied magazine writing and all that. I was about fourteen at the time, so I got interested in it. She could not sell a story, so she quit. But she also wanted to get the hell out of Indianapolis since there was not anybody there anymore and live on Cape Cod. So . . . 1) I became a writer, and 2) I moved to Cape Cod.

Both my brother, Bernie, and I worked at General Electric. While I was in Public Relations, he worked in a research laboratory. Now I was very good at public relations, I must say. And my brother was very good at research. He was nine years older than I, a physical chemist with a Ph.D. from MIT. At that time, General Electric hired scientists to do whatever they wanted to do. They don't do this anymore, but this was an enormous success, just to get people who would ordinarily be teaching at MIT or Cal Tech or whatever. General Electric got a whole lot of patents out of this arrangement. One day, while my brother was having lunch with a couple of other guys, they started talking about the weather. You know, "What makes it thunder?" "What makes it lightning?" "How come it rains some times and doesn't others?" They didn't know a thing about it. So, I guess they got out the *Encyclopedia Britannica* to look up about the weather and it didn't make a great deal of sense to them. They started talking about what would touch off clouds because sometimes the clouds would come over and it would neither rain nor snow. They got an idea. This was a week after they realized they didn't know anything about the weather and nobody else did either. General Electric had a little air field with some light planes and stuff there. They took a bag of dry ice and they got into one of these little planes and they flew over Mount Greylock, which is on the border of New York and Massachusetts in the Berkshire hills, and they threw the dry ice out the back of the plane over the top of a cloud. And they took photographs. What the photographs showed was a nice round hole. A nice round race track. So they got into whatever the hell else would touch off clouds. My brother discovered the silver iodide which has a crystal form very close to that of ice. Silver iodide will "teach" clouds how to rain or snow sometimes. He's done a lot of other interesting things, but this is the most interesting. I got the job at General Electric after Bernie had been there quite a while and was a big shot. I had been working for a Chicago city news bureau when General Electric decided to have their publicity done by newspaper people—professional journalists rather than people who had come up through the company, or advertising people, or whatever. So, I became sort of a reporter for the General Electric research laboratory because great stuff was coming out of there, and we did publicity stories about it.

The conversation turned to Vonnegut's novel, Player Piano, *and the fictional city of Ilium that stands in for Schenectady, the home of General Electric. And it is in* Player Piano *that Vonnegut developed a "war scenario," as it were, between individuals on one side of the river against those on the other—the technocrats and the labor force.*

Who are these two groups? Well, one one side are the engineers, the technologically sophisticated people on one side of the river, and on the other side are those who have no economic value anymore because the machines can think so much better for themselves than men ever could. I wrote *Player Piano*, where machines were going to throw people out of work because they could do the work better than people could, before the word "automation" was coined. "Automation" was coined by the Ford Motor Company, but at General Electric, with access to laboratories and talking to guys about what they were doing, I saw what the secret was. The company didn't think it wanted the story published and I don't think I ever got a story out about it because they were so troubled by what they had done. Some of the highest paid people at General Electric in the factory were the machinists who made these beautiful Brancusi forms for turbines. These guys were such great machinists they didn't need a union; they could just call in "sick" and somebody would send them money to come back to work. Some guys in the lab, not the research lab but the engineering lab at General Electric, got a machine to do the same damn thing with "punch cards" (because computers were very primitive then). And that impressed me because I could see it all coming *very* soon: factories were going to be without employees. I think now that is a calamity. Think about it: *here we are at the end of this century, and we are supposed to be celebrating being ailve when there are computers!* If it were not a way to make a person unemployable or worth only a minimum wage, there wouldn't be so much money poured into the development of these things. I don't know quite what the hell to do about it. You cannot fight progress, as they say.

The conversation began to address how artists make their statements. In the novel Player Piano, *a tension between technocrats and working men escalates until it has its own catastrophic moment. It appears that Vonnegut has as one of his themes in his fiction the outrage that develops when humans do inhuman things to each other.*

I look at anti-nuke rallies, anti-war rallies, save the rain forest rallies, and all that, and it's the same old bunch of moldy figs. It's the same seventeen moldy figs who show up every time. Why aren't there more people? I'll tell you, and don't let this get out of this room, please. I think people are so embarrassed by life that they don't care if it ends. We've poisoned the planet to such an extent that if Oppenheimer and Einstein were so smart, why didn't they tell us about the indestructible wastes? Why didn't they warn us to have some contingencies for these wastes. So we've done a pretty good job of wrecking the planet without a war. I think that the most hateful outcome of the communist experiment was the destruction of the environment. There was nobody in the Soviet Union who was responsible for conservation whatsoever. God, they killed the biggest of all the great lakes with industrial waste. In eastern Europe the trees are all brown and there's no life in the rivers. I think, in the long run, the Hiroshima bomb will kill as many Americans as it did the Japanese because the atomic wastes are around, and they are very lively.

We are not taking good care of each other now. I mean it's ridiculous to think of the federal government, or the state government, or a city government taking care of us. This used to be done by members of extended families. When I was in Nigeria, during the Biafran war, on the Biafran side, I met an Ebo who had six hundred relatives. He and his wife, with the war going on, had just had a baby. And they were taking this kid to visit all their other relatives, to tell these family members of the swell new member they had. You know I did this in one of my novels where I arbitrarily gave people the same middle names, just to connect them with somebody else. I say for a human being to do without an extended family is to do without an essential mineral or vitamin. What is it? What makes about sixty percent of marriages go bust? The problem isn't sex, the problem isn't money, the problem isn't power. When a married couple fight what each one is saying to the other is this: "You are not enough people!" My brother Bernie, for example, belonged to artificial extended families which allowed him to claim families all over the world. Why? Because he was a brother scientist to scientists everywhere.

Sometimes we can become desperate about wanting relatives. I had an uncle who did not have a drinking problem, though his wife said he did, but who forswore alcohol, joined Alcoholics Anonymous, and he did so because he found a family. And I do think that people stay with AA after they have begun recovery for social (and extended family) reasons. We are a terribly lonely society.

I'm honorary president for the American Humanist Association, and, as you know, we don't think much of organized religion. I succeeded Isaac Asimov as honorary president. Well, often I hear from people in prison, and there'll be a guy who will write me, "I've been in the prison system since I was 14 or 17 or whatever, and now I'm 31 or 42. I'm finally going to get out. What do I do?" And I say, "Join a church!" In other words, find a family. I had a relative who would address prayers, "To whom it may concern."

When I was on the plane, for some reason a poem I learned in junior high school came to my mind. You're liable to think of anything on an airplane. It's a terrible poem, and I wonder how many of you know it?

>Far, far, false alarm,
>
>Baby shit on Poppa's arm.
>
>Poppa went to get a switch,
>
>Baby called him "son of a bitch."

This sort of thing happens all the time in real life, all the time, but Poppa *kills* the baby, or Momma shits on the baby because it won't stop crying, or whatever. In the extended family there would be a lot of people who would rescue that baby and tell the parents, "That's no way to act!"

My generation, how different it was. The Great Depression and World War II generation had dreams of the future: "When the Great Depression is over, America is going to become *this*, or *that*." "When World War II is over, America is going to become *this*." And what we had in mind was either socialism or communism. Now these were reasonable schemes, or appeared to be. We had the Magna Carta, and the Declaration of Independence, and the Bill of Rights—remarkable declarations that were intended to create a more just society. We thought that after World War II, we'd make it more just economically, too—to distribute income more reasonably. Neither communism nor socialism was a wicked idea but it turned out not to work very well because people cannot be trusted with wealth, public wealth.

In the final moments of the conversation, the subject turned to Vonnegut's identification of the "one truly great writer."

Flannery O'Connor. Oh, Jesus, yes. What I think we both do is get our characters into big trouble as soon as possible. A lot of writers are slow doing that. In the industry, they call it "destructive testing," where some product is abused and abused until they finally find out what it takes to break it. Flannery O'Connor and I both do that. Put people in awful trouble, and then apply as much stress as possible to see what happens. To see what'll make them break. Actually, when I teach writing, I find student writers are too polite to do this. I say, "Look, you could torture this person. You could burn this person alive if you wanted to. It's not a real person. They're very reluctant to do this for a story. Guy de Maupassant's "A String of Pearls" is a perfect example. Nice, middle class couple and they have upper class friends. They are invited to a fancy dress ball by some of their rich friends. But she has no jewels to wear. These are darling people, and so she goes to a friend and her friend lends her a string of pearls. So they go to the party and they're beautifully dressed and everything. What's the worst possible thing you can have happen? She loses the goddamn pearls, right? Most writers, beginning writers, don't have the nerve to do that to somebody nice.

A New Delhi Romance

Ruth Prawer Jhabvala

Indu had married beneath her, but that was many years ago, and besides, she no longer lived with her husband. Everything else had changed too—her parents, who had so deplored her marriage, were long since gone, her brother and sisters had moved away, and the big house they had all lived in had been torn down and a block of flats built on its site. Indu herself still lived in the neighborhood, almost around the corner from the old house, in a complex of ramshackle hutments that had once been a barrack for policemen. She had lived here for twenty years and the rent was still the same, which was why she stayed on—who could have afforded anything else?—though it was far from her place of work. However, it did have the advantage of being near the University, so that her son Arun, who was a student there, could easily come home if his classes were canceled due to a strike or the death of some important politician.

Arun, taking full advantage of the proximity of his home and his mother's daylong absence from it, didn't wait for classes to be canceled but cut them whenever he felt like it. Lately he had begun to bring his girlfriend Dipti there—though only after a struggle, not with Dipti, who was willing enough, but with himself. For one thing, he had to overcome his feelings of guilt toward his mother for doing this in her home; and then there was the shabbiness of that home—he was ashamed of it for himself and his mother, and angry with Dipti for maybe judging it in the same way he did. But Dipti was so happy to be there that she formed no negative judgments of it at all, on the contrary.

Yet Dipti herself lived in a very grand house and was brought to the college every day in a chauffeur-driven car. Her father was a politician, an important cabinet minister, and the family lived in luxury. They gave lavish parties at which everyone ate and drank too much, they brought back all the latest household gadgets from their trips abroad, even a washing machine though they had their washerman living on the premises along with their other servants. Dipti's mother was always going shopping, for saris and textiles and jewelry, and she bought fresh pastries and chicken patties, so that if Dipti brought her friends home, there was plenty to eat, as well as every kind of soft drink in the refrigerator. Long before he decided to bring Dipti to his own house, Arun had been visiting hers. He didn't eat the pastries—he didn't care for them—and made no attempt to ingratiate himself with her parents. But they liked him—approved of him, and of his mother. Dipti's mother was very gracious to her, not at all assuming the role of VIP's wife that she usually played to its full extent, as was her right. She brought Indu home, ostensibly consulting her on a question of interior decoration, and she even pretended to take her advice, though Indu's taste was not at all consonant with her own preference for rich ornamentation.

Indu accepted Dipti's mother's respect as her due and did not return it. But she liked Dipti—how could she not, for Dipti was everything a young girl should be: sweet and pretty and very much in love with Arun. It had not taken Indu long to discover that the two young people spent afternoons in her house. Dipti's floral perfume hung in the air hours after she had left, and once Indu found a white blossom on her pillow, which might have dropped out of the garland wound into a girl's hair. Indu's feelings as she picked it up were mixed: pride in a son's conquest, as well as a movement of jealous anger that made her indulge in a burst of outrage ("and on my bed!"). But as she sat on this bed, slowly rubbing the petal between her fingers so that it released its scent, memories of her own obliterated all thoughts of the young couple. She hardly needed the fragrance of the jasmine emanating from between her fingers to recall the secret nights on her parents' roof with Arun's father, when the rest of the household was fast asleep. What more romantic than those nights drenched in moonlight and jasmine—or what more evanescent? The blossom in tatters between her fingers, she flung it away, her resentment now not against Arun and Dipti but against Arun's father, and also against her own stupid young self, who had tossed away all the advantages of her birth for the sake of those stolen nights.

Arun's father, Raju, had for years lived in Bombay, where he was involved in films. He had turned up throughout Arun's childhood, an unwanted guest who stayed too long, and far from contributing to the household or his son's support, borrowed money from Indu. Raju was good fun, especially for a young child—he sang, he played games, jokes, and magic tricks; but later Arun became as exasperated with him as his mother was. Dipti likewise expressed exasperation for *her* father: "Daddy works far too much! And all those people who come—does he have to see all of them!" But this was a pretense: she was proud of her father and the way crowds thronged to him. At certain hours of the day he sat enthroned on their verandah, an obese idol wrapped in a cloud of white muslin. Petitioners touched his feet in traditional gestures of respect; some brought garlands, some baskets of fruit or boxes of sweetmeats, poor people brought an egg or two, or milk from their cow. There were those who had traveled all night in crowded third-class railway carriages from his native state, in order to present some petition to him; others came only to be in his presence, imbibing his aura of riches and power. He addressed them in a tangy native dialect, and his homilies were illustrated by examples drawn nostalgically from the simple life of thatched huts he had long left behind. He had a reputation for salty humor and liked the sound of appreciative laughter. That was one aspect of him—racy, earthy, a man of the people; at other times, with other guests, he was different. Big cars drew up outside his house; if there were too many of them, special police constables had to be called to supplement the guard on duty at his gate. Then he himself became obsequious—he hurried out to receive the visitors, his big bulk moving lightly and with grace. He led them inside and into his carpeted drawing room where refreshments were served, not by servants but by his wife, her head covered as she offered silver beakers on a silver tray. Sometimes these visitors were led into a further room where a white sheet had been spread on the carpet; here they all sat crosslegged in their loose native clothes leaning against bolsters, some fat like himself, others scrawny from fasting and prayer. These powerful men weighed each other up like poker players, sometimes staying up all night while journalists waited outside: for the game that was being played involved millions not only of rupees but of lives. However, this was never a consideration in the minds of the players who, like all true sportsmen, were sincerely dedicated to their game for its own sake.

*

One day Dipti and Arun's afternoon was disturbed by the arrival of Arun's father. He walked into the living room that opened straight off the main compound around which all the barrack-like structures were grouped. "I'm here!" he called, like a most eagerly expected guest. In the bedroom, Dipti in a state of undress clapped her hand before her mouth and her wide eyes grew wider as she looked to Arun for rescue. As in all relations to his father, he was more exasperated than embarrassed. He got up and, winding a towel around his waist, went into the living room.

"Ah-ah-ah!" cried the father with delight at the sight of his son; and he hugged him tenderly, held him away for a moment to look at him, then hugged him again. Arun frowned all through this performance—he never liked to be embraced by his father and especially not now, for Raju was full of sweat and soot, as after a long train journey in an overcrowded carriage. But he pretended to have come by plane—"Indian Airlines is hopeless, hopeless! Two hours late and keeping us waiting without even a cup of tea! . . . How are you? And your mother—I tried to call her in the office to tell her I was coming, but the connection between Delhi and Bombay—hopeless, hopeless! . . . Did you get my telegram? No? That's funny. Why aren't you at college? Is it holidays? Good, we'll have a fine time, you and I, eh, what, ha? Pictures, coffee-house, and so on."

Arun said "I came home to study for my exam." He frowned more and added "With a friend."

"Ah. A friend. Where is he? . . . Understood!" cried Raju, his eyes dancing with pleasure and amusement as they roved over his son's handsome face and naked chest.

Arun went into the bedroom and, seeing Dipti fully dressed, told her, "You can come out. It's only my father. It's all right," he said in answer to her stricken look. When she still hung back, he took her hand and pulled her quite harshly through the curtain that separated the two rooms.

But Raju stilled her fears at once. Giving no sign that there was anything out of the way in a young girl appearing with his son out of the bedroom, he greeted her warmly, and with obvious though highly respectful admiration for her beauty. He became the host of the occasion, largely gesturing everyone to sit. Apart from the couch on which Arun slept at night, the furniture was scanty and makeshift; but Indu had made everything tasteful with handloomed fabrics draped over oil cans and egg crates, and hanging up reproductions from art books wherever new cracks appeared on the walls. Raju wanted to make a tea party of it, encouraging Arun to go for fritters and potato patties to the stall at the corner, even rummaging in his own pocket for money, but when he came up with nothing, the idea was dropped. He made up for it with his conversation, and while his son rolled his eyes up to the ceiling, Raju enjoyed his own skill as an entertainer and its effect on Dipti. She responded to him the way women, starting with Indu, had done all his life long—they didn't always believe what he said but liked his way of saying it. And he knew how to take the right tone with his audience: for instance, today, with Dipti, in telling her about the Bombay film industry, he did not stress its glamor but only its stupidity and vulgarity, adapting himself to what he guessed to be the opinion of someone like Dipti—a University student, and moreover, his scornful son's girlfriend.

"I *like* him," Dipti later insisted to Arun, and repeated it in spite of his "You don't know a thing." She did know some things—he had more or less told her the story of his parents' marriage—but she had not plumbed the depths of his feelings on the subject. And he had not described the scene on that night of Raju's arrival, when Indu got home from work. It was something that happened regularly whenever Raju reappeared in the bosom of his family. When it came time to sleep, he carried his battered little suitcase into his wife's bedroom, on the assumption that this was his rightful place. Arun was already lying on the couch, which had been his bed ever since he had grown too old to share his mother's. He had turned off the light and shut his eyes, pretending to himself that he was too sleepy to listen to the altercation in the next room. He didn't have to: he knew exactly what course it would take. First they would keep their voices down—for his sake—but when Raju kept saying "Sh-sh," Indu's rage rose till she was shouting, so that Raju too had to speak up to make his protests heard. That caused her to shout louder till she was shrieking, and finally—Arun waited for it—Raju's little suitcase came flying out through the curtain, and he followed, groping around in the dark to retrieve its scattered contents, while mildly clicking his tongue at his wife's unreasonable temper. Arun continued to pretend to be asleep, and with a sigh of patient resignation, Raju lay down on the floor mat. Arun then got up to offer him his place on the couch, and after some protests, Raju accepted. He was soon blissfully asleep, while Arun lay awake for hours, tossing and seething and aware of his mother doing the same in the next room.

Arun had grown up with such scenes, for his parents had been separated since he was two. Over the years, they had given him much occasion to ponder the relationship between men and women. Now he shared these thoughts with Dipti, though in a purely general way, careful not to give any insight into the particulars on which his theories were based. And that was the way she responded to him—also theoretically, with no reference to what she had observed between her own parents. For that marriage too, though enduring in the face of the world, had its own unmentioned, unmentionable areas on which no light was ever shed. Even in her own mind Dipti had veiled the scenes she had witnessed since her childhood—her father's outbursts when, for instance, a garment was not pressed well enough, or a stud was missing from his shirt: then her mother would cower in a corner with her arms shielding her head against the shoes he threw at her or the blows from his fist. Yet not half an hour later, when the defect in his toilet had been corrected and, starched and resplendent, he reclined among his guests, she was once more the modestly veiled hostess offering sherbet in silver vessels. It was only to Dipti that her mother sometimes whispered, in the dark and in secret, about the shame that it was the fate of wives to suffer: beatings and abuse, and also that other shame—she did not specify it further—that had to be undergone.

But Dipti knew, just as Arun did, that this was not how men and women should be together. They had formed their own idea on the subject, and it was the opposite of what they had observed between their parents. Their plan was to try out their theories on each other, and having already begun at the most basic, or essential, level in their afternoons together, they found that it was indeed a far cry from Raju's suitcase being flung out of Indu's bedroom, or that unspecified humiliation that Dipti's mother whispered to her about. Instead, they learned to grope their way around together in a completely new world that opened up for them, in infinite sweetness, at the touch of delicate fingers and the mingling of their pure breath.

"Yes and if she gets pregnant?" Having found yet another blossom on her pillow, Indu could no longer refrain from confronting her son. He shrugged—his usual response to any of her questions he did not care to answer. But his father, who was still there and more and more on sufferance, interposed: "Ah, don't spoil it for him."

Indu seized the opportunity to turn on her husband: "Oh yes—having ruined my life, now you send your son out to do the same to another innocent girl. . . . Not that I care what happens," she returned to Arun. "This time the shoe's on the other foot: it's not you who'll get pregnant and have to be married whether you want to or not."

If Raju had not been in such a precarious position in his wife's household—or if he had had the least bit of malice in him, which he did not—he could have pointed to himself as an unfortunate example of what Indu was talking about: for he, though still a student at the time, and from a very poor family, had been forced to marry Indu when she was found to be pregnant after their months of delight on her parents' roof.

This thought did arise in Indu, filling her with bitterness. "But, of course," she told her son, "you can always follow your father's fine example and never spend a single rupee on your child's support—well, what else have you been doing your whole life long!" she said to Raju, as though he had dared utter a word of protest. "Sitting around in Bombay, running after film stars, while I'm working myself into a nervous breakdown to raise this child and give him a decent education fit for my father's grandson—oh leave me alone, leave me alone!" she cried, though neither her husband nor her son had made a movement toward her. She ran into her bedroom—if there had been a door instead of only a curtain she could have banged it—and flung herself face down on to her bed.

Father and son remained together in silence. Raju would have liked to follow and comfort her but knew that his good intention would meet only with rejection. At last he said to Arun in a low voice, "Go. Go to her."

But Arun would not. It was not in his nature to dispense tender consolation to a woman in tears. He loved his mother fiercely and suffered because she did; but at this moment he also felt sorry for his father. Everything that Indu accused him of was true—Raju had got her pregnant and had never been able to provide for her and Arun but had let them struggle along on their own. But this was because he couldn't provide even for himself let alone a family, because he was—so his son thought with contempt and pity—just a poor devil. Raju would have liked to be generous, and if his pocket had not been chronically empty, he would have put his hand in it and pulled out bundles of bank notes to fling on his wife's table—"Here, take."

Dipti's feelings for her father were equally confused. Immensely proud of him for being what he was in the world, she could not forget what he was at home, behind closed doors with her mother. At the same time, she blamed her mother for the way she submitted to his treatment, crouching under his fury like an animal unable to defend itself: yet she was a proud woman, haughty and imperious with servants, with petitioners, with her husband's clerks, she passed among them like a queen, walking with slow majesty, as though her own massive weight and that of all her jewels and brocades were difficult to carry.

All this was before the scandal, which broke slowly, with a minor paragraph in one or two newspapers, and proceeded to mount with headlines in all of them, and photographs in the news magazines. At first Dipti's father brushed away the accusations against him, he joked with the visitors assembled around him on his verandah and made them laugh at the expense of journalists and other gossip-mongers who had nothing to do in their offices except kill flies and make up lies about him. Then, when the stories persisted and questions began to be asked in Parliament, he grew angry, he challenged his cowardly accusers—this too on his verandah amid his friends—to come out with one single fact against him. And when they did—not with one but with many, how he had taken money from industrialists, businessmen, and foreign investors—he blustered and demanded proof. This was forthcoming: there were letters and diary entries as well as the huge unexplained wealth he had accumulated in movable and immovable properties. Denying everything, he demanded an inquiry where he could, he said, easily prove himself as innocent as a newborn child. Cartoons of him in this latter role promptly appeared in the press. Although his resignation was demanded not only by the opposition but by his own party, he refused to submit it and hung on to his position, and to his official residence, until given the chance to clear himself before a committee to be appointed from the highest in the land.

During these difficult times, Dipti continued to attend her classes at the University, holding her head high. It was only when she was alone with Arun, during their afternoons in his mother's house, that she sometimes gave way to her feelings—and then only with silent tears, hiding her face against his chest. They never discussed the case and only referred to its essentials—as when she informed him that a committee of inquiry had been set up, or that her father had drafted his letter of resignation. Arun received the information without comment. Like Dipti herself, he had no desire to discuss the affair, and when other students did so within his hearing—and they spoke of it constantly, cynically, with jokes, everyone convinced of Dipti's father's guilt and gloating over it—he harshly reproved them. They nudged each other and grinned behind his back and called him "the son-in-law."

He also quarreled with his mother—his father was back in Bombay where he claimed to have been hired as a scriptwriter for a major production—for Indu had strong opinions about the affair.

"What do you know about it?" he challenged her.

"I know what I read in the papers plus what I've seen with my own eyes. You're not trying to tell me," she went on, "that they were living on his salary? All that vulgar display—tcha, and everything in the lowest taste possible of course, but what can you expect from people like that."

"People like what?"

She refused to be intimidated by his angry frown: "Uncultured, uneducated people. Peasants," she threw the word out with contempt.

"Oh yes, only you're very grand and cultured."

"Yes I am. And so are you." She tried to touch his face, glorying in his light complexion, his aristocratic features, but he jerked away and said, "And what about my father? Is he so very grand too?"

"Forget about your father. Think of your grandfather, who *he* was. God forgive me for what I did—dragged his name in the mud by marrying your father—all right, by getting pregnant from him, stupid, stupid girl that I was! . . . Arun, are you sure that you're doing everything—or she's doing everything—you know, so that she doesn't—?"

"Why, what are you afraid of?"

"That you'll ruin your life the way I ruined mine."

He wouldn't listen any more. He turned his back on her and went out of the house, through the compound, into the street, and walked for a long time through the lanes of the city, all the way to the old Mori Gate where he sat outside a tea-stall smoking cigarettes, immersed in his thoughts.

A few evenings later he had to take the same walk again. It happened after his mother had come home from work and was cooking their dinner in the little attached shed that served as their kitchen. There was a commotion outside, and from the window he saw that the children of the compound as well as one or two repressed little servant boys and the old sweeper woman employed by all the tenants had come running to see the spectacle that was unfolding outside Indu's house. A long shiny car with satin curtains had drawn up; a chauffeur jumped out to open the back door from which emerged Dipti's mother, in all the glory of an orange brocade sari with golden border and her full accoutrement of ornaments. Indu too had come to look but went quickly running in again to fix her hair, which was straggling over her forehead damp with perspiration from her cooking. She was in the somewhat stained cotton sari she wore for housework, and with no time to change, she had to maintain her dignity with a display of the breeding and fine manners she had acquired in her father's house and at her convent school. The chauffeur carried in a basket of fruit and several boxes of pastries and other sweets, then returned to his car to chase away the children scratching at its bright blue enamel paint. Arun too had to chase them off when they peered in at the window of the living room to see what was going on. This was not anything that required Arun's presence, so he went out and repeated the walk to the tea-stall outside Mori Gate where he sat for a long time, not wanting to return and hear what Indu had to say about her visitor and the mission on which she had come.

But of course he had to hear all about it for days on end. Indu was indignant—"Yes now they come running when they're in disgrace and think no one will take the girl off their hands. How old is she now?" Arun didn't anwer, so she answered herself, "Old enough to have been married long ago, I'm sure, only now who'll have her?"

"Dipti wants to be a college lecturer."

"She may want but her mother wants something different. . . . Who do they think we are?" She was incensed. "Who do they think they are?"

Arun did not tell Dipti about her mother's call, or its purpose. Yet she may have suspected it—even saw signs of it on her afternoon visits: for days the pastries that had been brought lay moldering in their golden boxes (Arun didn't like them, and his mother, who loved and could never afford them, was too proud to eat them). Dipti pretended not to see them. Secrets grew like a wall between her and Arun, making them often avoid each other's eyes. But as if to make up for the lack of words, their lovemaking became more passionate and they clung to each other as if fearful of being torn apart. They also grew more careless, and when Indu came home from work, she sometimes found an undergarment forgotten on her bedroom floor.

Now she changed her tactics with her son. She sidled up to him with sighs; she took his hand in hers, and when he snatched it away, she smiled and said that, yes, he was too big now for her fondling. Smiling more, she recalled their past together, when he had been a little boy and had crept into her bed and kissed her and promised her that, when he grew up, he was going to be a policeman and guard and take care of her forever. He squirmed at these memories—they were like little stab wounds in his soul—but she went right on, talking not of the past now but of the future she had always envisaged. No, he was not going to be a policeman, except perhaps a very high-ranking one who sat at a desk and controlled whole districts. A year from now, after he had graduated, he would take the entrance exam of the Indian Administrative Service, and he would pass with flying colors—ah she knew it! Wasn't he his grandfather's grandson and with the same brains? He would rank among the country's ruling elite, rising from one eminent bureaucratic post to the next. As for marriage—everyone knew that once a boy had passed into that corps, all the best families would come running with their daughters and their dowries. Well, he was free to accept them or not, as he pleased, just as long as he kept himself unencumbered and at liberty to pursue all his advantages.

Arun broke away from her—for while she spoke she had drawn closer to him, winding a lock of his hair around her finger—"What is it?" he said through clenched teeth. "What are you trying to tell me?"

He knew it all too well, for it was his own thoughts she was expressing, digging up what he was trying to suppress and hide from himself.

Last year on her birthday Dipti had wheedled Arun to come to her house—"Yes everyone knows you hate parties and all you do is sit there like a sick monkey—but you've *got to come!* Please? For me? Arun-ji?" He had sat at the side watching the others dance, their friends from the college and some other friends she had from prominent political families like her own. Dipti herself was a terrific dancer and she had often tried to teach him, but he stubbornly refused to have anything to do with it. He frowned while he watched them, but secretly he enjoyed seeing her spin around on her slim feet, wriggling and waggling inside her tight silk kameez, her hair and long gauze veil flying behind her.

After her father's disgrace, she stopped having parties. In fact, it was Arun who asked her, a few days before her birthday, "Aren't you going to invite me?" She didn't answer for a while but turned away her face; then she said in a low voice, "Would you come?" "What do you mean, would I come?" he answered her, doing his best to sound cross. "But of course if you don't want me—" Before he could finish, she had pressed her mouth against his, and he returned her kisses, pretending not to feel her tears on his cheek.

That evening he told his mother, "It's Dipti's birthday on Thursday."
"So?"

In the past, when he had gone to Dipti's birthday party, it was Indu who had bought the present for him to take. He relied on his mother's fine taste, and she always got a discount at the handicrafts emporium where she worked; besides, he had no money of his own.

"Don't tell me they're having a party," Indu said. "Surely they wouldn't, at such a time. And who would go to their house anyway."

"I'm going."

"You'll be the only guest then."

"Good. Get me a nice present to take, that's all I'm asking."

Later, while they were eating and she was serving him what she had cooked, she said: "I'll get her something very pretty, but give it to her at college. Don't go to their house," she pleaded, when he pretended not to understand.

He raised his eyes from his plate and looked at her. He had beautiful eyes, full of manly intelligence. She melted with tenderness for him, and pride, and also fear that he would not fulfill her hopes of him. "Oh I feel sorry for her, poor girl," she said. "And I've always liked her, you know that. But people are very cruel—the world's very cruel, once you've lost your place in it." She stared into the distance for a moment, as though into her own past, before continuing: "If you go, her mother will get a wrong idea. . . . Why aren't you eating?" for he had pushed his plate away and got up.

"Just get me a present," he said and walked away from her.

She did bring a very beautiful gift for Dipti—even better than anything she had brought for her before—and Arun took it there. Although, as Indu had predicted, he was the only guest to celebrate Dipti's birthday, her mother had attempted to reproduce the atmosphere of previous occasions. The servants had been made to shine the silver and wash the chandeliers, and the pink birthday cake she had ordered was as huge as for the previous contingent of thirty guests. But she did not manage to dispel the fog of gloom that had settled over the house—not even when the twenty birthday candles were lit and flickered on their pastel stems over the lake of pink icing with its festive inscription in green. Dipti did her best to be cheerful and smiling, in gratitude to Arun for having come and also to her mother for her efforts. These never ceased—the mother bustled about and gave orders to the servants and, a fixed smile on her face, tried to get her husband and Arun to join her in singing "Happy Birthday," and when they wouldn't, she sang it by herself. But most of her hard work was expended on Arun, for whom she couldn't smile enough. She had always been gracious to him, to demonstrate her acceptance of him as Dipti's friend, but now there was something desperate in her attitude, as if she were not bestowing but herself craving acceptance.

Dipti's father too had graciously patronized Arun in the past, sometimes singling him out among the crowd of admirers to address him with his pungently humorous remarks. Now Arun was their sole recipient, for there was no one else to hear them. And just as the mother had ordered the same size cake as for a large party, so the father, as voluminous as ever in his starched white muslin, spread out all his store of comment and conversation for Arun's sake alone. Supplying great gusts of laughter himself, he did not notice that Arun could only summon the faintest smile in response to his best jokes. And then, when he changed his topic and with it his mood, he needed no response other than his own mighty anger surging up in him. This was when he spoke of his case and of his enemies who had brought it against him: and from there he went on to announce what he would do to all of them, once he had cleared his good name and confounded all their schemes and dirty tricks. His voice rose, his face swelled out in a fearful way. Dipti implored "Daddy!"' while his wife laid a hand on his arm to restrain him: "Leave off," she said. Then his anger burst like a boil: "Leave off! I'll show you how I'll leave off when I've crushed them under my feet and plucked out their eyeballs and torn out their tongues—rogues! Liars! I'll show them all, I'll teach them such a lesson—" His hands fumbled in the air as though to pluck down more threats—and then fumbled in a different way like those of a drowning man attempting to save himself. His face swollen to a monstrous color, his words changed to a gasp, he keeled over in the throne-like chair on which he was seated. His wife screamed, servants came running; Dipti and Arun tried to prevent him from falling out of the chair, holding his huge throbbing body in their arms. Bereft of his guidance, everyone was calling out confused orders, several hands plucked at him to undo the studs on his kurta. "I'm dying," he gasped. "They've killed me."

Dipti's father did not die, but he had suffered a stroke and was taken to hospital. There he lay in a private room, monstrous and immobile, while his wife sat at his feet, moaning "What will become of us?" The sight and sound of her drove him mad, but he could neither shout nor throw things at her, and she refused to be driven away. His eyes swiveled imploringly toward Dipti, who had taken over the duty of caring for him. Fully occupied with her father, she could no longer attend her classes, and once or twice Arun visited her in her father's hospital room. But he had always been impatient of anyone's sickness—whenever Indu felt unwell, she suppressed it in his presence as long as possible—and the sight of Dipti's father in his present state was intolerable to him. And in a different way what was almost worse was the mother groaning "What will become of us?" and then looking with begging eyes at Arun, as though he alone held the answer to that question.

The final examination was drawing near, and Arun no longer had time to visit the hospital, or for anything except his studies. His mother was delighted with the way he completely devoted himself to his work, and she did everything she could to encourage him. She fed him with his favorite foods, and in order to buy special delicacies for him, like ham or cheese, she gave up taking a rickshaw to work and went by the public transport—though secretly, for she knew this would upset him, to think of her in the reeking, overcrowded bus, being pushed and even pinched, for she was still attractive enough to attract such unwanted attentions. It was her ambition—and his too, though he never spoke of it—that he should repeat the success of her father who, in the same examination more than half a century earlier, had stood first in the whole University. The gold medal he had won then was one of the most precious possessions. These days she took it out frequently and gazed at it in its velvet-lined case, and also left it open on the table where she served Arun his meals. She was in an unusually good mood, and was completely free of the headaches and depression that so often plagued her.

Unfortunately, Arun's father Raju again turned up unexpectedly at this time, completely broke, for the film script he had set his hopes on had fallen through. But he was as cheerful as ever, and although he tried to be respectful of his son's studies, could not refrain from expressing the thoughts tumbling around in his lively mind, or humming the tunes that came bubbling up there. He inquired after Dipti, and when he heard what had happened and how she had had to drop out of college, he shook his head in pity for her.

His thoughts reverted to her at odd moments—for instance, at night while he was lying on the couch and Arun sat over his studies at the table, he suddenly said, "But she was a pretty girl. Really special. Intelligent but oomphy too."

Arun looked up, frowning: "What sort of word is that?"

"Oh you know—like in 'She's oomphy—toomphy—just my moomphy,'" and he sang it, in case Arun didn't know this popular Hindi film song.

Indu thumped on the wall: "Are you disturbing Arun?"

"Oh no. I'm helping him with his physics!" Raju called back. After a while, he spoke again: "How you must miss her—oh oh, terrible! I know with Indu, when I had measles—can you imagine a youth of nineteen going down with measles—for three weeks I couldn't see her and I thought I would surely die with longing for her. . . . Yes yes all right!" he called when Indu thumped again. "I'm already asleep!"

After a few days of this—"He's driving me crazy," Arun complained to Indu. That night, when Raju already lay on the couch that was his allotted space, she called him into the bedroom. Raju raised his eyebrows at his son in pleased surprise; Arun too was surprised, and more so as the minutes passed and Raju was not sent out again. Arun found it difficult to return to his books. His attention was strained toward the other room; he heard their voices rising in argument till they shushed each other and continued their fight in whispers. Finally these too ceased, but by now

Arun was completely incapable of concentrating on his work. What were they doing in there? He could not hear a sound. He walked up and down and cleared his throat, to make them remember he was there; they continued silent, as though holding their breath for fear of disturbing him. He was no longer thinking of them but only of the room and its bed on which they were together, as he and Dipti had been together for so many afternoons.

Dipti's father was in the news again when the results of the inquiry against him were made public. He had been found guilty on every count—taking money from interested parties, acquiring properties, accepting imported cars, and going on shopping trips to Hong Kong in return for favors received—and the report expressed itself in the strongest terms on his conduct. Although he was named as the prime culprit, several senior bureaucrats were drawn into the same web of accusations, as were other members of the cabinet. The whole government was brought under suspicion, the opposition clamored for its resignation, while frantic meetings were held at the highest level to save the situation. By then he had been discharged from the hospital and lay helpless and speechless on his bed at home, with his wife at his feet and Dipti ministering to his needs. No newspapers were allowed into his room, and when he made signs to ask for them, everyone pretended not to understand. All this time Arun had not seen or spoken to Dipti. He had tried to phone her once, from the college—he had no phone at home—but he knew she was in her father's room, with both parents present, so that it was difficult for him to know what to say. And while he was groping for words, other students waiting behind him for the phone kept saying, "Come on, hurry up." After that he had not tried to contact her again.

When the report about her father came out, he had to listen to a lot of discussion about it but refused to participate either at college or at home. When Indu said she had known it all along, that one look at the way they lived had told her that it was all based on bribery and corruption, he cut her short with, "You don't know what you're talking about."

"It's all here—in black and white."

"Oh yes," he sneered, "you're just the type to believe everything that's written in some rag of a newspaper."

"*The Times of India*," she protested—but he was already out of the house and on one of his furious walks.

He had not yet returned when his parents were getting ready for bed. "He's thinking of the girl," Raju said to Indu in the bedroom where he was still allowed to remain. "He feels for her—poor child, what is her future now? He loves her," he concluded in a musing, sentimental voice.

"He doesn't see her. Of course he doesn't! He's much too busy studying for his exam to waste his time on a girl."

Raju smiled: "Time spent on a girl is never wasted."

"That's your philosophy, but thank God it's not his."

"Yes thank God," Raju echoed but continued smiling. His arms clasped behind his head, his eyes meditating on the ceiling, he began to recite in a soft poetic voice: "'My thoughts buzz like bees around the blossom of your heart—"

"Sh!" she said, putting her hand over his mouth. "He's come home. Arun?"

She had to call twice more before Arun answered: "What do you want? Why do you have to keep disturbing me?"

"Are you studying?"

"Well what do you think I'm doing?"

"He's studying," Indu said to Raju. She took her hand from his mouth: "Go on, but keep your voice down."

Raju continued: "'My sting is transformed into desire to suck the essence of your beauty.' Do you like it?"

"Is it something you made up? I don't know why you can never think of anything except bees and flowers."

"Should I turn off the light?"

She assented, yawning to show how tired she was. "I must get to sleep. I have to be up early to go to work, unlike some people."

But once the light was off, it turned out she wasn't so tired after all, and although they tried to make no noise, they became so lively together that Arun in the next room had to cover his ears, in an effort to muffle the sounds from the next room as well as those pounding in his own head.

Next day Arun had an important pre-exam tutorial, but instead of attending, he went to see Dipti. He prepared himself to find her house as silent and gloomy as on her birthday, but instead it was in turmoil. They were moving out—having lost his official position, the father also lost his official residence, and all its contents were being carried into cars and moving vans parked around the house. In supervising this operation, Dipti's mother had regained her former bustling, domineering personality. She was on the front lawn, fighting with a government clerk who had been sent to ensure that no government property was removed. Whenever he challenged a piece of furniture being carried away, she told him that, whatever was not theirs by private purchase, had been earned by years of selfless public service, and overruling his protests, she waved the coolies on with a lordly gesture.

Arun found her attitude to himself completely changed. She greeted him haughtily, and when he tried to enter the house in search of Dipti, she barred his way. She told him that her daughter was busy, and working herself up, went on indignantly, "My goodness, the girl has a sick father to look after, and here we are in the middle of a move to a big house of our own, not to mention other important family matters—you can't expect to walk in here whenever you please to take up our time."

Arun flushed angrily but was not to be put off. When she turned away to argue some more with the clerk, he strode past her into the house. He picked his way among sofa-sets, chandeliers and china services, through the courtyard full of packing cases and cooking pots to the family rooms at the back of the house. All the doors here were wide open except one: he did not hesitate to turn its handle and found himself in the father's room. The invalid had been placed in an armchair, with Dipti beside him feeding him something out of a cup.

Her reception of him made Arun even more angry than her mother's: "What a lovely surprise," she said in a bright, social voice. "And I was thinking of you only yesterday."

"I was thinking of *you*," he replied, but in a very different tone, his voice lowered and charged. "That's why I'm here."

"I was going to send you a note—to wish you good luck. For your finals. Isn't it next week? You must be so jittery, poor Arun."

"I have to talk to you."

"One more spoon, Daddy, for me." She put it in his mouth, but whatever was on it came dribbling out again.

"I must see you. Alone. Where can we go?" He didn't know if Dipti's father understood anything or not, and he didn't care. He thought only to leap over all the barriers between Dipti and himself—her huge helpless father, the house in upheaval, her mother, and most of all Dipti's own manner toward him.

Her mother came in. She addressed Arun: "You must leave at once. You can see we're very busy." To Dipti she said, "The jeweller has come. I told him it's a bad day, but now he's here, we might as well look at what he's brought. There's not much time left."

"Not much time left for what?" Arun asked Dipti, ignoring her mother.

Dipti had her back to Arun, and instead of answering him, she scooped up the food from her father's chin back into his mouth.

Her mother told her, "Don't forget those people are sending a car for you in the afternoon. I said where is the need, we have plenty of cars of our own, but they insist. They like to do everything right—naturally, they can afford it. I'll call the jeweller in here, he can spread it out on the bed for us to see."

"It'll disturb Daddy."

But her mother went to the door to call for the jeweller. Quick as a flash, Arun drew near to Dipti and bent down to breathe into her ear, "Tomorrow. Four o'clock." She still had her back to him, and he laid one finger on the nape of her neck—it was the lightest touch, but he felt it pass through her like an electric current, charged with everything that had always been between them.

But it so happened that next day Raju stayed home. Usually he accompanied his wife when she left in the morning and then remained in the center of town for the rest of the day, calling on friends, sitting with them in their favorite coffee-houses, enjoying himself. But that day he had a cold, and as always when he was sick, he looked at Indu with piteous eyes that said "What has happened to me?" Before leaving for the office, she rubbed his chest with camphor and tied a woolen scarf around his neck. She left tea ready brewed for him on the stove, and two little pots of food she had prepared. He stayed in bed, mostly asleep; but as the day wore on, he became more cheerful, and by afternoon he had almost forgotten about his cold.

Arun arrived just before four, and as soon as he entered, he heard his father singing a lyric to himself, in that swooning way he had when deeply moved by a line of verse. "What are you doing here?" Arun said, in shock.

Raju stopped singing and pointed to the scarf Indu had tied around his neck. He coughed a little.

"Oh my God," Arun said in such despair that Raju assured him in a weak voice, "It's just a cold, maybe a little fever." He felt his own forehead: "Ninety-nine. Perhaps a hundred."

There was a soft knock on the living room door, and Arun ran to admit Dipti. "Who is it, Arun? Has someone come?" Raju called from the bedroom. Dipti's eyes grew round in distress and with the same distress Arun said, "My father has a cold."

Raju came shuffling out of the bedroom, and when he saw Dipti, he held his hands to cover the crumpled lungi in which he had slept all night and day. "Oh oh!" he cried in apology, "I thought you were Indu come home early from the office. She was very anxious about me when she left."

But he quickly recovered and began to compliment Dipti on her appearance. She was dressed in pale torquoise silk with little spangles sewn on in the shape of flowers; she also wore a pair of long gold earrings set with precious stones—"Are they rubies?" Raju admired them. "All set around a lovely pearl. They say that older women should wear pearls, here, around their throat," he touched the woolen scarf, "but I love to see them on a young girl."

"You could go back to bed," Arun suggested.

"And leave you alone here with this pearl?" A flush like dawn had tinted Dipti's face and neck. "Anyway, I feel much better. Completely cured by the sight of beauty, which is the best medicine in the world for a poor susceptible person like myself. I don't have a heart," he informed Dipti, "I have a frail shivering bird in here, drenched by the rains and storms of passion."

Arun exclaimed impatiently, but when he saw Dipti, still freshly flushed, smile at Raju's extravagance, irritation with his father turned to anger against Dipti. "You should ask her some more about those earrings," he said. "Ask her if they're her wedding jewelry—" Her flush now a deepest rose, Dipti's hands flew to her ears. "What was he doing there yesterday with you and your mother," he challenged her more harshly, "what had he come to sell?"

"Whatever they are," Raju said, "she's come here wearing them for you. I wish I could say it were for me, but even I'm not such a conceited optimist. But I'm really feeling much better, and I think I might just lie and rest here a little bit on this couch! won't disturb you at all—I'll shut my eyes, and I shall probably be fast asleep in a minute. But if you're afraid of waking me, you could go in the other room and keep very quiet in there."

He did exactly what he said—stretched himself on the couch and shut his eyes, so that they could think of him as fast asleep. But they had no time to think of anything—before they had even got into the next room, Arun was already tugging at her beautiful clothes, and she was helping him. It was many weeks since they had last been together, and they were desperate. Their youth, their lust, and their love overflowed in them, so that their lovemaking was like that of young gods. It is not in the nature of young gods to curtail their activities, and they forgot about keeping quiet and not disturbing Raju.

He *was* disturbed, but in a way he liked tremendously. He lay on the couch, partly listening to what was going on next door but mostly in his own thoughts. These made him happy—for the young people in the bedroom, of course, and for *all* young people, and these included himself. Raju was nearly forty, he did not have an easy life—he told no one about the many shifts he had to resort to in Bombay, to keep himself going in between assignments, which often fell through, or were never paid for. Nevertheless, he had not changed from the time he had been a student in Delhi and used to creep up to the roof of Indu's parents' house. She often had to put her hand over his mouth to keep him from waking everyone up, for in his supreme happiness he could not refrain from singing out loud—he knew all the popular hits as well as more refined Urdu lyrics, and they all exactly expressed what he felt, about her, and the stars above them, and the white moonlight and scent of jasmine drenching the air around them.

But now the sounds from the next room changed: Raju propped himself up on his elbow. "I'll tear them off!" his son was saying. He was back on the subject of the earrings. The girl screamed—Raju sprang up, ready to intervene: he knew there was something in his son that was not in himself—a bitter anger, perhaps transmitted to him by his mother during the years she had struggled to make a living for both of them. But somehow the girl pacified him, or it may have been his own feeling for her that made him hold his hand. She pleaded—"What else could I do? Arun, what could I do? With all that was happening, and Daddy's illness."

"You wanted it yourself. Because they're rich. Ah, don't touch me."

"Yes they're rich. They can help Daddy."

"Who are they anyway?"

She hesitated for a moment before replying: "They're Daddy's friends." He had to insist several times for a more definite answer before she came out with the name. Then Arun said: "Great. Wonderful." And Raju too on the other side of the wall was shocked: for the name she had mentioned was that of a tremendously wealthy family, notorious for their smuggling and other underworld activities and involved in several political scandals, including that of Dipti's father.

Dipti said with a touch of defiance: "They helped us when there was no one else." But her voice trembled in a way that made Raju's heart tremble too; but not Arun's, who continued to speak harshly: "And you're madly in love with the boy. . . . Why don't you answer!"

"I've met him twice. Arun, don't! I'll take them off. Here." She unhooked the earrings before he could tug at them again. He flung them across the room. One of them rolled under the partitioning curtain into the next room. Raju looked at it lying there but did not pick it up.

Arun said, "It's like selling yourself. It *is* selling yourself."

Again she spoke defiantly: "As long as it helps my parents in their trouble."

"Yes and what about being a college lecturer? That was just talk. All you want is to be rich and buy jewelry and eat those horrible cream cakes."

After a while she said in a very quiet voice, "That's not what I want."

"Then what? Don't try and fool me. I know you like no one else knows you. Like no one else ever will know you. You can never forget me. Never. Never."

"No. I shall never forget you." Then she broke out: "But what can I do, Arun! You tell me: what else can I do!"

And on the other side of the curtain, Raju's heart was fit to burst, and it was all he could do not to cry out to Arun: "Tell her!" He was almost tempted to show him—ah, with what abandon Raju himself would have acted in his son's place, how he would have flung himself at the girl's feet and cried: "I'm here! Marry me! I'm yours forever!"

But Arun was saying something different. "I'll haunt you like a ghost. You'll keep reading about me in the newspapers because I'm going to be very famous. If necessary, I'll go into politics to clean up our country from all these corrupt politicians and smugglers who are sucking it dry. You'll see. You'll see what I'll do."

"I have to go. Let me get dressed."

"Not yet. Five minutes. Ten."

Then there was no more talking and almost complete silence in the bedroom, so that when Indu came home, she didn't know anyone was in there and said to Raju, "Why aren't you in bed?"

He laid a finger on his lips and glanced toward the other room. She followed his eyes and gasped when she saw the earring that had rolled from under the curtain. "Sh-sh-sh," said Raju.

"He's got that girl in there," Indu whispered fiercely.

"You needn't worry."

"What do you mean not worry? His finals are next week."

"Oh he'll do very well. He's your son; and your father's grandson."

And for the hundredth time in their life she said, "Thank God anyway that he hasn't taken after you. Let go of me. Let go." For he had seized her in his arms and pressed his lips against hers—she thought at first it was to silence her but relaxed as his kiss became more pressing and more passionate: as if he wanted to make it up to her for his shortcomings, and then, giving himself over completely, to make it up to all women for the shortcomings of all men.

Three Poems

Charlie Smith

Honesty

Maybe Anna won't arrive.
Maybe mordant self-concern will become love.
O you who know things
never change. I imagine
E. A. Poe kissing his childbride, thirteen year old girl
her mother standing in for his mother
sweet tempered raking roast potatoes from the fire,
and shiver with tension and morbidity.
He was appalled by loneliness
by scary apartness, shuddering with resentment
and an alarming sense of smothering.
He lived a while in a bee glade,
high on the island, in NYC.
Anna is
Anna Karenina. Maybe
she won't reach the station.
I used to think the fact my
crazy mother was still alive
meant there was hope. A fool's notion.
She became unreachable
long ago.
In the untidy southern village I come from
this is not unusual.
People are set.
Vietnam was so great, my friend says,
because folks who would never
get a chance to change their minds, did.
Like my friend's father fat ex-Air Force sergeant

who at last, weeping at the grave,
cried Please God end this, it's no good.
Not the *end this* important, but the *it's no good.*
A change of heart.
Not Vronsky saying okay
I didn't mean it, forget the war,
I love you let's get married raise a family,
but Anna.
It's no good. And Edgar Poe,
this weeping into my hat, tugging the sleeve
of a dead childwoman: It's no good.

Once in my junkie days I kept a cattle herd.
It was winter in the mountains,
prohibitive, rage like a canvas shirt caked in ice,
I pushed hay bales out of a truck.
The cows, fretful women,
their bony hips, moaning, snotty,
when they snuffled up
I'd punch them in the face.
I wanted to punch
my wife
and the side of the mountain
and my life snarled like a deer in a fence.
I was filled with longing
for joyful permanent fixations, and insight,
for play and a secular individualism,
a spiritual life and some unnameable
opportunity like a right I vaguely
remembered and couldn't get purchase on.
It was no good.
It took me years and one mistake
after another to realize this
and even then I simply got washed out,
put aside
I didn't really learn a lesson.
I know it's not so much the mistakes
not the divisions, or cultural impediments,
the threats and isolation techniques
we run on each other

it's the heart. The nutty way we grip
and won't let go, and the way,
despite what they tell us, My father went to his grave unchanged.
So did Poe.
And beautiful Anna Karenina.
And Ovid. Consuela Concepcion, too, my piano teacher.
They say in the end
Mussolini was so terrified his mind seized and he couldn't speak.
He sat there swelled-up and bug-eyed. This is not it.
Or anyone drowning or
lurching from the fire shrieking he didn't want this to happen.
There is so much gibberish. And imprecision.
No wonder we lock in.
Like you, I get scared.
I used to go to my friend's house,
sink into the old sofa on his back porch
and read all day. His family
and the ducks and dogs would pass by,
let me be—discreet love—I'd feel safe.
It was just after I stumbled out of my marriage,
grieving and
struck dumb, war paint still streaking my face.
My friend practiced a religion
remarkable in its narrow-mindedness. He inserted
his children into this olla-podrida
like a man stuffing leaves into a shoe.
It hurt to see it.
Broken saddle bronc of a beautiful face he had
and his wife a slim twist of blonde girl cunning
and fretful without shame
about anything—I spoke up eventually and got tossed.

I've spent years watching television.
I lie on the couch
eating chocolate and watching television,
arguing with some woman in my head.
Television says the world is not a mysterious place.
Don't worry, it says,
you don't have to change a thing.
And then I remember digging wild leeks,

buying eggs from a crippled old lady
who glanced into the next room sadly
as if a great novelist was dying in there,
and went on
talking, like Kissinger after the war.
And how scary things became when my wife
got up close. Change of heart.
Love leeching the lining away, exposing the pulp.
Stupidity and malice
and a fitful generosity,
shortsightedness and painful posturing,
tenderness, hope,
consideration like a coconut cake left anonymously,
and things continue just as they are,
nut cases, disputes,
overbearing stupid claims, modernity hamming it up,
life someone says only a device for entering other realms
—all these in the hopper.
And the tough decisions.
Poe dreaming of a cold finger
picking the lock. Anna stuffing screams back down.
Let go, or stay with it?
The Dali Lama saying *Sure, sure, I'll take the sprouts,*
including the Chinese in everything.
My girl friend stunned by the power of her own rage,
nothing she can do about it yet,
rebuking paradise, groping for the dog.

Beautyworks

. . . all kinds of beauty in the world dense pressed-down spots in grass,
crabapples scattered on a white sidewalk let me name them,
shadows draped across yellowing lawns, my wife
standing in a barrel to be photographed pretending to scream
is beautiful, my friend who paints with a table knife
endless solid scenes of light, light on the other side of red warehouses,
light in trees preparing the solution to life, light and misrepresentations of light,
and light behind the garage sale and stumbling down a ditch at dawn
such is beauty, and includes dependable father and son collection agencies
and my mother who went crazy, asking for "a little bit,
just a little bit," and a soldier's sudden refusal, copra plantations
and old bomb holes grown up in snakes and yellow flowers,
a lobbyist weeping over his father's cancer,
disputes that never get settled but go on for generations
as a kind of ethnic memory—Moslems never forgiving Christians
for Jerusalem 1099, for example—beauty's like this unmanned vehicle,
revamped and outhustled by sordid notions, capacious,
a lingerer at parties, last to get the taste of love out of its mouth,
a friend locked up for his own good, another
sketching naked men, wrestling with his conscience, consortiums
dispersing into colorful anecdotes, frailty of all kinds as if beauty
were erasable, walks on the beach
pondering the uselessness of existence, the endless variety of the natural world
always on the other side of conciousness, no way . . . this is beauty . . .
to understand a thing about it—

Flowers of Manhattan

. . . early morning petal-strewn sidewalks of Manhattan,
honey locust, buckeye, hickory flowers, exotic blooms
from the Korean groceries blown onto sidewalks,
small pale purple scoops and pink delicate purses,
shreds, loops, curled ribbbons of magnolia, spikes
and bells, scrawls, clusters of slightly hairy tiny yellow globes . . .
early morning advocacy of life . . . the left side of a walnut tree
glimpsed between ugly ochre buildings, starry petals
of blackberry flowers and the brushy swabs of horse chestnut.
Beyond a clump of Chinese privet with its white flowers
sporting antennae-like sepals topped with gold tabs,
a bush with papery slightly rumpled leaves, an import
never mentioned by comedians or other show business types,
a slender black man takes off his shirt. His skin is smooth
and unmarked has a deep dusty shine to it. He strokes his chest,
places his hands flat on his breasts and smiles to himself.
He stands under an empress tree just now shedding its
bell-shaped, unequally lobed pale purple flowers
that are slightly fragrant, slightly spicy, soft
to the touch (*a handsome, rapid growing colonial*)
speaking softly. I am overcome suddenly with a desire to
throw my body into the mass of hawthorn flowers
piled up in a bush beside the crooked stone wall. Elders
and black haws, frothy white, are in bloom.
The stately candelabra of the buckeye appear white,
but close up have a yellow cast and are spiked with gold
flanges and smeared with a slightly russet dye. Just now
a woman in wide blue shorts went by screaming. She
carried a sprig of tasseling pine, or this is simply
what I say she carried. I look away from life
for one second and it spurts ahead so suddenly I am bereft
a child abandoned on the trail. There's a whole tree
I don't know the name of shaggy and set upon by white blossoms
like a huge blanket or toupee draping the crest and crown
sliding down the wind-pliant sides, fluttering slightly along the edges

incidentally. Across the island now tuberoses and petunias
have established their first flowerings. Wind stirs
the surface of ponds in Central Park, catches slightly
in various pools dammed against curbs and in low spots
near Sixth and Bleecker. A flare of leftover wild azalea,
the last to be seen this year in Manhattan,
deep in woods beyond the Ramble, flickers and goes out.
Ecstatic thoughts, simple phrases spoken casually but
veering abruptly toward insanity, hearts broken in two,
the mind pushed beyond what it can take, continue as usual.
Spring pounds on the doors. A boy sweeping the sidewalk stops,
makes a fist and throws punches at the air. Love's no secret now.

Three Poems

Rachel Hadas

Recycling

If from ruined Tara's draperies
Scarlett O'Hara made herself a gown;
if at Bryn Mawr during the Depression
my mother's classmates used to sew their own

skirts out of curtains; and if the long rugs
Samian women used to weave for us
contained rag strips I'd cut out of my old
blue jeans or nightgown or flowered sun dress,

then I'm just carrying on a long tradition,
since everything I can reuse I will,
as long as it is paper: index cards,
jiffy bags, folders, bluebooks by the pile.

Any twice-used index card will tell
two stories, thanks to Janus, one per side.
Turned over, today's shopping list recites
the names of poems and just where I tried

to publish them in 1975;
Columbia admissions information
(my mother used to work for them part-time);
or bibliography for my dissertation.

Rough drafts of poems, essays, book reviews;
manuscripts sent by many a trusting friend;
contest entries, articles, exams—
of paper there will never be an end.

I give some to the super. Quite a lot
I keep as drawing paper for my son.
Some I dump into the recycling bin.
Some I cut up and put beside the phone.

Index cards, bookmarks, and matchbook covers—
any heavy stock—my father used to shred
to straw-sized markers for the text in use,
a practice I seem to have inherited,

recycling thus the habit of recycling,
approximating printed matter to
something like compost—an economy
by precept or example learned from you,

Daddy. Of course not every paper's sliced.
Jiffy-bags are sent back whence they came,
into the world to someone else's desk.
My favorite recycling, though, stays home.

Flocks of manila folders drift my way,
shedding the contents of their former selves—
courses I've taught, my mother's tax returns
but most of all from my friend Charlie's shelves.

His clipping files on writers he adored
no one could bring themselves to throw away.
His poetry collection came to me,
these folders tucked inside it like a stowaway.

I weeded through the clippings; earned the right
to toss each separate yellowing review,
but kept the folders, heavy, clean, and marked
in the loose clear printing that I knew

Sylvia Townsend Warner, Reynolds Price,
Williams and *Auden, Sarton* and *Vidal* . . .
Our tastes, not coinciding, overlapped
for far more folders than I can recall.

Here was recycling! Shorthand, slim, compact,
whole oeuvres signified by name alone,
each folder a synecdoche for worlds
my friend had loved to dwell in. He is gone

and incorporeal now, like literature.
Books too fat to fit in folders still
endure as reference, memory, and love,
recycled, feather-light, perennial.

Humble Herb is Rival to Prozac

In memory of my mother

An item in *Science Tuesday* happens to catch my eye.
A woman in Germany
(it seems that she is only one of many)
having been drinking several cups a day
of Saint John's Wort brewed into tea
reports *The fear*
that everything good would disappear
has stopped.

Reading this, I seem to see
something shiny, peeling: elderly
Scotch tape, no longer strong enough to keep
the little sprigs in place, maintain the shape
of wild flowers picked and pressed
(though not pressed long enough to be quite flat—
even at five years old I probably
found time too slow:
"Those flowers must be all pressed flat by now!")
and taped into the pages of a smallish spiral notebook,
whose khaki cover
bulges with still bulky flower after flower.

Open the notebook. Turn the freighted page:
buttercup, clover, yarrow brown with age
or else pellucid—fragile either way.
Time has not only thoroughly discolored
the contents of this makeshift album, but
has begun the task of disassembling.
Delicate petals grow
amber-veined and clear;
tough little stalks now show
their pith; the tiny, no

longer yolk-gold tubelets
that form the daisy's eye
have gradually begun to come apart
and one by one escape
the sagging tape,
meander down the page
like stray eyelashes, like fluffs of lint.
Black-eyed Susan, Queen Anne's Lace,
found, picked, pressed, taped, and labelled;
aster, devil's paintbrush, everlasting,
St. John's Wort. Even then
I knew—I think I knew—this last-named flower
was rarer than the others. Knew it how?
Because she showed me the reliably
five-petalled pale gold blossoms. Naturally,
knowing nothing, I had to be taught
every flower's name,
though probably I thought
Solomon's-seal, vetch, mullein, morning glory
were transparently my birthright,
as if all flowers hadn't come to me
through her who guided my unsteadily
printing pencil (1953);
whose disappearance (1992)
never made me fear
that everything good would disappear,
but teaches me, if anything, again
a lesson that each year I must relearn,
the renewable epiphany
of vanishing and then recovery.

The little notebook with my staggering
pencilled captions labelling
every blessed thing,
picked and pressed and anchored to the page,
recording the first summer I remember;
her long full skirts, their cotton prints, the florals and batiks,
my clinging at knee level,
or her bending over
or leading me to the cowfield, where clover

and thyme attracted hordes of noisy bees,
showing me where this and that plant grew,
their names, and how to write them,
enlisting me in the whole enterprise
of writing, how to press a summer flat
between the pages of a heavy book—
what storage! what retrieval! what an arc
from something tiny as a daisy's eye
to something vast, too nebulous to hold—
the trail from recollection to invention
blazed and reblazed of necessity,
since memory can take us
only so far before it lets us down.

That bulgy little notebook
vanished years ago
and I no longer care
whether or not I find it.
Probably it's gathering
(even as it turns to) dust somewhere.
But laws of leaf and stem and petal hold:
what seems sheer desiccation
unlocks its stored, distilled
power into this brew,
this brimming mug whose steam
wreathes the lonely air:
Courage. Nothing good will disappear.

Bedtime Stories

In Key West I visited D.J.
Naked, the old man smoked in bed all day.
And what was he to me?
I wept as I sat with him for an hour
chatting about the future and the past—
partly for him, but more
for someone he'd improbably survived.
Of course there was also the memory
of D's kindness thirty years before
in Athens, where he helped me find a job
and an apartment, even lent me sheets.
I sat with him, tears running down my face
for someone else. Oh, love is all displaced.

In various hospitals, in their apartments,
I visited four, five, six dying men.
And what were they to me?
Poetry students. And I to them?
Teacher, colleague, one more local friend—
the chitchat of the living. Even so,
conversation labored toward the end,
limping as unilateral dialogues do.
Talking to D.J. was like that too,
or yearly visits to my mother-in-law:
answering a question no one's asked
while a dumb monster presses its dull mass
against the window. Love is all displaced.

Dan, at Cabrini, talked and laughed and sang,
but that was several months before the end.
Diapered neatly, Tony lay at home
on the bottom bunk. I tried to tell him
about a play I'd seen. He tried to nod.
Or did he? Michael squeezed my hand. Or did he?
In Sloane-Kettering, James for the first time

sounded afraid. A bastion of pillows
propping Charlie up on my last visit
kept threatening to topple. As I was leaving,
his parents hurried in fresh from the airport.
I folded my grief small to give theirs space
as our paths crossed. Oh, love is all displaced.

His somber loneliness a smoky blaze,
an elderly heart surgeon falls for me.
He stares all through my talk on poetry,
asks me for Christmas cocktails at the Plaza—
how can I know—it's summer—I'll be busy then?
My middle age—my fragrant youth, for him—
is mesmerized months later, moth to flame,
by a man young enough to be my son—
teaches my son guitar, is twenty-four,
looks like a Quattrocento lutanist.
Romantic comedy? The prickly taste
of farce? Blind Cupid's arrow in each breast?
Whichever, love is once again displaced.

Am I saying all love wears a mask?
That buried motivations spur us on?
That our affection goes out to a ghost
and making do with substitution
restores the lost original? I never
sat beside my dying father's bed,
so maybe I'm condemned to search forever
for old, bedridden, or just any men
with whom to carry on the conversation
peculiar to farewells. My father teased
my mother for her flirting with old men
(other than him, that is). But she had lost
her father at age two. Love's all displaced.

Stuffed animals and guitar magazines
layer the bottom bunk where sprawls a boy.
I part the rubble, pull a chair up, read.
And what is he to me?
This dyad has a nametag: Mother/Son—

label so clear and simple it will soon
fade to a spurious transparency,
as if the natural were here alone,
as if all other ties were second best.
So that when he turns his back upon
this cluttered kingdom (amplifier, lion,
magic cards), it will be on a quest
in search of what if not this love displaced?

Three Poems

Pimone Triplett

Stillborn

Mother, here's what the night offers: silence,
        a tree with no bird, four unlit lamps, one sink's
empty bowl, and my closets packed with the spilt,
        open mouths of shoes. I'm up again at 3 A.M.,
one year past the age you made me. Inside
        my small apartment, a sleeve of winged
ants spun from the day's heat has expired
        by now. I brush their bodies, cramped as raisins,
from the windowsill. . . . A moment ago, hearing
        a rumbling truck's distant effort
to take the upgrade, and then nothing,
        I saw the black of an oak tree outside
set against the lesser dark of a city-lit
        sky, and hated its outline of absence.
Or not hated, *feared becoming*. Look, even if I want
        to write the names of everyone
I love on the dark, I still can't say

I know or understand the poverty
        of your grief that summer just like this one
when the doctor, knowing the baby inside
        you—the one before me—was dead, sent you home
without saying anything was wrong. Later,
        you said, he spoke to the husband—my father,
although that wasn't to be for years—
        because he thought the right man should break the news
gently. And tonight I keep picturing
        your interim hours, vacuuming

the carpet, turning the TV on, then off,
      then on again, reaching that much wider
past the couch, making way for your laden midriff.
      Meanwhile, the truth in the room with you,
not yet spoken, a nothing you couldn't know
      your body still wrapped itself around. . . .

Until he came home. Until the long car ride
      to the hospital for shots that could lift
your mind from consciousness and the final
      suction. Afterward, I can see you
walking through the sorrow of those days,
      threading the Washington parks. The late
August there spawns so many traces
      of gray that color's ghosted, a wish
you've given up on. I've thought of you each
      stepping through that mud, avoiding
the dropped pods of magnolia, the paths'
      thinning sprays of crepe myrtle,
not speaking of the phantom child
      you would also have named "Pimone,"
my sibling, my slanted self,
      already the unborn fact of his male sex
wasted by then, part seahorse,
      part flattened snail, a damp-rotted tuber.

I wish we could tell one another
      what it is the stubborn flesh asks of us.
For now, all the issue I can offer
      is to dedicate the silence of this night
to you and the shadow child who wasn't
      let to swim for the shore of his own voice,
the one who taught how little you could get
      from the botched scrawl of matter. . . . Mother,
on a blank page, in elegy, everyday,
      I could write my name and erase it.
It's six o'clock. A few new ants furrow
      the sill's cracks and outside, sunrise,

another one, leeches in through the oak limbs.
    If I look up, the windowpane,
transparent, gives me back my face.
    Enough, Mother. Almost enough.

Harriet Smithson Berlioz, a Letter to Her Husband

25 Oct 1844
Rue Blanche 43

My dearest Hector,

I take shame on myself that I was not
in any kind of tolerable health
to meet you Sunday last, as I stare now
in rapt constancy at your parting gift.
     Where did you ever conjure
     forth such a youthful likeness
of me, my one love, this Ardor clinging
to the solemn lines of gray lithograph?
Since lately, you'd admit, we seem to lose,
with our usual fury, each grace note
     we once had, how, or rather,
     who, could have entreated you
to keep such a thing? Of course, I'm grateful
for passion of any variety,
even sorrow, these days, and it's a fine
frame for the memory of who I was.
     I think I'll keep it beside
     the bed, next to the silver
combs and brushes you also gave me—when,
dear? At any rate, adding up so few
francs over the years, I do hate to think
of the many you've wasted for my sake. . . .
     Still, I can see in this print
     of me—Ophelia again—
quite the best note I ever struck onstage—
a kind of grief I'd rather not relive
these days. And as for losing one's Graces
well, I find coughing claims all of me now,
     though with no one to witness

my swift descent I half drown
in Doctor's potions by day, just to find
how loudly they clang me awake by night!
So Hector, for the sake of your music,
and my mind, you must be sure the next girl
        you take to yourself is good . . .
        Yes, in spite of my wishing
her dead, no doubt, before sealing this note.
But then, you have lived with such fantasies,
and know justice is not responsible
to nightmare, much less daydream. . . . And besides,
        no one would be there to see
        my last, grand, murderous scene,
and I quite agree with whoever said,
other countries assemble spectators,
while an audience comes only in France.
I know that has been your problem as well.
        You are terribly right in
        lamenting the twaddle that
passes for talent these days. I don't go
to the theater at all now, that vast
spectacle of third-rate imitators!
Instead, I've taken to sitting evenings
        in our library. Although,
        as you know, I never was
much of a reader, the books themselves can
be so decorative, and there is comfort
in having at least some of your music
volumes still here . . . How is your work, my dear?
        I do take blame on myself
        for all that's happened, Hector,
since no doubt my own jealousies drove you
to prove them true, or else my harangues' pitch
sent you to the damped quiet of your safe,
if unsaintly, infidelities. Still,
        I trust you know that for your
        real Genius I'd have you risk
everything. Even in your symphony
for me (the one that wedded me to you
entirely, long ago), in that spot

where the horns blast out of their infernal
        feathering, and the sweet dance
        turns into a witch's howl,
I imagine you can hear me there, dear,
and think how much that one crescendo lifts
to our lives' final anthem. I should say
I prefer the dulcet beginnings—string's
        note that shepherds in other
        ripplings—but I am not sure
it's true. They say music lets the soul know
time, but how ever were you able, love,
to find our undone future within it?
I suppose I owe all forms of myself
        lastly to you, and you're kind
        to bring me a splendid sketch
of the white bosom that once commanded
so much from you. Do make sure the next girl
you take on is quiet. I could help you
to keep her quiet. You know, I often
        sit through the long night's muffle,
        just combing my hair slowly. . . .
Tell me, am I a note stamped to the page,
or only the ringing of it, dwindling
off? Write to me soon, say why all the sounds
I once moved through, pursue me now, or you. . . ?

Your loving wife,

        Harriet

A Branch Between the Bones

1. Paul Klee in Exile

Caught, held between the joints, the sickness whispered
"no room," the once spun-silk of his tissues
tightening to less and still less, his own bones
brittle as branches riddled with the buildup

of days. Meanwhile, the cause went on within him—
sclerosis—its classic symptom "a hard
shiny skin, giving the face a masklike
appearance," that stilled. And in his mind, always

the memory of the frame's *once upon a time*,
a pencil skritch on a bare white page, always
the clock-faced clown laughing behind the witch's
house, skidding past the world's first fish . . .

In his fury, dozens of sketches a day falling
to the floor. Time, what he had left of it,
scrawling at him, quickly, etching a way in,
even as he did, making stick and line,

stripping the skin too clean, each saying to each:
"you are the gristle thinning, you are the silence I grind."

2. Mother and Daughter Reading

Happens just once, that fable, the taking of the mother's body,
    cells and their plot every daughter has to learn.

Her illness still innocent then, story within
    the story thickening, muscling up in the limbs,

a secret name you have to inherit. And I can see them,
    back in the small room I hold inside me—

sunlight's clot in the red carpet, the corner's
    stone white chest I once climbed into,

couldn't get out of. As she read, her leg's
    twist and curl, fatigue's command, joints

loosening, nerves scoured, her bundled fibers'
    writhe at end of day. And in the fairy tale,

her voice begins, saying *give me back my bone*.
    Time I asked who among us died and of what,

she named them all afternoon, couldn't stop the listing
    of hard words, the people they mastered, came to own,

each a bone rising from the gully of her mouth,
    up from matrix and marrow. She held her hand

to my arm. From the window, a tree's shadow
    now and then, the branch's claim laying skeleton

to her face, her mask, that stillness, shining. Then the voice,
    hers, louder, saying *give me back my bone*.

Then her hand held *into* my arm, harder . . .
    a clot in the red. . . . Until after a while I saw, underneath,

the shared joints between us, canals of blood,
    clefts denuded, striations amid the plates,

each of us falling through the room, its stain,
     through the heat of her hand, heat of her body scripted

in mine. Later, we made believe her frame was nothing to me.
     Later, made believe her shape was just another place.

3. Amputation

Happened because he wanted to move forward.
One foot on the brake, one on the gas.
First the tree, the high branch,
then his car rolling over.
Grinding blare of a moment, a cramp of metal on bone.

Then came the stop-time, second that owned him
forever after, that rip.
As in *once upon a time*,
a spot where the story keeps recurring, without ending . . .

And if we say this glaze of mind over place
is memory, then what?
There was a boy I knew, one that I'd held.
A window opened

and I climbed through it
because he asked me to.
I bundled the bed with a shape like my shape,
stole away.

Hours after I left him, the accident.
In his memory of the event, a voice saying
hide your arm,
saying, *hide that piece of meat.*

Later, I went to the hospital, wanting to see him.

Happened because he wanted to move

My wanting to see what we'd stolen that night, the proof.

(*No one* warned me, no advance)
The sponged shafts, the cartilage like ground glass.

Happened because he wanted to

I ran through the bare white halls,
past the nurse's station,
her pencil's skritch on a page. . .

Happened because he wanted

(*No one* told me the story)

I went in. There, in his privacy,
behind the screen,
the boy's face
like a clock, but laughing,

drugged, his arm hewn to stump

(*no one* told me)
the hand I'd held, shorn now,
the hand I'd held

(they had to leave it on the street)

And then the mask he wore,
a blank, shining,
asking to be touched when

I couldn't touch him by then.

The story, unswerving, trundles to its end,

takes the body
that must be taken away.

Still, the first face I held
(bone against bone).

Or it was the bone that held me
(*no one*),
Or else it was the bone that held us both
        (*and no one*).

4. Withstanding

In the sketch, here's where his angel can't stop
    remembering,
caught in a crux of white and its scrawl,
    a skinflint's
dance of ink around the empty.
    So what, Klee might have thought, if
somewhere his own country shawled its shoulders
    over an ash heap,
huddled to a fire's dung? In the end all he wanted
    were his skeletal lines,
the desert he made between them, the page
    almost barren, branch
hewn to stump, to stiver. As for the angel's face,
    he wanted her held
tight, held down, trying to trace
    the skin *beneath*
the skin, the hide of memory, the one that has no name.
    All day, sound of a pencil's
skritch on a bare . . . on a white . . .
    wall I once looked up into
while trying to make
    love to someone I didn't love but wished to,
staring down that empty story.
    Saw the naked face of plaster framing
our furious rubbing into one another and hated
    its blankness,
my wanting to force his face against it,
    press the white to white,
one mask to the first mask that he wore, hard, shiny,
    the mouth open, unreal.
In the morning, I woke to see
    a branch's shadow unbroken, its skeletal claw
laid to the wall,
    then its hand spilt on the bed between us. Dividing,
part thickening tendril,
    part outline of absence. He must have seen the same thing.
I couldn't ever master the art

of giving up touch, the line and its ending,
a skritch for each half-kiss,
  that faithful. Leaving, I tried to put the mask back on,
a face stretched
  clean of desire, unmoving, that stillness pillared
to itself. He stayed at the window
  above me, watching. As I stepped out into a day scrawled
wild with branches,
  canals, the channels all fibrous, the knots unnumbered,
I couldn't trace the limbs
  and their limits, the morning starting to burn,
couldn't stop walking,
  though it was everything not to look back,
everything not to look up between
  the branches, up into that sky going the color of bone.

Sayings of Ernesto B.

Judith Grossman

Your Thomas More was a failure—a failure, understand? Why? Because 'e let 'imself be trapped. Executed, understand? There's no point in teaching the failures of history: I, myself, never wasted much time on Thomas More.

Such passion in his mentor's voice, such a need to be heard, exacts from Terry a response at odds with the private one (Look, I *know* about More—I'm a historian too, remember? and anyway how are we defining "failure"?).

"Well," he says after a moment, "I can understand that."

Ernesto sits back in his chair, appeased.

The story goes that as a young man, Ernesto had to leave Spain in a hurry, after taking his Master's degree from Barcelona. Easy to imagine problems for a Catalan, with Franco in power: he must've learned a hard lesson.

But let's see, Terry thinks, aside from the general wisdom aspect, of what is all this *apropos*?

The reason he stopped at Ernesto's office, before the meeting upstairs, was to request funding for a second E.S.L. section next fall. Clearly they should offer it, since Willard Lake's actively recruiting more students from Japan, with marginal English skills. Likewise from the Middle East, Colombia, and the rest of Latin America. Typically these are kids from rich, but somehow déclassé families. Admissions has tapped into some Japanese "untouchable" caste network, ineligible apparently for home institutions. One of their exquisite girls floats about in beaded dresses under an ankle-length lynx fur coat—that's the kind of money they have.

As for the Latins, the crass speculation is they're from middle-management drug industry background. That's better, in any case, than this year's influx of home-grown psychotics, recruited from hospital exit wards. Among these there have been eight emergency commitments so far—even the psych. ward over in Laconia has registered a protest. It was Ernesto who let fall that the Latins often paid for the semester in cash, up front. They come right into his office and count it out in hundred dollar bills on the desk. The President loves it—and again, Terry can see his point, given the collection problems elsewhere, like from New York City welfare.

But with only fifteen E.S.L. spots available, the foreign kids are failing Eng. 101 at a terrible rate. He has the figures from Carole, the chair.

"Carole is *rash*, understand?" Ernesto resumes.

Oh now he gets it, Ernesto's reacting to the source of his request: Carole.

"You have to watch out in that quarter—she craves authority, so she makes decisions like that!" He snaps his fingers in a crisp movement. "With Carole, it's all on impulse. Not a wise person."

"Well, why don't I get the registrar's figures and check back with you?"

Terry has a sinking feeling. Nobody, not even Carole, is going to push for this. Yet it's so simple—just shifting around part-time assignments. At most, a tiny increase in cost, from the smaller sections. But the moment anyone around here mentions "cost," the shit hits.

Ernesto goes ahead to open the door, then pauses with one hand on the knob, the other beckoning him close. The Gaze locks on—another saying impends.

The amazing thing about Howard, Terry, is this (cough). *He's always thinking two steps ahead of the faculty. Not just one. Two steps ahead.*

Terry couldn't say it's a phenomenon he's noticed. But maybe that's the whole point: that after six months in this job he still hasn't caught on to the President's thinking-ahead powers. Assistant Deans are three-quarters faculty members, by workload—*ergo*, three parts moron, one part tea-boy. And Terry's the newest among them, promoted from History (European/World), where he was hanging on to a full-time job by his fingernails. Then Anita (Eng.), the previous Assistant Dean, took a sudden leave of absence last June, and Ernesto called him up. The promotion was Howard's decision, he emphasized, but he'd personally recommended it.

Since then, Ernesto has appointed himself Terry's mentor. First, Terry thinks, because they're both hapless Euro-immigrants, here in *la Nouvelle Hampshire profonde:* living free or dying. And second, in the hope of ending twenty years of solitude at Willard Lake, which must feel to him like the entire hundred, being (as he is) only too aware how the faculty despise him for his absolute subjection to Howard. The *padron*, a man so obviously his proper subordinate in all respects, jumped up from his blue-blazer slot in Admissions by right of marriage to Our Late Founder's granddaughter, Phyllis. A strange case, that. But it raises the likelihood that Howard thought two steps ahead of Our Founder, Spencer Devine, and also his son Spencer II (now "Chancellor" Devine). Hm.

They join the clot of Assistant Deans at the top of the stairs, Ernesto knocks at Howard's door, and they enter. Ernesto sits at the right hand of the *padron;* the rest line up on chairs against the wall.

And to be sure, Terry reflects, Howard despite that fiberglass-molded face may more closely resemble a Whole Man than the rest of them. Ernesto—well, like Terry himself only more so, he'll always be an alien, with that high, despairing Mediterranean profile, the hair combed straight back. And the rest of them: everyone knows George (M.Ed.), who runs Science/Health, was fired "for cause" from some high-school down in Massachusetts; and Kathy, Ed. D., is handicapped by braces from childhood polio. Bernard (who knows for sure, but he's Mr. Business Management) stands about five-two and must weigh three hundred pounds. Gary (Master's in Art/Design) has a riveting array of facial tics and, they say, survives on high-dose lithium between vacation visits to McLean's Hospital.

There's a memory hovering at the edge of his mind. Of course, it was Hitler who had a personal staff notable for its egregious oddities: club-footed Goebbels, the monocular Rohm, the stone-deaf PR chief, plus the various addicts. And wasn't Hitler's all-time favorite film *Snow White and the Seven Dwarfs?*

Howard starts talking. Oh but wait a second—he's got, yes, a *book* on his desk! Terry tips his head and reads the title. It is George Gilder's *Wealth and Poverty.*

Ernesto has raised a point, proposed something for the agenda. Howard exerts Instant Leadership and cuts him off. "No, we can't discuss that now."

"Of course not Howard, sure, just a suggestion, you know?"

Howard announces that he can only stay for ten minutes of the meeting, but here's the gist: enrollment estimates he's gotten from Admissions are down fifteen percent from February last year. Fifteen percent! Which, along with the projected ongoing decline in high school graduates across the Northeast region, means he's going to have to ask for faculty retrenchments, effective this June. Approximately, fifteen percent across the board.

George, sitting across from Terry, catches his destroyed expression, and purses his lips in mock commiseration, as if to say well, it's all a farce anyway, this academia biz.

"We'll have a follow-up meeting next week, with Bob here to represent Admissions. At that time, I'll ah—need your plans for achieving the, ah, fifteen percent goal."

Howard looks at his watch, has a private word with Ernesto, then leaves through the side door that only he and the Chancellor use. Terry notes he's wearing plaid trousers. Plaid? Looks like a golfing date.

There's silence in the room, until Kathy says, in a seething voice: "What's the matter, can't he stand us for even *ten minutes* now? Drops a bomb on us, like that? Then he just takes off?"

Ernesto sets a time for the next meeting, without comment, and hands round a sheet of announcements. They file out, thinking, Terry assumes, exactly what he's thinking: who'll have to go, who are the vulnerable?

The first name coming up from his list is the one that hurts most. Frank Larsen, whom he'd brought in on a one-year contract, to staff World History sections previously taught by himself and a part-timer who resigned. Frank has quickly proved himself the best teacher on Terry's staff, and the most active intellectual; plus he's a Vietnam vet with a wife and child. But the numbers in History 101 haven't held up—kids want the American option, 'cause they've done it in high school already, and there's less reading. A no-brainer.

How many victims must he find? What's fifteen percent of fourteen? He does the rough math, and makes it 2.1. But since the School of Liberal Arts has the largest faculty group, Terry thinks they could be under pressure to give up three. The more numbers, Howard'll say, the more fat. Bernie and George have been tight with Howard for years: he'll go easy on them. But Kathy's people, and Gary's, and his, they'll pay full price.

The second cut, he'll need to take out of Carole's hide. English has by far the biggest department, they can always slot in more Comp. part-timers, and he'll make it up to her by squeezing that second ESL section out of Ernesto. Who it'll be, technically she decides, but he knows it has to be Matt. Everyone else has an M.A. or better; Matt has only the B.A., plus a year for state certification.

On the path skirting the frozen pond, half-swamp, that must have given Willard Lake its name, Terry recalls some remarks Carole made about Matt, when the two of them were at lunch in a corner of the cafeteria.

"Why does Matt have so many *moles* on his face? It's too *weird* for me! He has more *moles* than anybody I know! I'd run to a doctor if I had *moles* like that—you've seen the one with hairs sprouting on it, under his ear? Incidentally, I wish you could let him know he needs a stronger deodorant. *You're* a man, you could tell him. Couldn't you?"

But he couldn't. So, farewell Matt.

At the edge of the pine-grove, Terry catches sight of the large boulder against which, a few years ago, an executive from the adjacent office park leaned the hilt of a hunting-knife, and with a thrust (or two? three?) impaled himself between the ribs, to the heart. Live free and die.

Then he thinks: Matt's invested seven years in this place; moreover, his thirteen-year-old son (he's been divorced for a while) has recently moved in with him. The timing there could not be worse. And it's already February 1—how the hell are these poor bastards going to find jobs for next year? Terry'll ask for a year's extension, and as a piss-poor alternative he'll make sure they get first crack at part-time, Frank too.

Any third name would be Terry's call. Mounting the stairs of Blockwell Hall, named for Our Founder's dentist, Trustee and donor, he's thinking, yes: Sociology. No college of seven hundred students needs four sociologists. Setting aside the two lifers, Mike and Wendy, there's Debra Walsh, who's A.B.D., and also dates from before the institutional convulsion (which nobody has explained to him) during which tenure was abolished, a dozen years back. And there's Mark Price, a recent Ph.D. like himself, hired three years ago. Potentially tricky issue here, but all the better—he can throw it into Ernesto's lap for resolution.

The offices, except for English which has its own cluster in the basement with the Language Lab, are a warren of under-constructed modules inside a long attic space. Mark's office is next to Terry's, and passing it he sees those extra-large feet through the eighteen-inch opening at the base of the wall-board. The door's open.

"Hi there," Mark says.

Terry leans cautiously on the doorway's edge. He gets along with Mark. The man's genuinely bright, no question, and he wears these interesting socks—jade green, mauve, sky blue—that even connect with some shade in the shirt, tie, or jacket he's wearing that day. In fact, Mark has better style than anybody in the drab halls of Lib. Arts, except for the divinely slim Donna, She of the Raven Ringlets, the Velvet Leggings, and Supple Thigh-boots!—their incomparable part-timer in English who, passing in the corridor, inspires the ten-o'clock erection he treasures behind his briefcase every Tuesday and Thursday.

But he's never had a conversation with Mark that didn't turn conspiratorial within seconds.

"Tough meeting, I'll bet?"

"Well, that time of year. Goddamn enrollment stats."

"Down?"

"What else? But they don't take into account that we always pick up a bunch of the rejects after May first."

Mark, stretching and clasping his hands behind his head, swivels his chair. "You know, Terry, Frank Larsen isn't someone who's liked, around here. Not sure why, but I get that feeling. Debra's the same—she has a knack of antagonizing people."

"You think? Well, they're both doing a good job for us. Anyway, gotta go prep my eleven o'clock class."

Mark bestows on him an understanding smile. "See ya."

There's an old Spanish saying, Terry: God throttles us, but 'e doesn't— quite—kill us.

Ernesto clasps one hand to his throat, and with a small jerk upward of his chin evokes that native Iberian tradition, the garrotte.

Decode: this is meant for a message of reassurance to Terry, before they go up to the staff cuts meeting. Assistant Deans have been warned to say not a word to their faculty, but Terry's gone ahead and prepared Carole, hoping she's passed the word on to Matt; he himself has told Frank Larsen that he'd better start sending out his c.v. It's shameful to delay notice this late, when the main hiring for next year's already over.

What Frank said: "Hey, thanks for letting me know in person. Doesn't always happen. I appreciate that."

But God, how else? Frank's being more than equal to the wretched occasion has depressed him more. If merit alone counted, Terry should be the one out of a job. As it is, he'll just write Frank the best letter he can.

They file in. Howard, with his usual dispatch, has his pen already poised over the faculty roster. He wants names, and calls on Terry first. Not good.

"Well, Howard," says Terry, "I'm sure you've seen the figures. There's some weakness in History, and I guess we'll have to lose Frank Larsen, although he's one of our best."

Howard looks down, scans the list, and draws a firm horizontal line.

"O.K., Larsen. And?"

Terry states the case for letting Matt go from English, but makes a point of mentioning his years of service, his new status as a single father. Hell, they're guys, Howard and Ernesto: let them face this.

Ernesto speaks up. "It's a sensitive issue, Howard. Matt has a *fine* record with us, a *good* record."

"Sure. But the fiscal health of the College has to be prioritized. In the present climate, the need to stay competitive—." He turns his palms out toward them: see how empty they are? "O.K. now, what about Sociology?"

Terry of course has looked at those numbers, and they're not so bad. What Howard must want is to substitute part-timers.

"O.K. I'm assuming Wendy and Mike and Deb all have tenure. On the other hand, Mark has the credentials we need, the doctorate. He'd be a real loss."

Howard calls in Ginnie from the desk outside; she brings with her a heady waft of perfume, along with the drama of a gold-buttoned red suit that puts Kathy's drab jumper to shame.

"Does Debra Walsh have tenure, Ginnie?"

While Ginnie looks up the file, Terry states that Deb, with her ABD status, is far more qualified than either Wendy or Mike—one with an M.Ed., the other a diploma in counseling. No comment from Howard.

Ginnie puts her head in. "Deb Walsh does not have tenure."

"So that's an option," Howard says, scanning the list and drawing another line. "We're gonna need a cut in that area. Plus, maybe two from English. You can give Ernesto the list Friday, O.K.? Now: Kathy."

Terry's left to absorb this new demand. *Four* cuts out of fourteen full-time faculty? That's not fifteen percent, that's—he jots down figures on a pad—*over twenty-five percent*. A fucking massacre! Immediately he starts the rebuttal memo in his head: One, a reminder *re* the original fifteen percent. Two, counter-proposal on Deb Walsh: why couldn't the college offer Wendy early retirement, given that accreditation comes up next Fall, and credentials are an issue? Three, need to hold the line at one cut in English, to avoid pushing the ratio of part-time staff above fifty percent. (See Regents' guidelines, as if Howard cares.)

And suggest ways for keeping Matt on, a final year. Memo to Ernesto, copy to Howard.

Late afternoon the next day, Matt's in Terry's office to hear the bad news. It's true, a persistent odor does accompany him, as of a shirt worn a few days too long, a suit that's gone a couple of seasons without dry-cleaning. Terry looks him in the face, says that unless they can find a way to persuade Howard to fund one more year, June will be his last paycheck. And Matt is so utterly shocked and furious—clearly Carole never gave him a hint—that he takes a couple of heavy breaths before speaking:

"O.K. So, you wanna tell me why *I, personally*, got the short end here? I mean, what's the *process*? In what way is this *fair*?"

He looks round Terry's barren cubicle, clearly a hard place to hide secrets.

"I'm not saying," Terry begins. But Matt breaks in.

"You know what I'm dealing with! I got my *son* with me, I had to rent a bigger place—*Jesus!*"

"I know, Matt, I'm not saying this is fair. What we're dealing with is Howard's ultimatum: fifteen percent cuts across the board. English has to take its share. And everyone except Lisa's more senior, so it's the credentials—the degree."

"I'm going in to talk to Ernesto. First thing."

"I'll support you on that. I already told him, at the very least you should have a year to look around."

Matt stands up. "Man, you've got some fucking nerve laying this on me! I've been here *seven years*—and you've been what, *two?*"

After he's gone, Terry stuffs papers in his Land's End briefcase, grabs his parka. And hears a shuffle of feet from Mark's office next door.

"Guess you heard," he says, pushing Mark's door half open.

Mark has that confidential smile on his face. "Yeah, well. Kind of obvious if I got up and left in the middle. That was harsh, though. Having to do that."

"Howard's pushing us."

"Yeah, I heard. But hey, aren't you *really glad* not to be on the receiving end of all this?"

Terry, at a loss, pulls his glasses off and rubs the back of his hand across his eyes. "Frank Larsen's worth two of me as a teacher. It's a fact. I'm sorry I can't switch places with him."

"Come on, man, you don't mean that. Be rational!"

We have a saying, you know. Approximately, in English, 'e thinks if 'e is well in with God, to Hell with all the saints!

Ernesto, all the way to lunch and back, has been churning over his feelings of outrage—at Mark, who's done a neat end-run around him, and up Howard's arse-hole (as they used to say back home) like a rat up a drainpipe. Mark prepared his move, and he's made it.

There were cues, Terry remembers now: Mark following Howard around, with that duck-footed little hustle of his; Mark asking Ginnie what Howard's schedule looked like for that afternoon; Mark popping his head in while a meeting was going on in Howard's office. What was it he said? That he had a draft of something. Draft of what?

Now the word is out: Howard and Mark have cooked up an idea together, for a new Master's degree in Social and Public Services. The

Social and Public Services Program—hereinafter to be known as "SPS." The genius of it is that it can use existing faculty resources in Social Science, Business, and Health Sciences: thus, recruiting can start next year even while the accreditation request goes in. And of course, though no-one's been named, Mark is poised to become its director.

Ernesto collapses into his office chair. His face has darkened to an ominous purplish-grey, his expression constricted with anguish. He takes a bottle of Maalox from his desk and pours straight from it down his throat. Terry tries to leave, but he gestures: no. Chronic gastritis, he explains—wait a moment and it'll pass.

"You know," Ernesto says, after a quietly massive belch, "I must admit I was not impressed with Mark, the way he behaved in this crisis. His one concern was for himself. Running to Howard, hiding behind the skirts. Special dispensation, understand? Well, it's been quite an insight, this past week."

He pauses, puts his hand over his mouth again. "Letters are going out tomorrow. You spoke to Larsen, and Matt?"

Terry confirms, adding that given the plans for the new program, Debra's case should be reconsidered. She's one person who'd be needed next year to develop courses.

Ernesto, distracted, says, "Possibly, possibly." Another pause, and he bursts out with what's really on his mind, a tirade against Howard and this project that Mark's sold him on.

"Howard's like a child with a new toy, a *child*, understand? But this is where 'e gets into trouble: 'e doesn't realize that whereas 'e can have everything his own way here, outside these walls *nobody's* going to care what 'e thinks. It's a joke!"

And it's Mark he blames, who's been feeding Howard this cocktail of Gilder, and Charles Murray, and E. O. Wilson's Sociobiology, persuading him toward the ideal of an alchemical marriage of Science and the Market—at which he, Howard, will be the priest, and Mark the best man. Then (and this, Terry sees, is the knife to Ernesto's heart), if the match goes through, Mark will leap right over and become Willard Lake's first Graduate Dean.

A coup indeed.

Carole hears about the SPS graduate program plan, and asks Terry who's going to head it.

"Well, and this is unofficial, in confidence, but it'll have to be Mark Price."

"Then I don't mind telling you, a lot of people are going to be very unhappy about that. See, I *know* Mark—I have a brother in *precisely* that mold. Completely out for himself, could care less about anyone else, just screw 'em!"

While she's talking, Terry clicks that this is a pure echo of the way he's heard Matt talk about Carole: "That woman is *exactly* like my ex-wife—completely focused on her own nutty version of reality. You can*not talk* to these people!"

So it's even with relief that, at the end of the day, he finds Mark sitting in his next-door office kicking back with a can of Diet Pepsi, openly contented with the world.

"Congratulations," Terry says in all sincerity. "Good call, there."

"Thanks Terry. I know there's a lot of people thinking, this is all about Mark Price. But Howard's right on this: we've gotta expand, and without endowment, we've gotta go the entrepreneurial route. Simple."

Terry, thinking out loud, says isn't Howard going to have to commit some resources to this? Seed money? They'll obviously apply for grants, but that takes time.

Mark takes a pocket inhaler out, and sniffs deeply once, twice. "Well that's gonna be our problem. Howard wants this thing *now*, read 'yesterday.' But, he doesn't want to commit the resources, money to it in advance."

When the initial meeting of Liberal Arts and Science/Health faculty on the SPS plan is held, Terry and George share the task of outlining curriculum proposals they and Mark have whipped up, on Howard's instructions. Terry goes first, then George—Mark sitting beside them, held in reserve. The moment they finish, there's a cascade of angry questions: "Where's the description of this proposed 'Social and Public Whatever' Master's Program? Does it even exist yet? Why haven't faculty been consulted earlier? What sort of compensation is Howard offering for people to work on this during the summer?"

Mark volunteers that Howard himself is "as we speak" putting the finishing touches on a draft of the SPSP proposal document. As for compensation—and here he's fumbling—at this time, a difficult question, he doesn't have the go-ahead from Howard—

Terry figures it's time to speak candidly: "No, we do not have any assurances on summer funding. But as you know, we're under the gun of declining enrollments. That's why, to put it bluntly, if there's any reward for our getting this program off the ground next year, it could just be that more of us get to keep our jobs."

Out of the corner of his eye Terry sees Deb Walsh turning to Carole with a pissed-off look, then jotting down notes on a pad. He's been delinquent there—hasn't told Deb her job's in question: why? Because he's still pretty confident of cutting a deal that would keep her on—but also because he dreads the inevitable explosion.

Still, he's brought the meeting back to order, or rather to a coerced submission in which he shares. The shoulder has been put to the wheel.

Meanwhile, it's already March, and Kathy's poodle has showed up with a green dye-job for St. Patrick's Day. Bio-degradable color, she assures everyone—doesn't hurt Baby a bit.

It's an old saying by a shrewd man: Faced with the choice of dealing with a fool or a knave, I would choose the knave. For the knave sometimes takes a rest from being a knave. But a fool's a fool twenty-four hours a day. There you have it.

Ernesto has Terry's latest memo in front of him. This is apparently the usual kind of mess that hits as the spring semester winds down. A couple of cute young work-study students, assigned to the enclave outside the President's office, have complained up there about these "insulting" D grades Carole's given them on their English papers. And Kevin, the *padron's* golf partner, the man who never lets Howard's coat hit the floor, has laid a couple of the papers on Terry. Lets it be known that Howard wants this looked into immediately as a potential grievance. Subtext, bring Carole into line here.

Terry knows one of the kids from class: Stacie, currently flaunting a white, see-through and plunging blouse, black mini, fishnet stockings, and heels. One of these little gal-pals Howard and Kevin pick up for themselves occasionally. He's kept his official cool and leafed through the two essays, one titled "Why Abortion is Wrong," the other "Protecting Our Enviroment" [sic]. Carole has scrawled *Development? Supporting details? Address the opposition? Spell-check?* in the margins. Fair enough. At best, he could see giving them a C-, but Carole's given these kids her time and attention for months now, and patience does run out.

He'd have quietly buried the matter, which he has learned is a key move in the administrator's repertoire, but Kevin has kept calling. So he's met with Carole—okay, take care and keep communications with these kids open. Then the memo to Kevin, copy to Ernesto, putting it on record that discussion was held as requested.

"The problem, Terry," says Ernesto, "is that you never know if Kevin's really acting as Howard's agent, or not. Sometimes 'e's taking the bit between 'is teeth. I say no more, you catch my drift."

Whatever, Terry thinks. Who gives a shit?

"Kevin is not—cerebral, understand? That man sees what 'e wants to see. You can put the facts in black and white, they'll mean nothing, understand? It's an old saying by a shrewd man: Faced with the choice of dealing with a fool or a knave. . . . "

Next day, Kevin's on the phone saying he appreciates Terry's efforts to follow due process, but "Howard still thinks something has to be done." About Carole.

Terry puts down the phone, having stonewalled politely but unmistakably. If Howard wants to harass or fire Carole, let him do it himself, openly. He'll have no part of it. But she won't be fired—why? because Howard won't want to pay any more unemployment money this year.

Then it comes to Terry, what just happened. He has personally failed the test of absolute loyalty. *Failed, understand?*

Deb Walsh stops by to talk; she mentions that she has a hysterectomy date set for late May, and will have to miss commencement. And recalls, at random it seems, the fact that Howard, eleven years ago, took one of her evening classes in psychology here.

"He did?"

"Absolutely. He was in Admissions then. A good-looking guy—well he still is, of course."

Good-looking. Has she *no idea* Howard's trying his damnedest to get her RIFfed?

"You remember what grade you gave him?"

"Oddly enough, yes. B+, it was."

Well, that'd do it.

At afternoon's end Terry drops again into Mark's office, for this is the hour when a knave may take a rest from his knavery. He finds the man in a rare troubled mood, popping Tylenol and taking out his nasal spray frequently for a snort. In front of him is the draft of Howard's official SPS proposal document. Mark kicks the door shut.

"Howard's vocabulary isn't, well, all it might be at times," he says. "See, here he's got 'enjoined' where he probably needs something like '*con*joined.' And this last section he's titled 'Epiphany'—that can't be what he means.

"'Epitome' maybe?"

"Well, I already gave him three pages of revisions I thought were important to make. And Ginnie sent the word down: no changes on this. Point is, if it has to go through the Regents, and then the accreditation team—"

"Yeah. Problem."

"I guess I'm getting a bit worn down, just now."

Terry has to feel for the man. Yet at the next meeting of Howard with Ernesto and the assistant deans, here's Mark tickled pink as his Oxford shirt, playing the new "His Master's Voice" as he briefs them all.

"So the schedule Howard wants us to meet goes this way. . . . as Howard's expressed to me, on that. . . . "

He leans forward while he's speaking, head tilted a little sideways towards the *padron,* so his glance comes up at them almost coyly. "Mark's faggotty style," Matt has taken to calling it. (For Matt has happily received a full scholarship to an M.B.A. program for next year; he applied just in time, and can't wait to be outta here.)

Then Terry looks over at Ernesto, casually, and is so shocked by what he sees, he wants to call out *Stop, for God's sake! The man is ill!* It's not just the insistent tremor of fury working in Ernesto's jaw, not just the dangerous flush under the skin, but his eyes, bloodshot and forced wide open, as if from a violent inward pressure. Terry's convinced that he's looking into the face of a man at imminent risk of collapse.

He does nothing. Because what does one do? The meeting ends; Ernesto rises and walks from the room with the stiff gait of a Nosferatu. Terry ought to follow him, take his arm, say something, say *Ernesto, save yourself!* But he has to catch Howard first, about the still-pending Deb Walsh case.

Briefly he runs his argument to Howard—that Deb's teaching a hundred-plus students per semester, they'll need her for the SPS courses next year; plus, the delay in deciding to renew her contract means that, professionally, they really must give her a year's grace to find something else. Finally, the issue of offering Wendy early retirement.

Howard acts surprised. Says he thought Terry would've notified Debra Walsh a while back that she might not be renewed. And surely, given Terry's excellent rapport with Mark, he knew Mark didn't see her as fitting into the SPS program teaching group.

"But Deb wasn't sent the letter that Frank and Matt were?"

"I'm not sure. You better check with Ernesto, or Debra."

He calls Debra the same night, who's heard nothing. She listens for a minute, then erupts in a blast of rage, disbelief, utter contempt. Who the *hell* does he think he is, coming in out of nowhere and wrecking everything she's built up in that goddamn place? When she's through, and he's said that he understands her reaction entirely, she adds, "You may as well know, I'm not going to take this lying down. I know it's Mark at the bottom of this. And I'll be in Howard's office first thing tomorrow morning."

Terry says he'd be very happy to go in with her.

"Howard knows my views. And the college at least owes you another year."

"And *I'm* telling *you, that's* not good enough either!"

He'll never know what went on in Howard's office the next morning, but Mark stops by at five o' clock to say there's been a turnaround, and Deb Walsh will be teaching one more year. Not his preference, he says, and Howard detests the woman too; but there were some kind of legal threats.

The look he directs at Terry includes a shade of distant compassion: something new.

The carriage of civilization rolled through Europe, and left its dust in Spain.

In late May, Ernesto is attempting a philosophical view of things. He reflects on the gradual but, he claims, unmistakable progress that Willard Lake is making, of which Terry's presence is one token. Even Kevin, he says, concedes that Terry is "a class person."

Well thanks, Kevin. They walk together past the flowering lindens and the lilac bushes to Ernesto's office. Once there, he finds a letter open on his desk, gives a short sigh, and pushes it across to Terry.

"Oh yes," he says. "Maybe this could be a nice little course to offer next year, hm?"

The time is after lunch, so he reaches in his drawer for the Maalox. And Ernesto has developed, Terry noticed while they walked, a perceptible listing to the left side: it's best these days to stay on his right hand.

The letter's on crested notepaper; it's from a state legislator in the local district, the Rt. Hon. William O'Malley.

Dear Dean,

It was a pleasure meeting you, courtesy of my very good friend President White.

Following our discussion, the course I have chosen to teach in Fall semester is The Politics of Participation. I append a short syllabus. I look forward highly to this opportunity. . . .

Yours, etc.

The syllabus is a half-page affair—no bibliography, of course. Ernesto makes a deprecatory gesture.

"He's a friend of Howard's, did a few favors for us, I gather. We had lunch, last week."

Terry's not going to make this easier.

"I know," says Ernesto, "it's unorthodox, but if you could perhaps find somewhere in the schedule—"

"Does he have a c.v.?"

"Of course, of course, he sent a full résumé. Ginnie must have it upstairs."

He phones, and waits while she goes looking. "No?" He puts down the phone. "I'm afraid Ginnie doesn't yet have the résumé."

"Also, I wonder if he knows how much we pay: just over a thousand for the semester?"

"Perhaps, Terry, you might write to him, give him the details, when you've looked at the schedule."

God throttles us, but He doesn't quite kill us.

Doesn't he, though, Terry thinks when he visits Ernesto in his hospital bed at home in late August.

Ever the professional, Ernesto waited until after Commencement before having the first of a series of strokes. Now he lies quietly, and after his devoted wife takes the bunch of flowers from Terry, he turns his eyes, and lifts his one usable hand and opens it in one of his small, eloquent gestures, as if to say, Look, this is what I've come to.

Trapped. Executed, understand?

"Everyone," says Terry, "feels it's not the same place without you—we really need you back, Ernesto."

"Like this?" He frowns slightly. "No, Terry, don't speak of it."

Yet what else have they to talk about? Terry doesn't know, and doesn't remember afterwards. At a certain moment, Mrs. B. comes in and stands at the foot of the bed.

"She wants me to rest," Ernesto says. He reaches out to grasp Terry's hand. "Something you should remember."

"Yes?"

One more time the Gaze takes hold:

If there's anything you need, Terry, anything at all, go to Howard, and ask 'im. Don't bother with those nobodies. Go straight to Howard 'imself, and just ask, understand?

"I'll remember, Ernesto. Thank you."

He grasps the hand with all the feeling he can muster, given his inner conviction that there's not a chance he'd ever bring himself to ask a favor of *el padron*. Not in this world: the world from which Ernesto is delivered, in October, by a final, decisive stroke.

The Monday after his memorial service, Ernesto's secretary calls Terry and says it was his particular wish that the desk in his office be transferred to Blockwell Hall, for Terry's own use. Later that week, astoundingly considering the heavy steel frame of the thing, a maintenance crew hauls it up to the landing outside the row of cubicles for History and Sociology. But the corridor between the partitions is too narrow to allow it to come any closer to Terry's office. He tries this angle and that; nothing works.

For a long time it stays where it is, a ledge for students to sit on, have a soda and swing their heels, waiting for some elusive instructor to show up. Eventually, Terry notices it has migrated into a classroom, where, as it happens, he's never taught a class.

Mango, Number 61

Richard Blanco

Pescado grande was number 14, while *pescado chico* was number 12; *dinero*, money, was number 10. This was *la charada*, the sacred and obsessive numerology my *abuela* used to predict lottery numbers or winning trifectas at the dog track. The grocery stores and pawn shops on Flagler street handed out complementary wallet-size cards printed with the entire *charada*, numbers 1 through 100: number 70 was *coco*, number 89 was *melón* and number 61 was *mango*. Mango was Mrs. Pike, the last *americana* on the block with the best mango tree in the neighborhood. *Mamá* would coerce her in granting us picking rights—after all, *los americanos don't eat mango*, she'd reason. Mango was fruit wrapped in brown paper bags, hidden like ripening secrets in the kitchen oven. Mango was the perfect house warming gift and a marmalade dessert with thick slices of cream cheese at birthday dinners and Thanksgiving. Mangos, watching like amber cat's eyes; mangos, perfectly still in their speckled maroon shells like giant unhatched eggs. Number 48 was *cucaracha*, number 36 was *bodega* and mango was my uncle's *bodega*, where everyone spoke only loud Spanish, the precious gold fruit towering in *tres-por-un-peso* pyramids. Mango was mango shakes made with milk, sugar and a pinch of salt—my grandfather's treat at the 8th street market after baseball practice. Number 60 was *sol*, number 18 was *palma*, but mango was my father and I under the largest shade tree at the edges of Tamiami park. Mango was *abuela* and I hunched over the counter covered with classifieds, devouring the dissected flesh of the fruit slithering like molten gold through our fingers, the pigmented juices cascading from our binging chins, *abuela* consumed in her rapture and convinced that I absolutely loved mangos. Those messy mangos. Number 79 was *cubano*—us, and number 93 was *revolución*, though I always thought it should be 58, the actual year of the revolution—the reason why, I'm told, we live so obsessively and nostalgically eating number 61s, *mangos*, here in number 87, *América*.

The Oversight Committee

Dean Young

It has always been our intention
that your stay among us be but brief
even though we may have chased you
through the hallways, promised you
our cubical, turned you into echoes
and trees and stars. Oh how you glowed
by the water cooler. As regards
earlier memos re: orgasm cultivation,
that should have read orchid cultivation.
Our apologies particularly to Cheryl
at processing. Still the smear
of your runkled sex steams
like monks' illumination upon our thigh.
The mind at such times works wonderfully,
it becomes its own employment which
research on the brains of gazelles
crushed in lions' jaws indicates
may be the result of a single neurotransmitter
reserved for just such moments
and finally, isn't it all about moments
jumping other moments, your love for us,
our love for your fur? But later, when someone
calls down the stairs, If you're coming up,
could you bring the tape? none of it
will seem remotely possible: tape,
finding the tape, stairs, climbing the stairs.
The brain has let you down, it thinks,
Why are you still around? Asked for a simple

accounting, many of you submitted poems
about abysses. Only one among you,
asked for a spanner, could actually
produce a spanner. This gives us little choice.
Think of all those flamingos that die each year.
Have courage. Think of all those colored stones
in aquariums. Who knows what happens to them
when the fish are flushed. Holding one's breath
is fine for hurrying through a room
full of poisonous gas but it's not something
we can take to the stockholders. Shiney conveyances
have been spotted in the sky, ditto swans,
all suggesting it is time you move on.
Not every motion falls under our aegis
but for those of you with difficulties
feeding yourself, a form is being prepared.
Now go, we will always be further and further
behind you. Never will we ride an elevator
without thinking of your ass. Finally, don't
forget to turn in your key to Cheryl
and remember, due to the flood,
the tornado drill has been postponed.

Two Poems

Bruce Bond

Digging up the Briars

Any stretch of rain will tell you,
the bulb is what you want, nothing less:
its spindled fist of roots and curses—
so rarely where you think. Which is half
the trick: reading your entanglements,
to work
        your way down without severing
your leads, digging past and around
all that discouragement of rock.
Once you're under, you're bound to lose
what's what . . . call it the unconscious
cunning of weeds,
            the way their fibers
twine and strangle, so when you get there,
when you catch the ganglia with your spade,
levering the shovel-handle like a jack,
it's not the weight of the prize you feel,
but some force
        of need woven into the nervous
system of things. For every bulb you claim,
there's one you don't—this much you know—
so that your arms grow heavy
in their sockets, in that ache
suspended between accomplishment

and failure, and the sleep that takes
them over, green with greed, sending
its shoots into the bedsheets below.
And crowning everything the disfigured

hearts of leaves, bearing you up:
more light, more light:
                    how far
to the little orange lamps of knowledge
in their orchard, in your sleep
no less . . . how far to the garden
gate at the end of the world,
where you just might look back
and wonder—
                    no surer than before—
what lies on the other side of all
that infusion of duty and desire, all
that work you worked your life for.
Those wiry scribbles in books
you gave your eyes to;
                    the illegible
Braille of bodies, wrapped in veins;
every deep allegiance that crinkled
on its coals and burst; what are they
if not the winding script of yards
you can neither finish
                    nor forget.
Which is why you take them to bed,
because they're hopeless and they let you,
they want you—so generous that way—
as if you could climb into them,
into every problem's helix and through.

And now you see whole groves of them
dripping in the merciful ropes of vines.
They are the other face of roots
startled into the sky's mirror,
blown into the erotic hand of letters
you burned,
                    the ones you didn't,
into the work of bodies braiding
and tearing, braiding and tearing;
and out of the ground—you can almost
smell it—the sharp green scent
of rain, ascending.

Alien Hand

It starts with the seizures,
the ones that grip her body
in their fist, so tight
they crumple life and limb,
and so force the surgeons' cut,

that manhole cover of bone
in her head—unspeakable,
their mercy, how far
they go, severing a bridge
at the core of knowing.

But it works. The fits subside.
At times they nearly vanish,
as if what brought them on
was the shudder of one self
in the mirror of the other.

Which is where the hand comes in.
She's not alone. It's a story
that flares up time
to time, ever since they started
in on the central tissues.

For her it's the left,
that bitter child of a hand,
her oldest conquest,
never so unruly and alive.
As if it has eyes—that's how

she puts it—the way it grasps
at the pointless spoon or shirt,
trespassing where it will.
She could be anywhere,
at a friend's place, say,

where it seizes up on the scruff
of his dog, just holding it
there, giving it everything.
And the more she resists,
the stronger it gets,

until she wakes one night
to the ridiculous horror
grasping at her throat.
It's as if her seizures
were now its dwarf province

and the bad dream that quarters
the mind again and again,
bequeathing fits to always
some lesser part, cursing
the odd moment awake.

Soon the whole angry tangle
of nerve—each bitten word
in a history of words—
becomes a broken empire, a night
sliced at the coldest hour.

And with each cut, each cell
divided, the swelling memory
of the blade.

A Day of Splendid Omens

Robley Wilson

I'm on my way to a September wedding in Scoggin, a small town in Maine not far from Portland. It's Webster Hartley—Webb, my closest friend since the days when we were at Bowdoin together—who's marrying Prudence Mackenzie. When Webb called me in Evanston to ask me if I'd stand up for him, he mumbled something about making an honest man of himself—he'd had a few drinks—and I felt a funny twinge of I don't know what. Envy, possibly; or, on the other side of it, maybe a curious sort of disapproval. Webb is 64, the same age I am, and I suppose some Puritan part of me rose up and clucked its tongue at the idea of a man as old as Webb marrying a woman as young—I think she's 28—as Pru. What if we'd known when we were in college, dating the girls from Holyoke and Smith and Jackson and Bradford Junior, that in fact we might eventually love and get married to someone not even born yet?

Webb is an artist—a good one, I think, but not a successful one. He moved to Maine after his last divorce and managed to buy a rundown farmhouse for back taxes. Then he spent the next few years making it livable—patching the roof of the house and the barn-like ell, shoring up the foundation, replacing broken window panes; he dug a new well, put in a septic tank so he could have an indoor toilet. He lived alone during all that rehabilitation, living a life so organized it hardly seemed possible this was the Webster Hartley I'd known at school. He got up with the sun, went into his makeshift studio carrying a cup of coffee spiked with Jameson's, and painted for two, three hours; he gave over the rest of the daylight to being a carpenter, an electrician, a journeyman plumber. Then in the hours after dark, before Prudence came into his life, he drank until he fell into bed. It was edifying—I told him this—to see a man take up the disconnected pieces of his life and use them to build a house.

I can only imagine what they live on, since Webb's income as a painter occupies a range from slim to none—though nowadays when he does sell a picture, he tells me he often gets something up in the four-figure neighborhood. Perhaps he sells two pieces a year, three in a super-good year. He doesn't have savings. He never did.

But the two of them are happy. I visited them a couple of summers ago, pulling into the yard on a Sunday afternoon in August, the day sweltering and hazy-gold. There were white chickens in the driveway, a fat, lazy orange cat asleep on the porch railing, a rusty pickup truck and a vintage Chevy sedan parked between the house and a rickety barn. Webb came out of the house in torn tennis shoes and swim trunks, Pru in the shadows behind him, barefoot, wearing a long-tailed man's shirt that might have been all she had on. The baby, Melinda—she was walking, but just barely, so she must have been what? not quite a year old?—was in cotton underpants, tottering against her father's hairy legs.

You have to spend a lot of time with Webb Hartley to know him. He's not tall, but he's big and he *seems* tall. He's broad-shouldered, stocky, with hands so huge that if somebody asked you, you'd presume that if he were any kind of artist, he had to be a sculptor, and ever since he entered his thirties he's worn a beard so red and so unruly he looks like a scruffy Viking warrior. Flamboyant—that's how you'd describe him, first meeting him. But it wouldn't be long before you realized you were in the presence of a truly shy man, and you'd forget you thought him flamboyant in favor of thinking him reticent, or self-effacing, or politely anti-social. He has a squint to his eyes that suggests the wariness he feels in the company of other humans; I've seen that squint disappear only when he's in front of a new canvas, or looking at Pru across the dinner table, or sitting on the porch steps by himself, petting the indolent orange cat in an absent fashion, his mind a million miles away.

It's late afternoon when I arrive at the farmhouse. The ceremony is scheduled for six, but the reception is before the wedding and I'm looking forward to some hefty eating and drinking and clowning around for the newlyweds' benefit. The day—in fact it's the first day of autumn, the equinox—is superb. The sky is absolutely unclouded, is perfectly, flawlessly blue; the air is warm and moves with the slightest of breezes, only enough to keep you from feeling uncomfortable; you can smell the grasses—not the humid scent of fresh-cut green, but a more subtle, drier odor, mingled with a distant suspicion of cow and horse from some unobtrusive neighbor's farm. A knockout day to declare love unto death, a day of splendid omens.

Oddly, there's nobody around. I sit for a few minutes in the rented car, surveying the farmyard, the house and the ell, wondering why no one strolls out to greet me. The car window is down—the breeze touches my cheek and brow—but no sounds reach me. No laughter, no clink of glasses, no background of a hired musician tuning his fiddle. No cars belonging to guests—only the Hartley pickup, rustier than ever. I'm surrounded by rare silence—or what passes for silence in a noisy world: a soft thunder we hear that science says is the rush of blood through our bodies; a thin whine alleged to be the electric current that drives the nervous system. Then other sounds disturb the quiet. The chirp of a cricket. A fly's buzz. A barely audible rustle of leaves in the birches. A crow calling, distant, like a rusty hinge. But no human noise.

I go to the farmhouse, cross the porch to the screen door, and knock. Knock harder. Open the screen door and tap on the glass of the inside door with the car key. The sharp noise of the key echoes into the birches, and the echo comes back sounding like someone far off swinging an axe against a tree, cutting it down. I push the door open—Webb has never locked anything in his life—and call Webb's name, get no response, close the door and turn away. I wonder if I have the wrong day, or only the wrong hour.

Walking around the house, I meet a first sign of human habitation: a pet, a small brown and white terrier who is overjoyed to meet me, who jumps up to lick my hands, whose tail wags non-stop. "Hey, little guy," I say. "Hello, boy. Where's the party?" I follow the dog around the end of the ell. At the end of the long, sloping lawn the farm pond shows a few dimples where dragon-flies touch and dance away; otherwise the water is quiet and unruffled.

In the backyard, finally things look festive. Three picnic tables, covered with red-checkered tablecloths, have been set end-to-end and laden with bowls of potato salad, macaroni salad, corn chips, raw vegetables, a variety of dips—all of them covered over with plastic wrap for protection from insects and air. At the end of one table are glass cups arranged in a circle that suggests they're intended to surround a missing punch bowl. On a pair of card tables nearby—also draped in red-checkered cloths—are paper plates, a few styrofoam cups, an aluminum coffee maker. On the lawn, pushed into the shade of a fair-sized oak tree, are a couple of galvanized iron washtubs filled with ice and canned beer, and I can see the corked necks of a wine bottle or two looking aloof among the cans. Tubular-aluminum chairs with bright-colored plastic seats and backs are scattered about; a few emptied beercans are in evidence, standing alongside the chairs or tipped over into the grass. On the top step under the back door of the house sits an old-fashioned wind-up Victrola, its lid open, its varnished horn aimed across the yard; a stack of shellac records is on a step below.

But no people. I stroll through the party scene with the terrier wagging at my heels, open a can of Narragansett, slip my fingers under transparent plastic to withdraw a stark cerebrum of cauliflower. I eat the blossom, toss the stem to the dog, who sniffs it and then gives me a puzzled look. I sip the beer and wonder what Webb is up to. Perhaps after a toast or two in champagne he has proposed to his guests a walk in the countryside, a procession, a one-time ritual—the wedding party tramping through the late-summer meadows to put on the last of the wildflower pollens, breathe the faint and fading perfumes of the dying season—that will lead back to the ceremony itself. That would be like him.

I sit on the steps next to the Victrola, drinking my beer, waiting for the party to return. The dog makes several circles, slumps into the grass at the foot of the steps and rests his head on his forepaws. I remember someone once told me that the point of the old RCA Victor trademark—"His Master's Voice"—is that what the terrier is sitting on, head cocked to listen, is a coffin, and the Master is dead inside it. Webb would enjoy this scene at the back of his house, the rearrangement of the trademark, its elements fragmented but the reference still clear; this is the kind of still-life subject he looks for in the world, that ignites his imagination and sends him into his studio. I pick a phonograph record off the top of the pile at my feet—*Vocalion* I can read, but the gilt lettering is too worn for me to read the fine print of the label—and put it on the green felt of the turntable. I lift the arm and turn it down to rest the needle at the edge of the record; the turntable begins moving, but too slowly to make melody. I crank the phonograph; the turntable speeds up, the music wavers and rises and becomes intelligible—a tenor voice, a sentimental song: "Believe Me, If All Those Endearing Young Charms."

*

The day cools, the sun has made its descent into autumn, the shadows lengthen and climb the shingles of the house, the breeze drops off to nothing. By now I'm sinking into concerns of my own. Where *are* Webb and Pru? Where are the wedding guests? I walk around to the front of the house, the terrier at my heels, and sit in a Boston rocker at the end of the porch—a vantage point from which I can look down the narrow gravel road, see what's coming toward me. For a long time I sit on Webb's porch, rubbing the ears of the dog at my feet, crooning nonsense words.

In the distance is a glitter of chrome—a car coming. I scowl down the length of the road, the low sun in my eyes, a cloud of dust behind the car colored like gold, boiling, molten. It's a blue Ford, a newish sedan that could stand washing, and it speeds past—its driver a middle-aged man, straw-hatted, with his hands holding the wheel at 10 and 2 o'clock.

"False alarm," I say to the terrier. I lean back in the rocker, close my eyes, try not to speculate. I wonder what happened to the white chickens. I wonder if Melinda—Mindy—is old enough to be the flower girl for her parents, and how they will dress her—or *if* they will dress her.

Now another car is approaching, not as fast, and behind it is a second. They slow as they come near, the dust clouds behind them diminishing, flattening in light no longer direct. I stand; the dog startles to his feet. I walk down the two porch steps to meet the new arrivals. Because it is dusk by now, the lead car has its parking lights on.

Both cars turn into the farmyard—the first stopping in the driveway, almost running up on the lawn in front of the porch, and the second going past it to park beside the old truck. The driver's-side doors open simultaneously, and two men appear. Neither one is Webb. The man from the car nearest me trots to the passenger side and opens the door. He offers his hand; a young woman takes it and he helps her to stand. Pru. She is dressed in a pale blue dress whose color is almost neutralized by the failing of the daylight, and her high-heeled shoes are likewise pale blue. She is bareheaded, but in one hand she carries a flowered hat and a sheer white scarf. She leans heavily on the man, who turns with her toward the house. Only then does she look up; only then does she see me, recognize me.

"Alec," she says.

"What's the matter?" I say. "What's going on?"

She puts her free hand to her face as if she is going to brush aside a stray lock of her long hair, but the hair is pulled severely, formally, back. The hand seems to flutter at her eyes, her mouth.

"Webb," she says.

"What about him?" I take a step toward her. I wish I knew who this man was who suddenly seems so proprietary, who stiffens and turns his shoulder so that Pru is shielded from my question. Pru anticipates me.

"This is the minister," she says. "This is the man who was going to marry us."

"Was?"

"Webster's dead," the man says. He steers Pru past me. "Let's get you inside," he says to her.

By now the man from the other car has come up.

"Alec," he says, almost jovial. He holds out his hand; I take it, a reflex, my mind still grappling with the words "Webster's dead," wondering if I heard correctly. "Bob Hartley," he says. "Webb's kid brother. We met once, a couple of Webb weddings ago."

"What the hell happened?"

"Heart attack."

"Jesus. On his wedding day?" I feel dizzy, and sit on the top step of the porch. Bob Hartley sits down next to me.

"Out of the blue," he says. "Right out of left field. One minute he was hugging Pru and bragging about his good luck; the next he was on his face, dead as the proverbial doornail. It was weird."

"Jesus." It is all I can think of to say. A prayer, a supplication—I don't know what. *Jesus.* Does the name give us some kind of relief from horror? "Are they sure?"

"Sure of what?"

"Are they sure he's dead?" *Jesus,* I keep saying inside my head. *Jesus Christ.*

"Yeah, they're sure. They tried CPR. They tried adrenaline." Bob produces a cigarette and lights it. "That electric-shock gizmo. He's dead all right."

"Where is he?"

"Kimball Hospital. The undertaker's supposed to pick him up tonight."

Sweet Jesus. I try to get a purchase on the day, to say anything that suggests I might have some modest control of reality. "How's Pru?"

"Destroyed; you saw."

"Where's Mindy?"

"My wife—you remember Theresa?— I dropped her and Mindy back at our motel. They were going to watch cartoons."

*

It seems to me it is the interior of Webb's house that is a cartoon—a caricature of what is expected to happen when someone dies. While I rehearsed my private blasphemies with Robert Hartley, two more cars pulled into the yard and emptied themselves, a parade of solemn guests passing around and between us, so that by the time he and I come inside, the front room feels crowded and there is activity in the kitchen. A screen door slams periodically; someone is ferrying food from the picnic tables to the refrigerator. Bob excuses himself, leaves me, reappears shortly thereafter staggering under the weight of one of the tubs of beer, which he slides noisily onto a kitchen counter.

"Who wants a beer?" he calls. "Who wants wine?"

This is a small room, made smaller by its furnishings. An old upright piano occupies most of the far end, bulking so large that it partially blocks a window. A claw-footed sofa covered with an afghan sits under the window that looks onto the porch, a long coffee table, littered with magazines and paperback books, slightly askew in front of it. On the facing wall: a leather chair, a brass floorlamp, a magazine rack. On the floor is a worn Oriental carpet, mostly dark red with extravagant grays and oranges.

It was the piano that was Webb's pride and joy. I was with him when he acquired it—gratis—from the Methodist Church of Holderness, New Hampshire, which wanted it moved out of the basement to make room for a projection-screen television set. Webb was beside himself; he hired half the football team of the Holderness School to do the moving, rented a pickup—he later bought the truck; it's the one that sits in the yard, rusting away even as we settle in to the evening's wake—and brought it here pretending it was a birthday present for half-nude Mindy. I've heard him play it, something he did whenever he'd had too much to drink and the light was too weak for painting. Honky-tonk; that was his specialty, and the piano—being out of tune, missing innumerable felts and having a cracked sounding board—was the perfect instrument. Had he not been so happy, so good-hearted, the experience of listening to Webb play would have been excruciating. As it was, you couldn't help but feel the pleasure of it all. He sang "The Darktown Strutters' Ball," his left hand boom-chucking away, his right hand trilling treble octaves, his voice—his awful voice—bouncing the lyrics off the room's walls and ceiling. He sang "I'll Take You Home Again, Kathleen," tremulo, while tears streamed down his cheeks. He played "House of Blue Lights" until the boogie-woogie bass gave you a headache. But how do you say to a man who's in a heaven of his own making that he should for God's sake give us a rest from all that racket?

*

Bob Hartley presses a beer into my hand, pausing to make sure I have a grip on it, since I must seem to him not to be paying attention. He says, "Okay, old buddy?" and I snap out of it and nod. The room is suddenly warm, crowded. The wedding guests talk softly, moving between the living room and the kitchen—the rooms are separated from each other by a countertop and a bank of cupboards—pouring wine, helping themselves to food. The screen door to the backyard creaks open and slaps shut incessantly.

I lean back in the leather chair and press the beer can against my forehead. The cold feels sharp-pointed, welcome. Bob returns and sits unsteadily on the chair arm.

"Pru's lying down upstairs," he says. "She'd like to talk with you."

"Now?"

"I think so; yes."

"Shouldn't she rest?"

Bob shrugs. "She took a couple of pills. I think she's about cried out for today."

*

Pru is leaning against two pillows in the center of a brass bed; a patchwork quilt is under her; she's clutching one of the matching pillow shams, holding it against herself like a security blanket. She's red-eyed, but not crying.

"Alec," she says, her voice small and sweet.

"Bob said I should look in."

"Please." She pats the quilt beside her.

I sit, gently, intending not to shake the bed. "Can I get you anything?"

"Thank you, no." She lowers the sham and lets go of it; she puts out her right hand toward me, but doesn't try to touch me. "Is that beer?"

"Yes."

"Let me have a taste."

"Should you? On top of—whatever?"

"They were only aspirin. Cross my heart."

I hold out the beer, but instead of taking it from me she puts her hand over mine and steers the can to her mouth. She takes a long swallow, then releases me. "I hate beer," she says. "It's such bitter stuff."

"There's sweeter stuff downstairs."

"I know. I helped buy it." She sighs, leans back, closes her eyes. "I made the punch too. With plenty of vodka."

I don't know what to say, or what she wants of me. I let my gaze roam around the bedroom: to her blue heels in the middle of the room, the scarf and hat on a wicker chair under a window, on one of the room's two dressers a beribboned plastic box with flowers inside it.

"You came a long way for nothing," she says.

Her eyes are open, and very green. On both her cheeks are faint, thin streaks made by tears, and her lipstick is faded almost to nothing. Her hair is loose; the combs are on the nightstand nearby.

"If I can help," I say, without the slightest idea of how to complete the thought.

"You can," she says. She sits upright, swings her legs over the far side of the bed. "But you have to turn your back while I get into something simple."

I hear her clothing rustle. A closet door slides, hangers jangle.

"All right," she says. "I'm decent." She's in tights, a loose pink sweater; she is tying her hair into a ponytail. "In the corner closet," she says, "could you get me that scruffy pair of Tretorns?"

"Where are we going?"

"I want to go to the studio." She finishes tying the tennis shoes, takes my hand to lead me. "Come," she says. "We'll use the back stairs so we miss everybody."

At the head of the stairs she stops so abruptly I almost collide with her; she turns, throws her arms around my waist and hangs on desperately. Her head is down, her face against my chest. "God," she says. "I didn't want all these people; I wanted you, and Bobby and Terry, just to witness."

"They'll be gone pretty soon."

"They don't know anything about any of us," she says.

*

After he'd picked up the old farmhouse from the Tax Assessor—long before Pru came into his life—I visited him here, followed him around while he boasted about what he was going to do, what he'd already done. The studio in those first days was an impressive mess: the ell windows had long been broken out by storms and vandals, and half the animal kingdom of southern Maine must have been wintering in it for years; scat and straw and nests of fur like tumbleweeds corrupted the space—the odor was unbelievably raw—and off and on during my stay various of the previous tenants tried to reassert their squatters' rights. One morning we burst in on a red fox couple, another time a family of raccoons like a band of gypsy thieves surprised around a campfire. Skunks were the riskiest, Webb told me, and when one Sunday he cornered one behind the pot-bellied stove he'd just hooked up, I opted out—went back inside the house and poured another cup of coffee for myself. "How'd it go?" I wanted to know when he came back to the kitchen. "Piece of cake," Webb said. "I think I've driven that one off before; he was friendlier than most—acted like he knew me."

That was the year I stayed all summer, and by the time I left, Webb had been painting in his new studio for almost three weeks. We'd put in a skylight, caulked all the old window frames, replaced a dozen broken floorboards. We even lugged in three cords of stovewood to take Webb through his first winter. Seeing the studio now, with poor Pru, brought all of that back, and it brought back the time I'd first met her.

The year was melting into springtime then, but the day I arrived there'd been a spectacular ice storm. The driving was ugly—I'd seen cars and trucks tipped off at the side of the roads, and I'd clutch the wheel to my chest like a life-vest, praying the rear wheels wouldn't break away every time I came to a curve—but Nature was glorious, encased in ice, glittering like cut crystal. Webb either saw or heard me coming; by the time I drove into the yard he was standing on the porch—Levi's, green-and-black plaid shirt, the same style of army boots he'd worn for close to forty years—waiting for me. He had a great black skillet—a "spider," he called it—in his right hand, and in his left a couple of brown hen's eggs he held up and waved at me.

"How many eggs in your omelet?" he said.

"Three."

I trailed him inside a house that was already full of the smell of bacon and too-strong coffee, laid my toilet kit on the magazine rack—it held magazines then—and sat at the kitchen table. The table was a recent find of Webb's; it was old and austere and heavy, made of oak and varnished to an autumnal shade of brown, and with its four high-backed chairs it crowded the kitchen. Webb poured me a mug of the coffee from a battered aluminum pot and went about his cooking duties, breaking a half-dozen eggs into an outsized measuring cup, adding a splash of water from a faucet at the sink—"Anybody tells you to add milk instead of water has never been intimate with a hen," he said—beating the mix with a fork and pouring half into the greasy spider.

"I'll remember."

"Cheese?" he said.

"Why not?"

He opened the refrigerator and brought out a fist-sized block of cheddar, grated much of it into the pan, ate most of the rest while he oversaw the omelet. "Sharp," he said. "Nice edge on it." The bacon was draining on a wad of paper towels on the counter, the coffee steamed above its low blue flame at the back of the stove. I remember how secure I felt; it came from being comfortable and attended to and needed. It had been years since I'd lost my wife, and I was still getting used to traveling alone, restless, moving in this direction and that like a hurt animal that thinks it can walk away from its pain.

"I met this woman," Webb told me. It was a statement that sounded abrupt—as if he'd been holding it in until it simply refused any longer to be contained. "In Boston a couple of weekends ago." He prodded the omelet, bent down to stove level to adjust the flame under it. "Goes by the old-fashioned name of Prudence."

"How'd you meet her?"

"Luck." He folded the omelet over, danced the spider on the burner for a moment or two, tipped it up so the omelet slid off onto a heavy white plate. He added several strips of the bacon and set the plate before me. "Karma. Life's reward for Good Behavior." He turned his back to me and went to work on the second omelet.

"Sounds serious," I said. "Is she rich?"

He seemed to study the question. "I think not," he said after a while. "Not by any worldly definition."

He set his plate on the table, brought over what was left of the bacon on its bed of greasy paper, sat down across from me.

"So you're in love with her," I said.

He took a mouthful of omelet, chewed, swallowed. "There's salt and pepper behind the mustard pot," he said. "I don't know your taste. Or your dietary requirements."

"So you're *not* in love with her?"

"I'm deliberating over the word 'love,'" he said. "There's a connection between us—I can't describe it." He tried his coffee, found it had cooled, went to the stove to add hot. "Like I've been only half human all this time, and Pru is the other half of me."

"Another marriage ahead?" I said.

"No," he said. "She's too good to be made by any man into a mere wife." He took a sip of coffee, scratched the beard at his chin. "You'll meet her." he said. "She's moving in with me on Saturday."

*

On today's sad visit the studio has the agreeable clutter it lacked when Webb and I first got it into shape to be used. One end of it is a kind of carpenter's shop smelling of the pungent, fresh-sawn wood waiting to be made into canvas stretchers and frames, and of the thick brown glue kept hot in its electric pot. At the other end, under the skylight stained from years of gray weather and mottled with bird droppings, the smell is sharper: of oil paint, lacquers and thinners, turpentine-soaked rags. Prudence wends her way through the canvases leaned against the workbench, the one-by-twos and one-by-threes of pine and hickory and oak; she pauses, picks up several corner fasteners and spills them with a sound like cracked bells into an open paper box on the bench. "Webb was never neat," she says.

Now we're in the studio proper, where Webb worked. A large easel directly under the skylight, finished canvases and Masonite boards leaned and piled against the end wall, a cabinet with open drawers that reveal paint tubes and brushes of every size. The floor, where years of colors have fallen, is like a Pollock painting. Squat cans of turpentine, spray cans of plastic, line the sills of the two windows that face east.

"It wasn't my idea to get married," Pru says. "If you've wondered. I was against it. I thought we were doing fine as lovers, as people with special 'significance' for each other." She leans against the windowsill. The light from overhead makes unflattering shadows on her face, accents her eye sockets, hollows her cheeks.

"He was no stranger to marriage," I say.

"I know." She looks down and her face is all shadow. "I'd have been number four."

"I'd lost count."

"He told me all about all of them, chapter and verse. I think he really wanted me to know him, make sense of him. He told me he'd decided never to do marriage again."

"What made him change his mind?"

"Oh, I think he was trying to be practical. I think that because he was so much older—and really, he was getting awfully conscious of his age— he wanted me to have whatever benefits the wedding ceremony might bring with it. Survivor benefits, insurance, tax breaks. I don't know what."

"Age affects people," I say. Not sarcastic.

"It never bothered me. I mean he never seemed to me to act old or talk old—or *paint* old." She sighs, looks out a window that faces the woods. "I suppose, too, he wanted to make things easier for Mindy."

"He said he wanted to make everybody honest."

"Something like that." She looks suddenly forlorn, and for an uneasy moment I think she's going to just let go, just collapse, as if it's easier to be unconscious and let the world go on without her for a while. My wife used to say: *I'm tired; today I'm just going to be a passenger.* Pru raises her hands, a gesture of futility.

"And he actually loved me," she says. "God—You can't believe how much I already miss him."

I hold her. "I'll miss him for the rest of my life," she says, and then she cries and cries. I hang on while the sobs shake her, my right hand pressed against her back, pressed against the light sweater through which I can feel her warmth, my left hand cradling her head to my chest. I wonder if she can hear my heart, or if her own grief drowns it out.

After a while she stops crying, her body begins to relax, she wipes at her cheeks with the back of her hand and steps away from me. Her face is mottled and her eyes swollen. She tries to smile.

"We were a strange and wonderful pair," she says. Then she goes through the motions of pulling herself together—adjusts the tights at her waist, pushes the unruly strands of hair back from her face, takes a facial tissue from a box on Webb's cabinet to dry her cheeks, blow her nose. "God," she says, "I almost forgot why I dragged you out here."

She goes to the pictures leaned against the wall of the studio and slides one out. A blue mailbox.

"Remember?" she says.

"It was my favorite."

"Mine too. It was the first work of his he showed me. Anyway, I know he wanted you to own it. He said you'd earned it."

"Maybe I have," I say.

"Oh, Alec." Now she comes back to me, not to cry but to let us join hands like the friends I believe we are. "You came here to stand up for Webb, and now you've got to stand up for me. You have to stay. You have to see me through whatever it is that's supposed to happen next."

*

"Webb wasn't a practical person," Bob Hartley is saying. "When I found out that he'd never made out a Last Will and Testament, and here he was with this string of ex-wives, and him planning to marry Prudence—God, I could see the complications. Nightmares for everybody, and Pru could end up in the poorhouse."

Bob is a lawyer by profession—something I might have remembered if I hadn't been so staggered by Webb's death—and we are sitting in the kitchen, at the oak table, with papers and envelopes strewn between us. Bob's glasses are pushed up on his head, and he's finally taken off his necktie. At my left elbow is a half-empty bottle of Jameson's, and he and I each have a tumbler full of ice cubes tinctured with whiskey. Prudence is still up with us—it's past midnight, Mindy has been put to bed upstairs—and she and Theresa are doing up the serving dishes and silverware.

"Though I'll tell you," Bob says. "She may end up there anyway. My brother didn't have much to give away."

"You can't take it with you," Theresa says. She's a big-boned woman with the kind of voice you can pick out of all the other voices at a restaurant or a cocktail party. "So why own it? I think that was the touchstone of Webb's life."

"Be fair," Bob tells her. "He just needed someone to remind him that he was going alone. That he might leave a survivor or two."

"Is there any estate at all?" I ask.

"Oh, sure." He unfolds the will stapled into its blue cover. "There's this house, which believe it or not is free and clear, and the seventy acres with it. This is a valuable thing—though this is a depressed area and it isn't an especially good time to sell. It's a terrible time, as a matter of fact."

"I won't sell it," Pru says. "Mindy and I live here."

"And there's his paintings."

"Ha," Theresa says.

"Cut it out, Terry," Bob tells her. "Picasso he isn't, but he told me the last thing he sold was for thirty-five hundred. And that was a painting by a *living* artist. Dead—"

"God, stop it, Bobby." Pru throws down the dishtowel she's been using and runs upstairs.

"Shit," Theresa says. She follows Pru.

"Just as well," Bob says. "Let them cry on each other's shoulders."

"Catharsis," I say. Something about Bob—or perhaps it's something about lawyers?—makes me say the obvious.

Bob looks at me. "It's peculiar. Terry didn't much like Webster, but she liked the *idea* of him. She'd like to have rolled us both into one person; Webb's Bohemian flair, my talent for making money."

"She doesn't seem to think much of his paintings."

"I've had divorce clients who act like Terry," he says. "They're still in love with the spouse but they know it won't work anymore, so they snipe at something they may very well be fond of—some habit of the spouse that used to be endearing and now seems to drive them bananas." He flips back the top page of Webb's will. "You know: denial."

I take a drink of the whiskey.

"It's a real stunner," Bob says, "to see a man drop dead before your eyes. One minute Webb was standing with his arm around Prudence, waving a champagne glass in the air, and he was saying something about how ordinary language was insufficient to express his feelings for this woman by his side. Very formal. The next minute he was on the ground at her feet." He tips back in his chair so it's leaning against the counter behind him. "You know what we did? We laughed."

I can imagine it. I can hear people saying what a joker Webb was. "Then, of course—" He rocks forward. "Well," he says, "the rest you know." He takes a long swallow of whiskey and sets the drink aside; he brings the glasses down to his nose to read. "Anyway, everything will go to Pru, the State of Maine willing."

He fishes among the papers in front of him.

"Except that rusted-out pickup truck. It goes to some farmer over in West Egypt. Don't ask me why." He shuffles the papers, gathers them, makes them into an even pile. "And I guess the mailbox canvas is yours."

"Pru's worried about funeral arrangements," I say.

"That's easy. I talked to old man Curtis from a pay phone at the hospital. We'll have to choose a casket—something you and I should do; I don't think Pru needs to be burdened with that."

"I think her worry has more to do with the body than with the box. Webb apparently said something once about giving his body to science."

"And his brain to Harvard," Bob says scornfully. "I think that's totally unacceptable. My brother isn't going to be some medical student's cadaver. You've heard those horror stories—they cut the body completely in half, for Christ's sake."

"So I've heard." When I was in graduate school, there was gossip about a med student who cut a heart-shaped chunk of flesh out of his cadaver's buttock, and sent it to his fiancée on Valentine's Day.

"Cremation seems to me the most sensible thing," Bob says. "No fuss, no grave to tend—maybe a marker in one of those commercial mausoleums, but no perpetual care fee to pay to some cemetery rummy, maybe not even a casket—and then if she wants to scatter his ashes in some appropriate place, someplace symbolic and special—"

"Like the Ganges," I say. "And then she could throw herself on a funeral pyre."

Bob stares at me for a long moment. "Fuck you," he says. "I'm only trying to deal seriously with my brother's remains."

*

Pru doesn't come back to the kitchen; Theresa rejoins us briefly, finds a bottle of Bailey's Irish Cream at the back of the liquor cupboard and pours herself a small glassful. Sitting at the table, she and Bob carry on a wary discussion: should the two of them go back to their motel, or should they stay—both of them measuring my presence—in case Pru wakes in the night and needs the consolation of another woman? My opinion isn't asked for. Finally, Bob gathers up his papers and they leave. I watch the car's taillights diminish in the trailing pink dust of the gravel road. Alone, I wander around downstairs, find a stray punch cup on top of the piano, a wadded-up paper napkin on the floor under the coffee table. I rinse the cup under the hot water faucet and throw the napkin into a wastebasket labeled *paper*.

Upstairs, on my way to bed I pass Mindy's room. Its door is partly open, and I pause to look inside. Among the dim shadows cast by a light that may be the moon's, I see Prudence. She is lying beside her daughter, one arm holding the child close, the small blond head nested under the mother's chin. Pru is talking softly—so softly, almost a whisper, that I can make out only a word, a phrase, nothing truly connected. I realize she is telling Mindy about Webb—about fathers and friends and, perhaps, about the ongoing complexities of love.

Fit As a Fiddle

Bruce Jay Friedman

It was a dark time for Dugan. Though he was hale, if not hearty, at sixty-two, his friends were dropping like flies. First to go had been O'Shea who had found the strains of a divorce to be unbearable and waded into a pond in Patchogue, never again to surface. Next came Taggert, a trumpet player who'd been hospitalized for frail lungs, then quickly released when he set a record for blowing up pulmonary balloons. Yet soon after, he expired all the same—in a commercial hotel, surrounded by weeping jazz musicians. No sooner had Dugan recovered from this loss than he received word that Lieberman, his long-time editor, had keeled over at his desk, as if he'd grown weary of reading introspective first novels. Lieberman had been Dugan's age, almost to the day and had appeared to be strong as an ox. Brilliant at shoring up defective manuscripts, he'd imposed a clever structure on Dugan's complex study of 19th century Balkan cabals. The loss was a grievous one to Dugan who couldn't help but think—it's getting closer.

Perhaps it was a cycle. He'd heard that such losses came in three's. But that theory was blasted out of the water when he received a call from his psychiatrist's wife saying that Dr. Werner had been taken by pneumonia—and as a result, Dugan's Wednesday afternoon session had been canceled. Dugan expressed his condolences—no finer man had ever walked the earth, etc.—but in truth, he was angry at Werner. At their last session, the doctor had produced a reference work of distinguished historians that failed to list Dugan's name. Thoughtlessly, and perhaps because of his advancing years, Werner, in referring to Dugan's work, had used the term "intermediate." Dugan was crushed. At the end of the hour, he had raced to the library and searched out reference books in which his name *was* listed—but now he would never get to brandish them at Werner. The widow gave Dugan the name of another man he could see, but although

Dugan dutifully scribbled down the phone number, he knew he would never use it. Werner was the second psychiatrist who had dropped dead on him; he had lost faith in the profession.

Dugan hoped for a let-up in the parade of grim developments, but none came. Soon after, he was notified by fax that Smiley, the owner of his favorite saloon, had died in the back room of the popular watering place. In this case, the news came as no surprise. Not only was Smiley a heavy drinker, there was also a drug habit that was supposed to be a secret but that everybody in the world knew about. In Dugan's dwindling circle, the concern was not so much for poor Smiley—but whether the saloon could function without him. And before Dugan knew what hit him, he lost his accountant, who was barely fifty—although he did smoke a great many cigars. Dugan had given some thought to firing Esposito—who never really understood the peculiarities of artists—but fortunately the accountant died before Dugan could let him go.

He looked on with dismay as friend after friend bit the dust. And if that wasn't bad enough, even his enemies started to go under. Chief among them was Toileau who had accused him in print of shoddy research on his massive Bismarck biography—an attack so vicious and unfair it took Dugan a decade to regain his confidence. He had hated Toileau—how could he not?—but the man was, after all, a contemporary—and it was only small consolation that the nit-picking critic was safely in his grave.

Despite the circling ring of doom, Dugan saw no other course than to press on. After all, wasn't his favorite hero Marshall Joseph Joffre, whose answer to every battlefield situation, no matter how dire, was: "J'Attaque."

Dugan lived in the country where he had carefully surrounded himself with youth—a wife who was twenty years his junior, an adopted son of twelve, and young dogs. In truth, his wife took fourteen kinds of pills to make sure her disposition was cheery. But his son excelled in ice hockey and could lift Dugan off the ground. Dugan was not particularly hypochondriacal, although an occasional twinge in his chest got him nervous. But to be on the safe side, he wolfed down fresh vegetables and made sure not to eat anything he enjoyed too much. His one exception was the large pair of greasy eggrolls he treated himself to on his occasional forays into the city. The hell with it, he told himself, as he took a seat at the bar of Ho's. I've got to have something.

At the moment, he was working on a DeGaulle biography (the youthful DeGaulle, of course) and it troubled him that Lieberman hadn't trained a skilled underling to take over as Dugan's editor. But he forged ahead all the same. His routine was to lose himself in the book for two weeks, then come up for air with a drive into the city for lunch with a friend. But even his surviving friends weren't setting the world on fire. His choice of lunch companions included Burke, a poet who'd been fitted up with a pig's bladder, Karen Armstrong, a brilliant copywriter whose leg had been chopped off to stem a circulatory ailment, and Ellis, the healthiest of them all, a jade collector who wore a pacemaker and had a penile implant to help him with impotence. Another candidate was Grebs, his former attorney, who'd been in and out of mental institutions. In this case, he could imagine the repartee: "They've suggested volts, Dugan. How shall I instruct them?"

His friends were all fine, upstanding individuals, each one a credit to his or her profession—but Dugan lacked the courage to meet them for lunch. Considering the circumstances, how could he be expected to concentrate on food. So on his trips to the city, he ate alone, checked a few bookstores and drove home in cowardice.

An argument could be made that the condition of his friends had nothing to do with Dugan—there were healthy people all over the place. A case in point was his brother Kevin, the picture of wood-cutting vigor in far-off Maine. But Dugan didn't buy the argument. The numbers were against him. The wagons were circling. Even Kevin had begun to send him childhood mementoes, explaining that at sixty-five, it was time to "pare down his life a bit."

Dugan's one consolation was that of all the friends he had lost, there wasn't one who had a claim on his heart—someone he could call in the middle of the night for a discussion of his darkest fears—of death, for example. Could he survive the loss of such an individual? And then one day he found out, when he learned that Enzo Cavalucci had lost a secret and uncomplaining battle with Mehlman's Syndrome, something new, a spin-off of Alzheimer's. (Cavalucci had once joked that it was unwise to catch a disease that had someone's name attached to it.) When Dugan received the news from Cavalucci's mistress, he wept into the phone without shame. And when Cavalucci' s widow called later on to confirm, he wept again. He'd loved his friend, but hadn't realized to what extent— until it was too late. A rival historian, Cavalucci had enjoyed far greater eminence than Dugan and had even sold his Boer War trilogy to the movies. Cavalucci had gotten rich, but such was Dugan's love for the man that he hadn't begrudged him a dime. At a troubled time of his life, Dugan had set out with a lead pipe to kill his first wife's lover; it was Cavalucci who had gently stayed his hand, saying "You don't want to do that." Actually, Dugan *did* want to do it, but that wasn't the point.

Cavalucci had rescued him from a potential shitstorm. On another occasion, sensing Dugan was in financial difficulty, Cavalucci had wired him $10,000, along with a note saying there was no rush to pay it back. And if he needed another ten, that could be arranged, too. Dugan barely slept until he had settled the debt, but he never forgot his friend's kindness. And when Dugan's Bismarck bio had been raked over the coals, it was Cavalucci who stood up bravely at a gathering of historians and recited selections from the work—focusing on the ones that had suffered the greatest abuse. Cavalucci lived in St. Louis, and the two men rarely saw each other, but they spoke regularly on the phone, each conversation picking up seamlessly from the last. Of late, Dugan had noticed a tendency on Cavalucci's part to lose his focus on the phone, but he attributed that to a preoccupation with his planned Cardinal Richelieu masterwork.

In the weeks that followed Cavalucci's passing, Dugan was inconsolable, and could think of nothing else. Acquaintances were one thing—but the loss of this wise and friendly bear of a man—a rock he could always cling to—was more than he could stand. Dugan's wife, an independent woman who dabbled in the sale of waterfront property, barely noticed his extended grief. For the time being, Dugan slept in the guest room, which she didn't notice either. His son trailed him around, hoping his father's melancholy would pass, then gave up and went outdoors to jump up and down on a lonely trampoline. Work was no longer Dugan's salvation. How was he supposed to get excited about DeGaulle's childhood? He sat at his desk, mindlessly reciting the phone number of his boyhood apartment in Jackson Heights, reflecting on his parents, his brothers and sisters, all of them gone except Kevin who was making preparations to join them.

One day, unaccountably, his spirits came awake. Momentarily cheerful, he reached into his pocket to pay for gas at a service station and pulled out an expensive goatskin credit card holder—a gift from Cavalucci. The sight of it put him right back where he started. At the fish store, the following morning, a woman he barely knew gave him an update on her husband's condition in a nursing home. "Mel's incontinent," she shouted across the shellfish counter. He returned home with his flounder fillets in time to receive a call from the representative of a family of blind Hispanics who'd all been fired from their basket-weaving jobs on the eve of Thanksgiving. Before the man could ask for financial assistance, Dugan, to his everlasting shame, shouted into the phone.

"I can't take any more of this. Speak to my wife."

On that note, he packed an over-the-shoulder carry-all bag with pajamas, underwear, toiletries and a Helmuth Von Moltke memoir he planned to finish reading, no matter what. Then he drove to the hospital, although in truth, it was so close to his house he could have walked. Of late, his wife had hinted that she'd had her fill of small town intrigue and wouldn't mind moving back to the city. Normally, Dugan gave in to her every whim. But on this occasion he stalled and failed to list the house with a broker. He loved his spacious Colonial which was in such sharp contrast to the cramped apartment he'd lived in as a boy. Also, he enjoyed the proximity of the hospital. In the winter months particularly, when the chic vacationers were partying in the city, he had the facility virtually to himself.

Dugan took a seat in the waiting room and was alone, except for a bartender who had suffered a clamming injury on his day off. When Dugan's name was called, he flashed a Fast-Track card and was whisked right through to a preliminary examining room where a nurse silently recorded his temperature and blood pressure. As luck would have it, the doctor on call was Alvin Murdoch, Dugan's own physician who'd recently moved to the community, quickly attracting a strong following among the locals. Murdoch had once stopped Dugan outside the post office and gotten him to sign a petition having to do with encroaching health providers. It probably made sense, but Dugan felt he'd been bullied into putting his name on it and mistrusted Murdoch ever since. But the doctor had a reputation for thoroughness and it was difficult to get an appointment with him—so Dugan stayed on as a patient.

Murdoch checked the nurse's findings, then called up the results of Dugan's recent physical on the computer. He made some notes, then crossed his legs daintily, folded his hands on his knees and flashed the boyish smile that everyone except Dugan had found engaging.

"You *look* great," said Murdoch. "Your sugar's a little high, but we discussed that. What's wrong?"

"Not a thing," said Dugan. "Actually, I'm fit as a fiddle. But as we both know, it's just a matter of time. So I thought I might as well check in and get an early start."

Fishing Naked

Kevin Stein

Bent knee within the cathedral
  of Indian Summer, I canoed Crooked Creek's
  great nave adorned with Paduan gold

rich as Giotto's *Lamentation*, where
  Christ-become-man becomes spirit again,
  one body broken among angels' keening.

Alone, I was bamboozled by the sheer
  luxuriance of decay, opulence of loss
  as robed as Catholic pageantry

I'd skipped out of, having swallowed
  Emerson from ullage to last dregs
  of final exam. I was adrift,

lost amidst Emerson's theorizing
  all language is fossilized metaphor,
  pondering the sere bone source

of a word upon my tongue—"paddle"—
  which, in the world of the real,
  simply blistered my hands

as I slogged from here to there,
  where the old couple was fishing,
  their bodies as naked and drooping

as the bent catalpa they lay beneath,
  its brown pods dangling limp dicks.
   I cleaved to the bank. Sure, to look:

I didn't know the crotch grayed,
  breasts withered and hung,
   his sex dark as old hemp rope.

I didn't know much.
  How to get by them, for instance,
   fishing naked in sluiced light,

without plundering their pleasure,
  or hooking the eye of my enlightenment:
   backwater-transparent-eyeball-Peeping-Tom.

             *

What is there about pleasure and its
  perpetual imperilment, the clock
   tick ticking, the hand about to knock,

a galaxy of telephones and yours
  bound to ring as soon as you slip
   in bed, in bath, in the folds of some

all-afternoon casserole whose cheeses
  grow bitter when cold? What is there
   about pleasure brevity makes sweeter,

the way Saturday's blushed pears
  become Sunday's dozen gone to mush?
   Why is the water slide's wait

decades longer than its ride,
  time enough to dot-to-dot
   every freckled shoulder?

What is there about pleasure
  best-sellers must counsel us
   slow down, take it easy—

the dance with silken hand,
  good wine beside tall candles,
   your lover unzipped by pursed lips?

     *

Pleasure, like speech, makes us human.
  Or so we like to think,
   forgetting we choose pleasure

less often than it chooses us.
  To choose or be chosen:
   either way's delicious,

though guilt's greedy fingers
  clutch the scant throat
   all pleasure sallies in and out of.

We call cats' purring mere reflex,
  dogs' humping simply Darwinian—
   because we do the deed when not in heat,

thus confusing pleasure with the story
  of who couldn't refuse the proffered apple.
   Neither one, lest you forget,

as did a friend who phoned us over
  to witness paired primordial bugs
   mating behind her stove clock's glass,

oblivious in their Bermuda
  of honeymoon dreams
   made tropical by hot pot roast.

Blissful, if bliss is something
  bugs can feel, they went at it,
    secure beyond the timer's needle arm

until the lady of the house ballpeened
  her stove clock—glass shards,
    severed legs, two red armored heads

spicing the uncovered pan
  of corn she tossed out back
    for the dog to cut his tongue on.

                    *

Who says the real fount
  of pleasure resides below the waist
    or among the mind's crinkles, and not

on the tongue—who gets the best
  of both—lord of his temple,
    honored guest in others'?

Think of sodden places the tongue goes,
  brave emissary of our heart,
    sampling others' breath and spunk

to bring back unspeakable riches.
  Think of all who visit bearing wine
    and ale, flesh of pear or apple,

assembled culinary delights
  whose sight and scent promise nothing
    without the blessing of taste.

This, our simple ceremony
  of the ravished and thus exalted.
    This, the communion of tongue

and other by which a world
  enters us. O, isn't this the spot
    we enter the world—

not in body but in thought
  given body? Speak a word
   (simple chemical, firing neurons)

and idea bodies forth beyond our lips.
  If not in language, where else
   the juncture of mind and flesh?

That's why, cloistered in a doctor's
  stifling office, I admit to heady pleasure
   just looking at jarred tongue depressors.

Once oaken trunk, supple maple,
  stolid ash branch—now autoclaved
   for safety—they yearn for the sordid,

fecund life of my tongue or yours:
  one quick touch, a throaty *ahhhhhh!*,
   that unceremonious toss to trash.

             *

Degas at mid-life, roughly where I am,
  tossed Impressionism in the can.
   He loathed his worldly reputation

as "Degas, the painter of perfect dancers,"
  and so undid himself. He drew nudes
   gravity had had its sweet way with,

plump and rounded, lumpy-thighed:
  years of pan drippings,
   goat butter, cheeses as pungent

and unforgiving as any rival's eye.
  Now, now, his pencil consoled,
   sketching models at bath with sponge,

hair spooled in curtains of velveteen
  curls—women rapt by the toilette's
   casual ritual of appraisal and repair.

Such was Degas' pleasure, sketching
  from the rear so every rump bloomed
  without the furious complications

a face unfurls. In "After the Bath,"
  a charcoal figure (I'll say, Degas)
  flips a towel's oceanic waves toward

a bather, her body's flushed vessel at rest
  on the tub's cool lip. Both his hands,
  nearly erased, and hers, blurred

with motion, plead *This isn't me*—
  amid cross-hatch ticking toward night,
  the liquid dark all things drain to.

                    *

"All is water," Thales pronounced,
  the first recorded philosophical
  utterance. Who will disagree,

cast amidst October's waves,
  leaves swelling from elm and locust,
  a priestly ash, one squat burr oak

the kids' swing sails upon?
  Listen, the principal foundation
  of Western thought is itself fluid,

wanting nothing more than to change
  its state—vapor, cloud, rain,
    then river and ocean again, again.

Wanting nothing more than to get
  from one place to another
    as wildly as we run to catch

a leaf before it touches down,
  grounded and thus claimed
    as we must be, will be, are.

Wanting nothing more than to be
  the fallen who does not fall,
    one carried with fanfare

to the great table—itself, in former life,
  oak-with-leaves. Wanting to be
    propped among frost-stung mums

beside paired candles, the one
  anointed by bees wax and the sour
    hurried breath of dinner prayer.

Wanting nothing more than to be
  the one saved who sprawls
    to dust in our own good time.

                    *

From dust you came, the story goes,
  though I think it's more likely water,
    this pivotal confusion wrought by a single

sadly flawed translation. Or maybe it's
  all ornamental, the source and end of us
    less in the thing than in the changing of one

to another, pleasure as blessed
  as any stranger become lover become
    wife become poem about same.

"Blindfold a metaphysician, and he'll
  lead you to water," brooded Melville,
    who nonetheless hated Emerson's

insufficient appreciation of evil.
  That was before Emerson's mind went,
    and solids like *table, cup, chair* became

Platonic things he had no words for,
  no tongue to speak them. It was Plato,
    after all, who thought male and female

once joined, now severed, thus sex our quest
  to reunite. Lead a metaphysician
   to water, blindfold him, and he'll drown

in pleasure of a thing neither solid nor gas
  though partly both. This is pleasure
   we have no language for, only articulate bodies

yearning for change, vertiginous
  along the shifting line water and shore unmake,
   all of us fishing that pleasurable edge.

The Inheritance:
A Lamentation

Michael Chitwood

Here it is at last, the indistinguishable thing.
Schooled, well-read in grief,
even in gnashing and wailing, the women driven weeping before the chariots,
and I do not even cough out a dry cry—

just a phrase is all—a goddamn phrase, silent and repeating
in my inner voice, you know the voice you hear,
though hear isn't the right word
since it's never spoken,
but the voice that says your words
when you are silently planning what to say.

Look how far off the subject I've already gotten.

I want to blame this on heredity.
It's a Hall, my mother's people, trait.
Sarcastic, more than one genuinely funny
in a jerk-your-pants-down-and-embarrass-you-in-front-of-everyone kind of
    way,
but all strangely quiet in calamity.

For example,
see even in the midst of what began with weeping
I can say "For example,"
there was the time I was driving toward them, grandmother just dead.
I was ready to be born into family sadness,
mother, the aunts, crying, I imagined,
when I emerged from my car.
They sat on mother's front porch.
"Here, Michael, have a seat," Mom said.

And suddenly now I'm seated beside grief
and everything in the room is equal,
the gray and black ultrasound screen
with its masses and blobs like a high pressure weather pattern,
a greeting card propped open on the desk,
it must be from the technician's husband,
I can read *ove you, honey* in a jerky cursive,
the tube of gel the tech slathered on the wand,
my wife weeping,
the first time I've heard genuine, driven-before-the-chariots weeping.

It was a Hall response.
The emotional fuse blows,
I never knew it came with a distracting phrase,
and we're left silent and dark.
The technician's diploma is elegantly framed.
It says, I'm sure,
the print is too small for me to read,
she is qualified.
She knows a dead child when she sees one.

*

When I would ask him a question
on the way to a job site,
my uncle, mother's younger brother, would turn his ruined eye,
blinded when a piece of steel flew from a struck survey spike,
so I could see it
and say, "You writin a book?"
Once I got smart-mouthed enough to answer "Yeah."
"Well, kiss my ass and make it a love story."

I squeeze Jean's hand,
try to press enough to comfort her.
The technician wipes the gel from the wand,
and then from where she had smeared Jean's abdomen.
The phrase, ridiculous, surreal, inappropriate,
repeats aloud in my head.
But it is unheard in this room
with the blue pocket book under the desk.
The ultrasound pipes and squeaks.

When a piece of heavy equipment broke down,
my uncle, Flukie is his nickname,
would emit a high-pitched, feedback-type shrill
before he would pour out the most eloquent, well-delivered
oration of cussing I, to this day, have ever heard.
It was inspired, a regular lamentation.

Hard to believe a man so gifted distrusted, even openly disdained,
anyone who made a living with words,
salesman, reporters, DJs, preachers,
especially preachers.
But listen to him,
on an August day, in a rage at a backhoe,
shaking a socket wrench over his head and shouting
"I would just as soon carve a wooden bill
and go peck shit with the ducks
as try to make a living with this goddamn yellow motherfucker."

The ample shade of maples.
I squeeze Jean's hand.
The technician balls up the coarse paper wipes.
The ample shade of maples.

"Wish in one hand
and shit in the other.
See which one fills up faster,"
Flukie would say
when I wanted what wasn't
or what was to be wasn't.

My child that was, now wasn't
and in my hand I hold a hand
so full of grief, yes it even fills her hand,
that it can not be touched
even as I clutch it.
The ample shade of maples.
The ample shade of maples.
The tech peels off her skin-tight gloves
and tosses them, inside out,
into an orange plastic trash can.
She's done with us.

135

What will we do for the rest of the day?
Where will we go?
What will my job be?

Flukie turned slightly
so I could see his unseeing
bad black eye, grinned, took pity
and didn't ask this time if I was writing a book
which I was, as we all are, in memory,
a love story.

Two Poems

Neil Shepard

Chameleon

Green fading yellow fading gray—
barely denting the photo-plate
of consciousness until it's too late,
as green lawn goes cold-yellow, or gray

rain all day becomes gray evening.
Imperceptible . . . and wholly predictable.
Your green eyes withering as you hold my gaze.

Your clothes slightly sexier, the colors
jauntier, each morning as you leave for work.
Your return home lengthening from rose sunset,
to purple dinner hour, to gray night-cap.

In the scotch-haze of evening, our words expire.
So I mutter one story: when a pet chameleon
bit me I fed it no more crickets. But

there's something more, old as a sister's love.
It was the summer she smeared
mascara and rouge, her face changing
hour to hour before the mirror.

I hardly knew her. She whispered her secrets
to the shifter, its long sticky tongue
shooting out to trap prey. *What color*

will my eyes be for him tonight, she'd ask.
what color will my lips gloss across his,
what blush will convince him he's won?
No, I tell you, I crushed the crickets

in my hands and would not feed him.
His color changed, green
fading yellow fading gray.

Dramatics

"Hate you, hate you, hate you!"
"Let's not get dramatic. It's over."
I stumble over arrowhead and bitteroot,
traverse the meadow's slim waist,
climb the hill's spine to the crown
of stones poking up between yellow
poplar and twisted acacia, and there the sky
opens around me. Crepuscular rays
thin to nothing and the first
constellations spin into view: the steadfast
Northern Cross, not to be confused
with the migrating Swan. Much later,
Orion's jeweled dagger, his heart
a clouded nebula, his arms outstretched,
endlessly pursuing the Seven Sisters.
I sit for hours and watch the drama unfold.
I trust it, like nothing on earth, small
and insubstantial though the light may be.
A hundred years away, it's the time
lovers never have for perspective
before the cruel words come.
At some dark hour, I go back down
through sassafras and jewelweed, find my way
to the thinnest woodsmoke and window-light,
and all the variety of narrow, human doors.

It is the ripe red

Alan Shefsky

It is the ripe red
plum she prefers,
she tears into it with
the sharp fingernail
of her right thumb.

She loves even
the mess of it, the red-yellow
juice that washes
her hand and wrist,
falls to her dress.

She tears at the plum;
though peeled uneasily
she must peel it;
its small pieces give
and the plum is revealed.

Flesh and beneath—
she divides it further
into pieces she can
grab between finger
and thumb, she hides

the dark peelings
of skin in the folds
of a white cloth,
brings plum flesh
to her mouth, draws it in.

All is yellow-red
and tart, all is sweet
and wine-red; all is
flesh and tender
and plum and heart.

Choose Your Garden

Erin Belieu

When we decided on the Japanese—
foregoing the Victorian, its Hester
Prynne-ish air of hardly
mastered urges—I thought
it would be peaceful, thought
it would relax my nerves,

which these days curl
like cheap gift wrap: my hands
spelling their obsessions;
a nervous tic, to wring the unspeakable from
a speechless alphabet. I thought

it would be like heaven, stern, very clean
virtuous and a little dull . . .

But we had to cross the bridge
to enter and in the crossing came
upon a slaughter of
camillias, a velvet mass
decapitation floating on the artificial lake,

and there the bloated goldfish frenzied
at the surface, 0-ing their weightiess urgency with
mouths too exact to bear

O My Beloved
they said to the snowy petals and to the pink

petals soft as wet fingers,
O Benevolent Master
they said, looking straight up at

us, where we stood near
the entrance, near the teahouse
half-hidden in a copse of gingko, where

even now, discreetly and behind
its paper windows, a woman sinks down
on all fours having untied the knot
at the waist of her robe.

Luminaria

Jeanne Foster

The bougainvillaea lets go a few
papery lanterns, luminaria of day
gracing the hard earth of autumn

      *

Filaments of hair
torn by a mother's hand from a daughter's head

time slows nearly to a stop

she watches them settle through the surface
to the bottom of the tub

the worst child

      *

Fish mouth opening
closing

giant sea bass behind glass
awesome dirigible

like the school principal

when I raise my hand, I mean
absolute silence

*

Men have the luxury of breasts
they can suckle, women have
a poor second in the male chest

his nickel nipple
a small comfort

*

Her blood coming down irregularly now
purple black
clots

daughter without daughter

*

At night she goes into the tunnel
the others pressing sticky palms against her back
high on fear, they strain to see the old woman
who lives in there with the dog that looks like Ali Baba
her grandmother's spaniel who never learned to stay home
sailed away on an aircraft carrier with some sailors
who took him for a stray and made him their mascot
the old woman sends the dog out to do her work
drag one of them into the labyrinth that opens in the dark
from a child's second story bedroom
and floats by day invisible
in the china berry limbs outside the window
when the little friends catch a glimpse
they turn and run, shrieking, shoving
she, the first, is the last
treading against the wall of backs
this happens again and again

*

In the change of life
she knows the mother's curse

*

Sometimes taking giant steps
sometimes walking on her toes

she avoids cracks in the sidewalk

*

The trigonometry teacher
does a hula in the middle of the street
for her

she speeds up the car
gives him a little scare

the best student

*

She hears the voice
there is no dream beyond this one

seeds of loveliness past their prime
fallen in the garden

*

He practices meditation
is initiated, guards the body
of the master, helps him dress
silently in street clothes or in robes

he hates
his mother, but instead
hates her

*

His father

*

She leaves school before noon and walks home alone
It's not fair she says to herself over and over
avoiding the cracks, the snakes in the grass
The teacher said I ran, I didn't run
I walked fast

her mother believes her
it would have been easier had she been
all bad

      *

At first he used to say *I love you*
but became more like her mother

      *

She dreams a mosquito hawk
bites her on top of the head
she swats it, it falls
she kneels down and sees its golden wings
my mother she says

he says *it is a good dream*

      *

She offers him her breasts

      *

Her mother wanted bougainvillaea in the garden
but in her part of the country it freezes

      *

She once fell in love with a Father
God loves you he used to tell her

the shape of his face reminded her
of her father's brother
he was the only lover approved by her mother
around him she became giddy as a girl

*

A mother's dream
planted in a daughter's garden
where it doesn't freeze

*

No matter
how faithfully he practices

*

Call them brave
practicing *perfection*

not *without mistake*
but *the through making of something*
the way her mother
shapes clay on the wheel
laying hands on
living with

a friend who died too young
who may have been a saint
used to say

*

Bougainvillaea
last lights of the dry season
flashing on earth
before the rain
autumn lengthening into winter
the blossoms
fragile paper lanterns, luminaria
turn brown and melt

148

Two Poems

Forrest Hamer

The Different Strokes Bar, San Francisco

Maybe I knew it wouldn't last long, that the joys of us
could vanish like ghosts having lost interest.
Maybe I knew there would be more
than the early twenties of this life, the body quicking.
Maybe I could see men dancing themselves invisible,
one by handsome one, that year before they began to go.
So when I told my friend to stop dancing,
stop with me in the middle of the floor and remember this,
how wondrous already it was, I must have known
how easy it is to forget, how easy it is not to notice,
the dancing going on all about
your new and hungry body, you taken away with it.

Crossroads

Crossed over the river and the river went dry
Crossed over the river, the river went dry
Saw myself drowning and I couldn't see why

Come up for air and the day said noon
Come up for air, said the air read noon
Day said, Son, you better mind something soon

Sink back down, felt my spirits leave high
Sink back down, I felt my spirits lift high
Didn't know if I was gonna die

A man give his hand and he pulled me to the shore
Man give his hand, pulled me over to the shore
Told me if I come I wouldn't drown no more

Me and the man walked and talked all day and night
Me and the man, we walked, we talked all day and night
We startled wrestling till the very lip of light

I put my mind on evil sitting in my soul
Put my mind on evil just a-sitting on my soul
Struggling with the devil make a soul old

I looked at my face and my life look small
Looked hard at my face and this life it look so small
All of a sudden didn't bother me at all

Returned to the river and I stood at the shore
Went back to the river and I stood right at the shore
Decided to myself needn't fight no more

Little Dead Uglies

Joshilyn Jackson

Arlene could've got Aunt Mag just as easy, we both pass by the home on the way in to Possett, but no one was about to ask Arlene, what with the nose ring and her dragging home one long-haired smokey boyfriend after another and anyway they all make such a deal about her being in college for seven years getting all these degrees about nothing, so never mind that she's three years older than me and never mind my sick baby, no, they ask me because no one is going to trouble Arlene's big old Northwestern brain with something as piss-ant Alabama little as picking Aunt Mag up for Gran's birthday, or the family reunion before that, or Susie's wedding before that, or any Christmas.

And of course when I tell Bud he gets all up in my face about it, asking why we have to do it every damn time and saying I can just forget about him even going for the damn birthday and I say I'm not dragging my sick baby and Mag around by myself the way she gets all crazied up in the car, not that he's ever been with me to help, and what with Owen coughing and his little chest all full of snot, and he says that's my fault anyway for dragging the damn kid out in the pollen, but I'd like to know what he thinks he's going to get to eat if I can't go to the Kroger, and him saying all the time we can't afford a sitter just so I can do things that normal women do all the time with ten kids, and if he is so set on sitting on his butt like a lump at home, ignoring my family just to be spiteful, that is just fine, but when did the sweet boy I married die and when the hell is his replacement getting out of my house?

Bud says fine, and he hates my family anyway, and then he goes into the whole long thing about how they think he don't take care of me and Owen good, and my Grandpa being such a holy F word, and he's right about my Grandpa, who hates everyone but God and at my mother's wedding said right out loud, looks like a nigra in that woodpile, when he saw my father's mom's dark eyes, and I don't like my Grandpa either but that's for me to say and not him because its my family so I just run off from his contentious self to me and Bud's bedroom to take him and Owen's things out of the overnight bag I already packed for going to Gran's, hollering back over my shoulder that Bud can stay home and drink beer and scratch himself the whole weekend, but he can darn well keep Owen home with him while he's doing it. He laughs all nasty and hollers back that my F word Grandpa won't like that, keeping the only boy away, and I say Susie and LeeAnne won't want their girls around Owen's mess anyway no matter how many times I tell them you can't pass allergies, so Grandpa can just shut up and like it. Then Bud is yelling something else so I kick the door shut and Owen is squalling from the noise but Bud will just have to fix it because I am busy putting Bud's stuff back in the closet and taking all of Owen's little things out of my bag.

It's a two hour drive to get Aunt Mag, who is not really my Aunt, she's my great great Aunt, but Lord, the woman is past ninety, and if you tried to call her all that she'd be dead before you finished saying hello, and then an hour's drive after that to get to Gran's. So I go get her, and there's this smell in her room, like medicine and old lady, and on top of that Aunt Mag's roommate's poop bag. And there is Mag in the rocker looking up at me with the lines around her mouth all crusty with snuff and already calling me Emma.

Hey there, Mag, Now Aunt Mag, you know me. I'm Clarice, remember? Clarice? Emma's my Gran?

But Mag is already pushing up on out of her rocker and shuffling over with one hand out and as soon as she gets close enough to breathe her old lady jello breath in my face she's saying, *Emma, you come to get to get me out of here Emma, you gonna take me home Emma?* and digging her old bony hand into my shoulder and it's her death grip, she won't let go till we get to Gran's and she can attach to her. I keep telling her I'm Clarice, Gladys' girl and Emma's grandgirl, but it doesn't do no good because of course she's senile and before that she was a retard, so I just get her hand bag and we go on out to the car. I already checked her out because the last time I came and got her out of her room before signing her out with the nurses she got all nervous at the nurses' station and peed all down herself and I was wearing these little cloth shoes with flowers on them I had just bought at Target and she was right behind me clutching on to my shoulder and I didn't know she was peeing herself until the puddle spread out and all of a sudden my foot was warm and wet and those shoes were just ruined and it took an hour to get her redressed and then I had to drive the whole way smelling my pissy foot. The nurses station scares her because she's got this thought that the nurses are from the devil, but I don't think she really used to believe that. I think it was a trick to get my Gran to take her home, she can't stand to be away from Gran so she had all these tricks, she was pretty crafty for a retard, like saying the devil part in front of my Grandpa, who believes that doctors and nurses and even movies are infested by demons, was pretty smart, but he likes Mag even less than he likes Satan, so it didn't work, and then she got all senile and she probably believes that stuff about the nurses now.

We get back on the road and Aunt Mag is just talking on at me in this old whispery voice with her hand clamped on my shoulder just talking on, saying, *Emma, you got to get me out of there, you got to take me home with you Emma, you don't know what they act like there when you ain't around they hit me Emma they hit me with me a stick across my bottom, they lay me up on the bed and they pull up my night dress and they hit me with a stick, and they put things in me Emma, little dead things, they put things in the food, sick-making things, I'm sick like a dog all the time, and my bottom is all over welts I can't even sit up on it sometimes, Emma, you got to get me home with you I want to be home with you.*

I just keep telling her I'm not Emma and just pay no mind to the other stuff because if a person even acts like they hear all that stuff Mag says about the home then Mag'll start doing things, like when Grace picked up Gran and Mag just for a day trip on Easter Sunday and met up with all us family at a real nice steak house, the kind that has the big salad bar with all kinds of things on it that aren't even salad like biscuits and hot potatoes and you can go back as many times as you want, and Mag started saying her piece about the beatings and the sicking up poison and Grace went all sanctified over it and started asking Gran how she could even leave poor defenseless old Mag in such a hell hole and Gran kept trying to shush Grace, but Lord, nobody can do that, Grace had to stick her big head all the way up in it and Gran kept saying, *Just leave it be,* but Grace wouldn't of course until Gran finally had to come right out and say that it wasn't true, which just made Mag all the more stubborn—Mag is pure mule—and Mag stood up and yanked her skirts up and dropped her drawers and showed her butt right there in the steak house. So there is Mag with her old puckery butt hanging out over Grace's salad plate, yelling *See? See?* so that every person in the place looks and there's not a mark on her. Grace keeps saying, *Mag, Nothing is wrong with your butt, now put it away,* but Mag won't, she keeps running her hands over her bare cheeks screaming that she can feel the welts and why won't Grace at least take a feel. Well, the manager came over and we had to leave and I had only got to visit that salad bar one time and you have to pay up front.

So I just keep telling who I am but it never stops her talking like I'm Emma, she always thinks I'm Emma, because I look like Gran in the eyes, and the red hair, and because she raised my Gran up from a baby because my Gran's parents were lampers and they was walking two hours each way to Dale's Eggs, which is still in business, Grace lamps and she has lines all up around her eyes big as spider webs from squinting, holding eggs up to the light looking for dead baby chicken bodies instead of a yolk and it's an eight hour shift there, enough to drive a person blind, and then Gran's mamma and daddy sharecropped a little piece of land on the side so with the shift and the walk and the cotton they didn't have time to raise any baby, and so they gave my Gran to Mag to keep because Mag distracted too easy to be a good picker and Dale's Eggs wouldn't hire no retards back then because they didn't have no laws like about who you have to hire that Bud says made that black guy from up over to Leyton get that foreman job but I know it's because Bud called in sick nine times and sat around under my feet driving me crazy.

Now if Mag couldn't keep her mind on picking how she was supposed to not lose a baby or kill it, one, I just don't know, but I do know I would never just pass Owen to a retard and go, but Mag got all crazy about my Gran and never did put her down somewhere, or bake her like this one retard did over to Flomaton. Fact, my Gran didn't learn to walk, even, until she was past two because Mag never once set her down. Now, my Owen is just three months and he has these new little pink feet like little fat wads of nothing, just perfect little pig feet that've never been used, and my Gran had feet like that for going on three years. Even after Mag let her touch the ground she barely let go of her. Mag was always that crazy over her, like when my Gran came to tell Mag that she was marrying my Grandpa who was twice her age and really just a lamper no matter how many times he screamed about hell for free down at First Southern Baptist who couldn't afford a real preacher and my Gran barely fourteen, Mag fell down on the ground screaming and biting at the dirt and she pulled out two big handfuls of hair and then tried to tear her own eyeballs out, until my Gran said, *Mag, you can come live with us,* and then Mag got up with her mouth all full of mud and grass and was fine. She almost didn't get to live with them, though, because when my Grandpa saw that she had these two bald scabby patches on the top of her head from where she'd torn out the hair he thought she was from the devil and had got her horns clipped off to fool him.

Now I start watching Mag real careful the minute we turn onto Highway 41, it's just a little shit road that goes nowhere but Possett and then on to Leyton, and all Possett is is the Baptist church and a general feed store, and three tin sheds like you would put gardening tools in with a big board that goes across the top of all three with the words "Police Department Jail Fire House" painted in black, and Leyton ain't much bigger, but this road just gives her the screaming crazies for no earthly reason I can see. There's never no cars on the road, and the only thing to see on both sides is high summer cotton, but when we turn onto it she goes all quiet and her fingers kind of dig in my shoulder harder and I think this is going to be one of her times so I clench up tight on the wheel and I'm thanking the Lord I don't have Owen in the car this time but then she starts groping her free hand around for her snuff and starts up with the *Emma Emma take me home*, just droning on and working herself out a dip and with her just rattling and the road looking the same I start not paying as good of attention as I should, knowing how she gets and all, and I am just thinking about will Bud remember to give Owen his medicine when Mag suddenly crabs up and pounces faster than anyone almost a hundred should be allowed to move and she grabs the steering wheel and pulls right so hard and strong we bounce off 41 and the cotton closes all around us.

I slam on the brakes but just then the cotton in front of us give out and we hit a dirt road and start skidding and fish tailing so I have to ease up or we are going to slide right off the little road back into the field. The road is winding all over and I can't turn around on it without smashing some more of somebody's cash crop so I just keep going slow hoping the road will wind us back around to 41. Mag has her hand back clamped to my shoulder and she is screeching and carrying on and I'm still sliding around on every turn when up ahead I see the man with his back to us walking down the road wearing that old fashioned broad brim, that same damn man except I could swear last time Mag pulled us off the road a good thirty miles west of here. Mag's voice stops like it's been cut out and I swerve to miss him and almost drive back into cotton as high as the car, and then I straighten out and we're past him and he's moving over to the side of the road almost in the cotton and this time I'm almost calm and can look back at him because Owen isn't in the car so I do look back but he's shading his eyes to look after us and I can't see his face for the hat and his hand, but Mag spits brown juice at him like she hates him and it goes dribbling down my window. Well, we keep driving and the car says we're doing twenty but it feels like fifty but in slow motion with the cotton green and white all around us and the road is red dirt, and around the next bend coming towards us is that pretty wormy looking girl, like she don't have anything better to do but be walking on any piss-ant dirt track Mag pulls us off on, and she's got that woman walking behind her with one hand clamped down on her shoulder and then I see how they walk together, I forget about finding 41 and really see them how they walk and then I look at the girl's face and its my Gran's little girl face that I've seen in a brown picture that's been on the mantle at my mother's house since I was born. Mag sees her too, and she starts hollering, *Emma, stop and get her, Emma,* but the other two times I thought she was calling me Emma, but now I see how they walk together and the car is going really slow now and I just in that second know she is walking down that road, she is about to meet him, and he is twice her age and he will stop to preach and lamp in Possett after he sees her thin pretty face on this road and he will marry her when she turns fifteen and in nine years will give her four baby girls and seven little dead uglies who should have been boys, and he will tell my mother that she should have been one of the uglies who fell too early out of Gran into the toilet seven times, so that a boy could have made it all the way safe, and my mother will marry my daddy to get out of that house alive and I will be born, and I know all these things just in that second.

Mag is still screaming, *Emma, stop and get her, Emma, Emma,* and it's like Mag can't even see herself behind my Gran's little skinny self, and I can't think or decide if we should stop and pick my Gran up and turn around and drive her past my Grandpa to wherever she is going and then maybe I would be dead or not born or some other person with hair not so red and who maybe went to college or went to Europe but then maybe no Owen, but no Bud either, and we are almost past and passing and Gran is turning to watch us go by and then I look back at her as we go by but she isn't there, just the empty fields and Highway 41 is just ahead and Mag is for once quiet, and she stays quiet all the way to the turn off for my Gran's farm, and then she starts up again at the beginning with the beatings and sticks and the take me home with you.

We get there pretty early, but I can see Arlene is already out in the yard cutting open a melon there and talking on in her her new fake Yankee voice and trying to make everyone call her Lena, and she has a black guy with her with his hair in little braids all down his back and my Grandpa must be just shitting and I see he has a gold hoop bigger then the ones Bud got me for our first anniversary, not that he ever takes me anywhere I could wear them.

I open the car door and Arlene walks up with Grace and before I even get out the first thing out of Grace's big mouth is, *Lord, Clarice, you getting so big I could sit on your butt and ride to town,* like I didn't just have a baby, and Arlene just stands there like a little slice of nothing in all black smoking at me and my Gran comes and gets Mag out of the car and then leans in to give me a kiss with Mag's hand already clamped down on her shoulder and I bet if you was to peel Gran's dress down off her shoulder you would see these dents that fit those fingers perfect.

The Coroner's Report

Jason Brown

At 333 Willow Road a thirty-five year old woman sipping tea in her back yard falls off a picnic bench and stops breathing. A six year old boy in kangaroo pajamas opens the door for us when we arrive.

"You've come to the right place," he says. "Everyone is in the back yard."

Two medics and three blues stand in a semi-circle around the body waiting for us. They're not allowed to touch the body until we arrive. My trainee Andrew removes the cap from his pen and writes: "Body supine."

"That's my mother," the boy says, his hands hanging at his side. "I called 911 and no one answered so I called again and told them she was dead." He stares without blinking at the body.

"Where's your father?"

"He lives in California. We don't know where. I'll never see him again."

Andrew interviews the medics while I walk back through the house taking mental notes I will write down after we have delivered the body to the morgue. In the living room: a blank TV, smell of Pinesol, rug recently vacuumed. In the kitchen: a half-eaten turkey sandwich, an unfinished glass of milk on a counter, a napkin folded over, the sliding glass door open to the deck and back yard. The time the boy called the dispatch: 11:42 A.M.; the time they arrived: 11:55; the time we were called: 12:10. It is now 12:20.

"Asphyxia," Andrew says leaning down over the body's open mouth and eyes. She wears running shoes and nylon shorts, a thin gold watch and a small silver ring.

"No purple." He nods and runs his hand along the muscles of her neck and shoulder. Rigor already, I can see from the stiffness. The morgue guys arrive in their white overalls and shortly after them Patty from child protective services. The position of the bench indicates she fell directly onto the grass. Obviously no foul play, though sudden death requires we take pictures.

After Andrew finishes with the camera, he stands next to the boy on the porch. "What about him?"

I point to Patty standing by the sliding glass door in her blue slacks and tan blouse. She places a hand on the boy's shoulder and slowly turns him away from the scene to a new life none of us can anticipate.

"What happens to him?" Andrew asks. They always ask questions like this when they're right out of the academy.

"He goes with her for now."

In the back of the morgue van in the dark with the body we review the case.

"No abuse to the body, no sign of struggle, no sign of forced entry," Andrew answers my questions.

"Something happened. If she didn't choke, what happened?"

He is silent. A good sign. Above all I want him to focus.

In America the course to become a coroner lasts no more than a few weeks. When I first started there was no course. The chief coroner was appointed and he chose deputies. There was no one to learn from, no books to read on the subject, just a brief outline describing our duties, a badge, and a gun. In those days most of the guys came directly from the police, but I joined from the ambulance service where I had grown tired of arriving too late.

The scene of a crime does not remain static for long. The blood starts to settle, the muscles stiffen into rigor mortis. Pieces of evidence, even the body itself, are often moved by inexperienced officers. After twelve hours, for instance, the temperature in the body is no longer significant. Before that time we can discover, by jabbing a needle into the liver, how long the body has been dead. Doctors report hospital deaths to us, but we do not investigate. If they do not die in the hospital or in the presence of a physician we are required to respond. A large percentage of deaths are self-inflicted. Without conclusive evidence they are labeled *natural*.

Most of the calls during the day involve accidents. A few involve suspicious death. Those calls, when they come, come at night. It is fine for other people to believe what they want, but it is important that Andrew *dispense* with numerous misconceptions: drowning victims do not come up three times before going down for good; a shot through the head or heart will not kill someone instantly; and exit wounds for bullets are not always larger than entrance wounds.

"One night two years ago," I tell Andrew, "a sixty-year-old man living three miles from our office picked up his coat at eight P.M. and announced to his wife that he was taking a walk. Instead, he got in his car and started driving down route 89. Two miles south where we found skid marks, he parked, pulled a thirty eighty out of his pocket, and drove a bullet through the middle of his head. He slumped against the steering wheel and passed out. Sometime later he woke again, started the car, and drove home. His wife met him at the door. He took off his hat and coat and handed them to her.

"'You're bleeding,' she said.

"'It's nothing,' he replied and climbed up the stairs for his nightly bath. He filled the tub, took his clothes off, sat down in the water, and died. We found him later. No matter how fatal the wound may seem at first, it is impossible to tell how long the person will live or what they will do in that time."

Andrew nods.

"Another man, a police officer involved in a gun fight, was shot directly through the heart after shooting his assailant dead. He reholstered his gun, walked two blocks to his cruiser, climbed inside, and died. This took him several minutes, and he did it all with no heart. You have to accept when you approach the scene that these kinds of events are possible. Another man, cut in half below the ribs by a train, lived for five hours. We arrived expecting to find him dead. He was having a lively conversation about the Boston Red Sox with the paramedics. They rushed him to the hospital where the doctors pulled out their tubes and machines. They tied things up. There was very little bleeding by then because his blood pressure had reduced, but despite the shock he still talked to the doctors and nurses.

"We waited outside for three hours listening to his gibberish. We had found the bottom half of him on the other side of the switch box, where he had obviously been preparing to commit suicide. It took us an hour to collect the rest which was spread over the two hundred yards it takes a train to stop. Despite the irrelevance of these body parts to the individual or to the investigation, we must recover all human flesh from the scene. We stood outside the emergency room with a bag filled with this man's bones, flesh, long pieces of stringy muscle, and gelatinous fat, and we waited for him to stop going on about baseball and about overhauling the engine on his Camero. He didn't sound depressed at all. His mind rushed frantically from one topic to the next. Then he was silent. He was finally dead."

Neither Andrew nor I are doctors and know nothing, really, about how the body works. I am not even an expert on the ways a body fails. I am an amateur. They call us when everything has happened, and we make close observations and tentative suggestions. We observe and oversee the transportation of the body. We ask a few questions, but mostly we are the custodians of the body and all of its effects from the scene of its last moment to the doorstep of the morgue. A dead body requires us to protect its legal rights.

Later we issue a report based on our observations. Nothing we say is ever conclusive. The detectives and the medical examiners make the decision. Finally we make a much harder report to the family. Sometimes they see our badges and all we have to do is stand there with our hands crossed in front as they scream. I give the basic facts: on his motorcycle, or in a car, or crossing the street, or shot. They ask why, but they're not asking me, nor do they expect an answer just because I am wearing a badge. If necessary I will repeat the basic facts to them.

The medical examiner and later, possibly, the judge may ask our opinion, but our job does not usually require that kind of speculation for which we are not trained. At most, our observations may lead the medical examiner in the right direction. We may save him time.

Our observations are far more relevant concerning the circumstances of death. We may observe, for instance, that the fingers are tightly wrapped around the gun handle. It is impossible for a murderer to simulate what we call the cadaveric spasm of muscle at the instant of death. This can be observed before rigor mortis occurs and can help in determining suicide versus murder. The position of the body in relation to the instrument of death, marks on the clothing indicating dragging, the angle of the wound—all of these are relevant. If lividity centers on the right side but the body lies on the left, we know that someone for some reason moved the body after death. There is also a narrow stretch of time during which the skin will register a probable cause of death, either by asphyxia, purple coloring, or poisoning. One woman who appeared to die of a heart attack had been killed by a relative using a safety pin. The murderer jabbed the pin into the chest between the ribs while the woman was sleeping. Investigators later found the blood stained pin in the same house, in the room of the dead woman's daughter.

*

Today my shift ends at 3 P.M. On Indian Summer afternoons like this when the leaves have already turned and started to fall, but the air warmed by the sun feels thick and stagnant, I walk in the sand at the beach where people fish or lie on their towels looking out over the waves. My toes curl into wet grains as I push forward following the line where the wash ends and the sand is cool. People know the snow could come tomorrow or next week, so they have left work early to walk their dogs or simply lie on their backs and turn their faces up to the sun. A woman standing knee deep in the swells raises her arms up above her head. I stop and stand behind her, listening to my heart pound in my ears. She turns around and walks toward me. If I were going to introduce myself, this would be the time. Instead I lower my head and wait for her to pass by.

As soon as it dies, I think, the body begins to erase itself and return to its original elements: CO_2, H_2O. I should tell Andrew that the things I want I will not get because of the way I have to live. The same will be true for him. Our job never varies. I hope Andrew understands that. I hope he is not seeking adventure. For us, every week, every year, is the same.

At three in the morning I am reading history. I know the year the city that employs me was founded. I know the history of my profession—coroner from corona, crown, second only to the king in thirteenth-century England. I am not reading in my apartment but have come to my brother's apartment to watch him sleep. It is the only time he looks peaceful. After he has been drinking he never hears me turn the key in the lock, if he has bothered to lock the door at all. I come across town and climb the four flights up just to hear his breathing. He told me he had quit, but his apartment is a pile of empty bottles, dirty clothes, and unwashed dishes. He sleeps on the bare mattress spread across the pull-out couch. When he wakes to vomit at seven I am still sitting in his chair thinking. On top of the rug sit a few boxes of clothes and a tape recorder. The cars roar down State Street toward South Portland without interruption.

*

Every Monday some of the files from our office move back to the warehouse for storage. We can only hold a certain number of files current. I have Andrew carry the stack and we exit through the back of the building across the parking lot to a metal-sided structure guarded by a man in a plastic booth. He knows me, but asks for Andrew's ID. Inside the shelves extend two stories up to the ceiling. The rows on the right contain boxes of personal effects used as current or former evidence in trial or simply unclaimed effects—wallets, watches, rings of people who did not have a next of kin or could not be identified. The rows to the left contain files of John and Jane Does going back to the time of the Portland Fire in 1891. Andrew climbs up the ladder and places each file, according to number and date, in the right slot. As we walk out our heels click against the concrete and echo throughout the metal cavern.

At 10:25 this morning Andrew and I are sitting in the car sipping coffee he bought across the street at Green Mountain. The smell of almonds rises in my nose and the heat steams the window blocking my view across Fore Street to Gritty's Pub where my brother, Brian, knows one of the bartenders.

After five days I will write a report on Andrew. We have our own way of training and determining qualification in this office. A person who sees a dead body for the first time may know they have made the wrong choice but not being willing to admit it. If we don't like them or feel they can't handle the job we send them back to the police where they see us as nothing but pay check workers. Support staff.

The best people do not become coroners. I have seen trainees turn around in the middle of the street and walk away from a body. In other, less extreme cases, the trainee forgets himself and starts to shake the body by the shoulders shouting, "Get up!" For this reason, I am more suspicious than usual of Andrew because he seems just out of high school—too young not to believe in saving lives as I was when I became a medic at his age. No one that young requests the coroner's office unless they are hiding something from themselves. He squeezes the bridge of his nose and runs his palm over his forehead and closely cropped blonde hair. His red, Irish cheeks burn from the coffee's heat.

He will have to learn that the people in our office are not friends, though we are not unfriendly. We know very little about each other. Some of them live with another person, a lover, but few are married and fewer still have children. Andrew doesn't seem willing to tell me about himself. I only want to know the relevant facts. In the same way we try to avoid knowing more than necessary about the deceased. Beyond names it is only necessary to learn about the circumstances leading up to death. That the dead man beat his wife is only pertinent to us, for instance, if she may have played a role in his death. Whether or not she was justified in killing him, in self defense, is not up to us.

We carry information. We assist in the tabulation of the facts.

"What were you doing before this. High school?" I ask. He looks eighteen, nineteen.

"Before the police academy," he says, "I was in the 82nd Airborne for two years. Did hundreds of jumps, all of them practice. Dozens of guys in each plane, hundreds of planes, thousands of guys all pouring into the air. The chutes popped open in hundreds of tiny explosions."

"Tell me about your coroner training. How much do you remember? How many people died last year?" It is an important question.

"In the world: 52,514,000. More people in winter, less in summer."

"How many from disease?"

"17,199,000."

"How many hearts failed?"

"11,931,000."

One person kills themselves every twenty minutes in America. 30,000 a year. There are 400,000 unsuccessful attempts. 92,000 accidental deaths. 45,000 car accidents. 13,000 people fell. Poison: 8,000. Fires: 4,200. Drowning: 4,000. Suffocation: 3,000. Guns: 1,800. Gas: 700. 23,700 murders reported. 10,612 by guns. 3,043 from knives. 1,000 from blunt objects.

Sometimes, however, facts do not tell us the full story and statistics are misleading. Appearances at the scene are often misleading, too, which is why I tell Andrew to observe without drawing conclusions. I held a piece of someone's brain in my gloved hand, looked at the picture on the license of a twenty-year-old boy who had just ridden head-on into a brick wall on his motorcycle and wondered about the 7,300 days of memories, thoughts and fears contained inside. His death was eventually labeled accidental, as those kind often are, though his was definitely a suicide. He was driving eighty five miles an hour through a parking lot straight at a wall on his birthday.

In our job timing matters just as much as accuracy. After a suspicious arson I was present during the questioning of a burn victim whose hours were numbered. His eyes burned red—even the skin on his lips was burned off. Though I stood behind the investigating officer, the burned man saw my badge and tried to raise himself up. "Get him out of the room," he mumbled through his bandages. I had come too early.

Across the street a man coming out of the bar stumbles on the bricks and catches himself on the light post. Two bigger guys follow him out and stand back. Brian turns from the light post and rushes at the stomach of the bigger man. I open the door and start out of the car but think better of it and slam it closed.

"Who's that? Do you know that guy?" Andrew asks.

"My brother."

"Shouldn't we do something?"

"There's nothing we can do."

Andrew looks at me, steps out of the car, and runs across the street. He flashes his badge at the two men who back off and walk away. Then he helps my brother to his feet, brushes his jacket off, and pulls him by the arm toward the car. There's blood coming out of Brian's nose, but it's not broken, and his left eye is swollen shut. He turns his face away from me to hide the scar on his cheek as if I were seeing him for the first time. My beeper goes off and a call comes in over the radio. Brian steps back as Andrew lifts the beeper off his belt and looks at me. I wave him in the car. Sitting beside me, Andrew rubs his hands down over his thighs, and I can tell he won't sit still until he looks back. He does and I do, too, glancing into the rear view. Sure enough, Brian crosses the street back to the bar.

Accident on I-95, the overpass. Someone hit the guard rail, according to the dispatcher. We drive through the sudden cold downpour and blowing leaves along Forest to the on-ramp and north until we reach the red and blue lights clustered at the roadside flashing into the gray mid-day sky. The white caps rise in the bay out beyond the brown stacks of the old bean factory. No brake skids on the pavement. The individual did not try to stop from driving into the guard rail, but the position of the car tells the story: the first car bounced off the rail, turned sideways to traffic and skidded. Another car hit the passenger door and shot the person into the street where another car dragged the person to a stop. Two other cars smashed into the first car. It could be, I think, looking at the upturned Buick Skylark, that the person was careless. It could be that the person drank too much or did not fight sleeplessness. It's hard to know why it happened, though we can see from the remains and the skids what happened.

"Bottle of Scotch between the seats," John Harvey, a cop from the station, says. Andrew writes it down as if the statement were fact.

"Erase that," I say to Andrew. "Write only what you observe not what you are told."

"Two dead," Harvey says and nods to one of the cars that crashed into the Skylark. Rescue guys have inserted the jaws of life to extract another man, fully conscious, out of the fourth car. A dead man lies on the ground with his face smashed in, and a woman, the wife of the man being extracted, paces back and forth behind the rescue guys holding her head. One medic tries to calm her, but she pushes him away.

Just as I expected, the body of the first person is spread out in many pieces, dragged by the second car that came along. "First it crashed against the guardrail," I say to Andrew pointing out the twisted metal. "The door was torn off there. The car skidded sideways and rolled. Individual was pitched onto the road when that second car up ahead came along. The other body seems intact, so let's help the morgue guys collect the pieces of number one before the rain washes it away." Already the guys in white jump suits are combing the street and dropping pieces of flesh into plastic bags. The torso and one of the legs lie in one pile. The person's head lies where it first hit the pavement. The skin is rubbed off and the skull cracked in two. The grayish pink contents have smeared over a distance of ten feet. The rain erodes the streak and evidence of what has happened.

"Write this down and snap it," I say. Andrew pulls out a water proof camera and snaps the photos, jumping from one side of the piece to the other to capture both angles. I hand Andrew a pair of rubber gloves and send him with a plastic bag in the direction of the two arms, separated from the torso and lying several feet from each other in the middle of the road. I want to see if he hesitates, but he leans down and picks them up by the wrists dropping them in the bag one at a time. He walks back and stands in front of me, his face blank and calm.

"What else?"

"Male or female," I ask him, pointing down at the collection of parts we have collected lying at my feet. He looks down at the bags and back to me. He opens up the bag containing the head. He closes his eyes and the bag, too.

"I can't tell."

"Check the rest."

He opens the bag with the torso but the skin was ripped off when the body dragged underneath one of the cars.

"There's nothing left. How am I supposed to know?"

"Check the curve of the pelvic bone or the sciatic notch. Both are sticking out."

He uncovers the torso and runs the gloved hand beneath the flaps of flesh along the exposed bone, but I can tell he doesn't remember.

"It's too narrow there for a woman," I say. "You should know that a body is only ever impossible to identify for two reasons: either its remains are incomplete, without teeth, skin, or retinas, or the person was indigent and without connections. This kind of person vanishes without anyone noticing. It is rare, though, that a person like this will pass into the ground without revealing their identity. The body owned a car. Even though we have not found ID and the car has caught fire, the burned plates will reveal the owner. From there we will investigate. It is our job to identify the body, so learn to identify characteristics," I say. "This will give you the name of the body. A scar, a tattoo, dental work."

"Yes, sir."

I know how hard it is. After eight hours or less even an uninjured body ceases to resemble the person. It is much harder to identify a body that has been altered. After a fatal fire in a building, I identified the partially burned body of a friend who I knew lived there. We attached his name to the body and took him to the morgue. Two days later I saw him walking toward me along the street. He had been out of town. "Wasn't that lucky?" he said.

The woman who was pacing by the wreck has come up beside us and started to drag the charred corpse of victim number two north along the road. I rest my hand on her shoulder.

"Excuse me, ma'am. This body does not belong to you."

"Yes it does. It's my husband," she wails. Probably she thinks she is taking him to their home miles away.

"No it is not, ma'am."

"I should know my husband."

All the skin has melted tight against the bones, the face smashed in.

"Your husband is still alive. They've just taken him out of the car now, back there."

She stops, looks south to the twisted metal of the cars and the endless line of backed up traffic. She drops the body like an old bone. The red and blue lights flash off her soaking and bruised face, and she runs.

This is why we keep family members away from the scene—they will see what they want to see, and often there is very little about the body to remind them of the person they loved. We will take it to the morgue. We have this man's ID from his pocket. Only the head and torso were burned. It is best for the family involved to hold the image of their loved one unspoiled in their memories.

This time Andrew rides in back with the body alone to the morgue while I follow behind. When he steps out I examine his face for signs of changes, but he holds the same steady expression. The color has left his cheeks, but he goes about the business of helping the guys carry the body and the bags of parts to the door. We don't follow inside because I have obtained the address of the burned man's wife, in South Portland.

"This is your first time, so when you speak to this man's wife," I say as we cross the bridge, "always restrain your tongue if you have any doubts. It is not only important to speak in a calm voice, it is important to be calm. Death does not concern the body. It concerns the survivor. She may appear anxious, distracted, she may cry, break into a frenzy, or simply be unable to move or speak. If she starts flailing her arms around, pounding her fists or screaming, wrap your arms around her, locking your fingers behind her back, and squeeze tightly. Whisper her name over and over until she calms. When you have her attention, give her a task if you have to. She can pack, if it is necessary to leave the house to visit a relative. She can call relatives. You can ask questions which may have no relevance to the case. It is critical, at this moment, for her to believe in the importance of her answer to your questions. You must frame the questions in a tone of voice that conveys urgency, as if the results of the discussion could even bring back her husband. This kind of lie has to be very subtle to be effective. The deceased's name should not be mentioned. You may ask her to recount, in detail, the previous day's activities. Look her in the eyes. If her eyes wander, ask her again until she looks back at you. Then, when she recounts beginning in the morning, interrupt her, asking for more detail, minute by minute, if possible. Pretend to write down everything she says, flipping the pages of your notebook every few minutes.

"After a short time a relative, neighbor or case worker will arrive, at which point you break off the conversation. Your responsibilities concerning the survivor have ended, unless that person needs to be interviewed concerning a suspicious death. Don't ever look over your shoulder as you leave the home. She may be watching you as if you are the dead person come back to life. It is important that she understand that you will not look back and that she will never see you again. You will feel the impulse, in the doorway, to turn around. You will feel responsible and empathetic, as the course manual explains, but this is not your actual responsibility."

I drive over the bridge crossing the Fore River to South Portland, where I rent an apartment. Occasionally the bridge opens when an old tanker is dragged by a tug to the giant white cylinders jutting out of filthy banks. The rents used to be cheaper on the South Portland side, but now a scrap metal yard rises on the banks across the river from the oil tanks. A giant barge floats up river once a month, loads a pile of crushed cars and appliances, and floats back out to sea. I live on one side of the river and work on the other. It used to make a difference, passing from one city to the other, but not anymore. Blue and gray swirls of gas and white patches of foam swirl beneath us in the current. We make our way to Thorton Street, just a mile from where I live, and stop at forty-five, a blue, vinyl-sided bungalow. A woman comes to the door. Probably Mrs. Leblanc. She guards the latch on the screen door with her hand. It is dinner time and I can smell roast chicken. I lean over.

"I'm from the Coroner's office, Mrs. Leblanc. May I come in?" She obeys, and I walk into the living room. Andrew is at my side poised with his yellow legal pad.

"There's been a horrible accident and your husband is dead," Andrew says looking right into her eyes just as I told him to.

She looks away, out the window to the drips falling down in front of the bay window and a group of kids splashing home through the puddles. Maybe she is thinking he was supposed to clean the gutters this weekend.

"Your husband is dead, ma'am," he repeats. "He was killed in a car accident."

When possible I will also report that the victim did not suffer, unless, as in this case, it is not true.

A long silence ensues as she pulls her robe tightly around her waist.

"Is there anything we can do for you? Do you want to pack, to visit relatives?" Andrew lowers the pad and takes a step as if the woman might tumble forward into his arms.

"No," she says. "No." She backs away into the darkness of the house. I lean against the screen for a moment before steering Andrew back outside.

Andrew looks back at the front of the house. "That's it?"

"Come on," I say. "We'll call Human Services from the car. She doesn't want to talk. You only talk to her if she wants to talk or appears hysterical. We have no idea what kind of relationship she had with her husband or if they even lived together. We will call it in and inform one of the neighbors."

The neighbor, a woman in her late sixties, comes to the screen door carrying her cat like a weapon. "We're from the Coroner's office, ma'am. Your neighbor, Mrs. Lablanc, just lost her husband. We thought if . . . "

"Who?"

"The woman who lives next door."

"I've never met her. I don't know anything about her."

"Thank you for your time," I say.

"The woman next door lost her husband!" Andrew says.

"Who are you?" The woman backs up, lowering her head as if Andrew were threatening to hit her. I pull him away from the door by the shoulder.

"I'm very sorry to have disturbed you, Miss." She vanishes into the back of the house with her cat.

We walk to the other neighbor's house. Here we find a younger woman, in her thirties, with two children behind her playing on the living room rug.

"I'm very sorry to hear about this," the woman says, rubbing her forehead.

"Would you mind going next door at some point to check on her. Someone from Human Services will arrive soon."

"Yes, I will. Sure. I've never met her. I don't know her. I mean I've seen her coming in and out of the house, and him, too, of course. It's a horrible thing."

Andrew doesn't take his eyes off Mrs. Lablanc's house until we have rounded the corner out of sight.

*

Twenty-five years ago Brian and I were sitting in a bar with our mother. His pale and still chubby fingers were spread out on the table top, and he looked down at his knees. I looked from him out the window where the cold rain blew sideways across the parking lot. She poured the last of the pitcher into the glass, swallowed it down, and stood up. The bartender met us at the door. He knew our mother.

"Sara. I don't think you should drive home. Not with the kids."

"Leave me alone," she said, pushing past him. I watched for him to stop Brian and me, but he didn't. Brian raced ahead, jumping over the puddles in his sneakers. I walked right through the water in my rubber boots. She had started the car by the time we climbed inside, Brian in the front, me in the back. Brian inserted a finger into a hole in the soft-top roof where the water dripped down onto the dash. Our mother pushed him back onto the seat and snapped his seat belt closed.

The bartender reappeared tapping at the driver's side window. She rolled it down until I could see his red dripping face turned sideways, steam pouring out from beneath his mustache.

"I'll call you a cab," he said. "I'll pay for it."

"Leave me alone," she said and shifted the car in reverse. He looked in through the window for a brief moment before stepping away. Gravel snapped up from the wheels and thumped against the rusting floor. She jammed the shifter down and thrust us forward onto the road.

In the rearview mirror I could see the tears rolling down her face—not an uncommon sight for us to see on the way back from school after a stop off at the Grill. All the windows were fogged over except for a small circle she had cleared away with her palm. Brian stretched his hand up to my mother's cheek to clear away the drops. The crying was worse but Brian stayed put and stared straight ahead into the space cleared away by the defrost. I watched the speedometer move from fifty to sixty-five and higher. The heavy green fir trees came slowly into view then rushed by. We reached eighty-five, approaching ninety, and I knew there was a turn ahead. We drove home this way every day. She reached over and unfastened Brian's seat belt, and this is the moment he cannot forgive.

The car would go no faster. Her eyes closed but she wasn't asleep; her lips shook. I did not see the forest flying toward us though I felt the car leave the ground for a second. By the time I opened my eyes we were upside down, and I was hanging by the waist belt with blood dripping from my nose into my eyes. I pushed my way out through the side and stood ankle deep in the slushy snow. Brian stood nearby. Somehow he had lost his sweat pants. His skinny pale legs seemed like two small birch trees. A piece of glass had cut open his cheek when he was thrown from the car. He refused to blink, as if the world would vanish if he stopped watching it. "Flying," he would call it two weeks later. "I want to fly again."

Our mother crawled out of the car and stood, seemingly unharmed, beside Brian. She reached her hands down and rubbed his legs, and I could see blood matted on top of her head.

"Oh, honey," she said. "You lost your pants." She took his hand. All three of us walked down the side of the road in the direction of our house. Our mother began rubbing her head. She stumbled once, kept going at a slower pace, and finally stopped walking. I had just begun to believe that we might make it home, that we were strong enough to hurl ourselves into the woods at a great speed in a one ton steel bullet and walk away unharmed. Our mother had created this illusion, and of course we believed her. She was an expert at making us believe we could continue living as we had been with little food or clothing, listening in the cold at night to the sound of her throwing up in the bathroom. She stopped walking, as if someone had suddenly called her name. I even looked around to see if someone was passing by. By the time I looked back, she had lowered to her knees then tumbled on her side.

Brian never let go of her hand. He sat down next to her and stared back into the woods at the spot where we had left the road as if he were trying to remember the spot in order to return there someday. She had unhooked his seatbelt—he would never forget that she had wanted him to die, too, and at that moment he seemed to stop living.

Our mother's eyes were open and her body shook. A moment later was the first time I saw an eyeball without life, fixed in the skin like a miraculous, glistening stone. I pulled on him, but Brian would not let go. He expected her to rise any moment, and he still expects it now.

*

There is nothing we can do for a person who is already dead. In that second they no longer exist. Without this understanding it is impossible to collect the pieces of a young woman who threw herself in front of a train and was scattered over two hundred yards and not believe that we are already in so many pieces ourselves. A hand-sized piece of skull, hairy on one side, pink and fresh on the other, is no more alive than a stone. I can drop the object in the bag, remove the glove, place my hand up to my face and smell nothing but soap and rubber.

I came here from the ambulance service knowing about the job, but Andrew is just out of the academy, a clean kid from North Deering, the Irish neighborhood where I grew up. Maybe, with the long shifts and off time, he hopes to have a second job as many firemen do who become carpenters and plumbers. Most of the people here don't pursue those second jobs. On their days off they like to go for long drives. To take a second job you would have to want to get ahead. This is the wrong place for that.

As a member of the ambulance service, I saw many people die in front of me. When their bodies relaxed and their eyes became still, I felt a warmth in the air that lingered for a moment before vanishing. It is not uncommon for people in that profession to develop similar superstitions. Sometimes for weeks after this kind of event I would be violently sick with what felt like the flu, and I began to imagine in the midst of fever that the dead person's spirit was inside me struggling for life. In the ambulance service I learned that there was little I could do to save someone, and in this job I have learned that there is nothing I can do to bring someone back.

Andrew sips from his coffee as we wait for a call. I know he's still thinking about the woman we visited yesterday to report her husband's death. When they finally do believe you, they will remember your eyes and your unwavering, monotone voice. They won't believe it because it's true, they will believe you because of the way you told them. Sometimes these people will find your name and phone number. They will call you at home to scream at you. Remember that you are not to blame. These people calling in the middle of the night no longer deserve or require your attention. If statistics are true and eight out of ten cases are accidental, then they are calling you because there is no one to blame.

As we are leaving the office, the secretary gives Andrew a message. He reads it by the door and walks back over to his desk to pick up the phone.

"Who's it from?" I ask.

He pretends not to hear me.

"Who's it from?"

He stops dialing and hands me the note saying the woman from yesterday whose husband died called and wanted to speak to him.

"You don't speak to her," I say. "Your job is completed. You brought her the information. That does not make you responsible for her later. It cannot become your problem if she has no other people to whom she can turn. You are a stranger. Do you understand?"

He nods as we walk out to the car. Ten minutes later a call comes in on the cellular.

"Who is it?" he asks. "All right. Put her through." Andrew closes his eyes and listens as the person speaks. "How did you get this number? That's all I know. I have to go." He hangs up with the voice still pouring out of the receiver.

"Who was that?" I ask. "Her?"

He just shakes his head.

As we pass up Congress Street, Brian's standing outside the AA meeting slightly apart from the others in his green polo shirt and basketball sneakers. He doesn't want to talk to them and they have given up on him. I know from when I quit myself that if you go back drinking too many times the AA people stop talking to you. One guy walks a wide circle around him just to avoid getting near him, as if Brian's bad luck could be transmitted through the air. He steps off the curb and looks both ways to see if I'm coming. He cups his hands together in the golf grip familiar to his year and a half on the college team, raises them above his head and swings through. His hips and shoulders twist and his head looks up. You might think he had just come from the golf course if not for the black eyes and stitched chin.

"Where are we going to take him?" Andrew asks.

"Just down the road. He's staying at a halfway house."

Brian opens the door and climbs in the back seat. Andrew turns around and offers his hand.

Brian's square jaw seems to hang loosely by threads. He nods and stares past Andrew to the road, the red light, and the people in suits crossing the street to Fleet Bank.

"You used to play golf," Andrew says, rubbing his chin nervously.

Brian's eyes flicker for a moment in Andrew's direction, but he doesn't seem to hear. I've been watching him in the rearview mirror, but I'm driving now, climbing up Commercial Street. When I stop Brian gets out of the car and doesn't look back to wave.

"Your brother doesn't want to answer any of my questions."

"Maybe he didn't hear you."

"Is there something wrong with his hearing?"

"I don't know."

He walks across the pavement with a slight limp. The heat from the sun rises in waves around his legs so that he seems to float—the shirt and pants, even his arms seem to waver in ripples.

"Should we let him go like that?" Andrew asks staring out the window.

Even if there was enough of him to bring back, he would soon slip between our fingers like water cupped in the hand. If Andrew doesn't see that already, there's no way I can make him see. Brian may show up on my doorstep tonight and he may keep walking to the back of the halfway house, to the edge of town never to be seen again. He has vanished before.

It is partially my responsibility to ascertain if the trainee remembers the necessary information. In some remote areas where skills have not been passed on, the coroner has no guidelines for handling the death or the surviving family. Sometimes families find out through the press. Sometimes murder victims are cremated before their bodies are examined, and quite often deaths are not reported to the coroner at all. Bodies may even be wrongly identified and buried under false names.

To prevent this from happening I must decide if the trainee is capable of the job. He has no idea, during this period, that an evaluation is taking place. Now that the course is over, he believes the job is secure by right and qualification. I am taking a left on Forest Avenue now, driving by the giant yellow and orange McDonald's sign. Andrew's face turns orange in the light as he looks toward people still inside mopping the floors.

"Can you tell me the seventeen kinds of deaths that must be reported to the coroner?"

The next generation of police, nurses, doctors, and morticians may not receive this information from their superiors. It is the coroner's job to periodically inform them and it will become his job when I am gone to inform the coroners who train under him.

He closes his eyes and points his face forward. This may be one of the easiest questions.

"Homicide or suicide?" he says with his eyes still closed. "Accident or injury. Suspicion of criminal act. No physician in attendance."

"You rearranged the order."

"Medical attendance less than twenty-four hours of death."

"That's enough."

"I thought those middle three should go at the end. They seemed less significant."

"Once the person is dead, there is no gradation."

I pull into the McDonald's and park. He gets out, crosses to the door of the restaurant, and steps back. I hold the door open for him. Inside, the lights blind him. I squint, but he closes his eyes, bends his head, and raises his forearm as if to block a punch. At the counter I order coffee and a danish. He has walked to the far corner of the room and leaned against the dark window.

"I'm not hungry."

"What happened to you?" I ask.

Maybe he remembers something that happened, maybe something happened he can't remember, and maybe he remembers something that never happened. It hardly matters which.

"Nothing," he says.

"What is wrong?"

"I don't know. I don't know."

A call comes in on the beeper. Suspicious death on the Eastern Prom, the dispatcher tells us in the car.

"What time is it?" I ask as we step out on Bryant Street.

"Nine fifteen."

"Don't tell me. Write it down." He takes out his notebook and marks the time.

Only investigating officers have arrived. I let him go first so I can watch his approach. Our first priority is the body but not at the expense of the scene. Signs of the criminal's path, if there was a criminal, must not be disturbed. We do not touch the door, nor walk through the middle of the passageway, nor the middle of the room. The alleged assailant may have walked through the middle of the room to where the woman sits in a chair with a gaping wound in her neck, exposing the esophagus.

"Putrefaction?"

"Not yet."

"Temperature?"

He takes the needle out of the case, lifts the woman's shirt, locates her liver, and jabs into the skin.

"Ten degrees."

"More than an hour."

He cups his hands gently under the woman's jaw and moves it back and forth. Her entire head, fixed eyes and filthy brown hair, move also.

"Rigor," he says and notes on his pad. "More than three hours." He moves his hand along the muscle of her neck to test the muscle tension there. "Less than five."

The woman's mouth is open, the tongue stuck out. Common.

The investigating officer has found the woman's purse and ID. Kathleen Danby, aged forty-three. These items go in a small plastic bag.

"Throat cut on left side—three inches," Andrew says. "Knife sits in her lap next to left hand. No bleeding at the throat. Cut after she was dead."

He looks at me.

"What about the hand?"

He looks from the hand to me and back to the hand.

"The knife sits next to the wrong hand."

"And the neck?"

"No hesitation marks. A straight cut. No angle. And no cadaveric spasm in the hand. The hand muscles would still be gripping the knife."

He jumps up suddenly and steps back from the body. His eyes race over the face and neck.

"Coloring?" I ask.

"Normal. She didn't die from the knife wound."

"What haven't you checked?"

He steps forward and carefully removes her shirt. Her back and shoulders have turned bluish purple where the blood has settled. Lividity on the back. She was moved, sometime after death, to the chair from the floor. The detectives discover a blood spot on the floor suggesting this. Andrew checks her head.

"She was shot. Entrance wound, more than two feet away, three centimeter diameter. Slightly concave. Exit four centimeters, back right. Minor bleeding. Instant death."

"Tweezer the fibers, photo, and bag the hands."

Andrew removes the tweezers from the case, collects several fibers and wraps paper bags around the hands to protect them. The M.E. will want to check the nails later. The morgue guys arrive. They stand in the corner in their white overalls with their stretcher and body bag. Andrew stands on a chair above the woman, photographing. He moves five feet back, shoots, five feet to the side, shoots. He hands me the plastic bag of fibers. The morgue guys step forward to bag the body. Andrew's eyes watch their every move.

"Be careful of the hands," he says.

One of the morgue guys I have known for years scratches his chin and looks from him to me. It's a new guy, he knows. Nothing worth mentioning. Andrew is correct, though. He accurately recalls his instruction. From this point until we reach the morgue, in a suspicious death like this, our eyes cannot leave the body. We will both ride in the back of the van in the dark with the body. The morgue guys ride up front. Two benches have been provided in the back for this purpose. The gurney is secured in the middle between us. Before they close the doors I can see Andrew's eyes illuminated by the street lights staring down at the bulge of the woman's head against the black plastic. Then we are in complete darkness. No windows. The van bounces along Commercial, down the hill to the "butcher shop," we call it. I know the sound of every street in this town. Some of the potholes on this hill haven't been filled since I learned how to drive. We rise slightly before continuing down. Now at sea level on cobblestone by the empty warehouse, and into the underground garage. Fluorescent lights burn as the doors swing open. Andrew's eyes haven't moved from the body the entire time, even in darkness.

"Come on," I say. "Let them work."

He backs off and we follow the gurney down a gentle slope to a pair of electronic doors. These are not the significant doors. The important doors come next. They are blue and can only be opened with the card the morgue guys carry in their pockets. Beyond these doors the body is technically now the jurisdiction of the medical examiner, but we follow down the plain white hall, no windows, still descending. We turn right at the bottom. The building goes no deeper than two stories. There at the desk we sign our names. The morgue guys sign their names. Another man appears from a door behind the counter. The woman sitting at the desk never looks up. The man who has just appeared will take the gurney the rest of the way down the hall to the morgue. The others are friendly. The morgue guys will drive us back to our car, but Andrew won't turn around. He watches the body roll down the hall to the silver metal doors twenty yards away.

"Andrew," I say. "We're done."

"Are we allowed to follow?"

"There is no reason for us to. The body is their responsibility."

"Are we allowed?"

"You are asking the wrong question," I say. The gurney pushes through the metal doors, and both the body and the attendant in white vanish down the white hall.

At the scene the investigating team has taken over. They will search every inch, find the bullet, and probably find the assailant. Eighty percent of murders are committed by the victim's relations. Her ex-husband, an ex-felon, will be one of the first people paid a visit. He will be the right person. Nothing in the room was taken. We found her purse, full of a hundred fifty and a gram of heroin. This crime like most was committed for more complicated reasons than theft.

The blue lights flash across Andrew's face; his eyes race over the building as if expecting to find the clues written on the clapboards.

"Now we go back to the office and write our reports. We may write brief, conjectural recommendations at the end, but our duty is to report what we observed, nothing more."

Andrew purses his lips and closes his eyes, lowering his head. "Don't we have to do something to find out who did that?"

"No, we don't," I say. "That's not our job."

In the car he leans forward and holds his stomach.

"Are you all right?"

"I'll be fine."

But I pull the car over. "You tell me what it is," I demand.

"It's just that it happened so recently," he says. "A friend I grew up with next door. He and I joined the army together after high school. He was behind me on the line during a day jump when something went wrong. His chute didn't open. He reached out his hand as he passed by. I could see his eyes as if he had paused in the air. I tried to get loose from my chute. I wanted to go after him. I found him on the ground. He was pressed into the dirt, his body limp like a sack of sand. No matter how much the CO yelled at me, I couldn't get up. They had to carry me out. It happened during the end of my time. We were about to sign up for another hitch. What gets me is that he had several minutes to think as he fell. I can't stop wondering what went through his mind as he fell. I watched him fall all the way. It was a clear, bright day. He shrank to the size of a tiny dot before hitting the ground."

I start the car again and continue driving.

After our shift I wait outside in the parking lot for Andrew to climb on his motorcycle. No doubt the woman gave him a call this afternoon because she had nowhere else to turn. She remembered his face, and he says to himself that he will just stop by to see if she is safe. I know what he is going to do. He looks at his watch, pulls the helmet down, and heads out up State Street and left down the hill and across the bridge to South Portland to Thorton Street, the home of the woman who lost her husband. He pauses for a minute as he steps off the bike. I have parked down the street in a shadow. Hopefully, he considers what he has learned in the manual or what I might say. He tucks his helmet under his arm and walks up to the door.

She has been waiting for him. She comes out onto the landing and wraps her arms around his chest—not as a lover, around his neck, but as a child. She sobs and rests her weight on him. He drops the helmet in order to hold her up. She has moved her hands inside his shirt and closed her eyes. She's not with him anymore but with her husband who no longer exists. He thinks he's in love with her, but he's just become a ghost. She presses her lips against his, and he hopes she will bring him back to life. This struggle not to vanish is what takes him inside the house where he removes his clothes in the front room to press his skin against hers, to feel her heat. I know what it is like to want that.

My mother used to run across the lawn as if she did not know what to do with her hands. They would hang at her side like leaden wings. Brian would follow her, his arms raised in the air. He imagined himself a winged fighter pilot protecting her.

A year after the accident I found him on the second floor of our grandparents' house in his Superman cape crouching in the window, ready to leap. I should have grabbed him from behind. I should have run across the room screaming his name. Instead I just spoke. He heard me, and turned his head. I saw the magic marker "S" on the cape and walked easily across the room to sit down on the edge of the bed. I knew there was a fence and metal stakes just below the window in the yard.

He never looked down but up toward the seagulls and the tips of pine trees.

"I am," he said.

"What?"

"I am. I am. I am!" he screamed.

I lunged forward grabbing him around the waist, hauling him to the floor, burying my head against his chest and squeezing as he beat his fists on my back, still screaming. I have always known when he was about to jump, and I imagine I can feel what he feels falling to the ground in the middle of the night after someone has hit him halfway across town from my apartment.

Years later I waited up at night staring at the ceiling. Sometimes he would not come home at all and I would see the sun rise in the window. Other times he came home with his feet stumbling on the porch. Only my grandfather was alive then and he was too old to do anything. I rushed downstairs to the front porch where he was either passed out or trying to find his keys. I put my hands in his armpits and hauled him backwards into the house. His heels bounced down along the floor. His eyes, if they opened at all, rolled around the dark room. Often his clothing was soaked with beer, sweat, and vomit, so I stripped him in the shower and turned on the water. His hair matted down on his eyes. The pale skin stretched tight over the thin frame shivering under the cold.

"Come on," I said, and he lifted his chin to the stream for a moment before lowering it again. He was wrapped so deeply in his mind that he could not even feel the drops on his skin or my voice in his ear. Only his glistening ribs rising and falling against the skin confirmed that he was alive.

I've driven back from South Portland and parked outside Brian's apartment just to see what he will do. I take a few notes, sitting in the car, concerning Andrew's situation. When I speak to Gerald Dworkin, the Chief Coroner, I will tell him, without mentioning details, that Andrew is one of us. It is impossible to tell yet if he will develop the necessary discipline for the job. Those who find that discipline comes naturally do not make good coroners. Nor do those who find no self-discipline at all.

Brian leaves the house at nine P.M., walks down State Street, and takes a left on Fore. I step out of the car and follow on foot, staying a block and a half behind. He throws a cigarette into the gutter and lights another. At the corner of Fore and Market he walks into Gritty's. I sit across the street on a bench. From here I can see him sit at the end of the bar, in the corner by himself. He has shaved, combed his hair, put on his best clothes—a golf shirt and blue jeans. The people there are his age, so they wouldn't know at first unless they looked closely at his dim, vacant eyes. He orders one drink after another, beginning with beer and moving to vodka. After an hour and a half a woman sits down next to him. He turns his head and I can see the jaw moving. He wipes his chin. After just five minutes the woman points across the room. She won't come back, and he probably knows that. Two hours pass. The woman has left with someone else. Most people have left. The young couples and groups of women in summer skirts have vanished, gone home. Groups of guys in football jerseys or muscle shirts tumble out of the bar and make their way back to their cars. The police cruiser passes by. I lower my head so they don't notice me. Four guys still in their softball uniforms pass by. One of them comes back to stand in front of me. His buddies don't notice at first.

"What gives you the right to sit on this bench all night?" the guy slurs. Slobber sprays onto my cheek. I sit back, cross my legs, and look up. "I seen you sitting here before." His friends have joined him by now. "I want to sit down." And he collapses next to me. For a moment I can see Brian again. The bar only has a few guys playing darts.

Another guy demands, "My friend wants to stretch out. Who do you think you are?"

I take out my coroner's badge and hold it up for him to see. He leans down and reads. When he looks from the badge to me I can see his eyes darting frantically over my face. He leans forward, grabs his friend by the shirt, and hauls him to his feet.

The bartender runs a finger across his throat when Brian asks for another beer. Brian doesn't react but he also doesn't let go of the mug. I'm up crossing the road. I have to wait for a car to pass. He stumbles across the room. He raises the glass over his head and hurls it against the dartboard. The five guys playing there circle him, and I jump out into the road without looking. A car screeches to a stop, the person leaning forward on the horn. I'm running now past the bouncer with my badge in my hand. He holds his hands up as if I might arrest him for not doing anything to stop the five guys pummeling Brian to the ground. Now they're kicking him in he stomach. I pull two guys back and one guy by the throat just as he is about to swing a stool into Brian's kidneys. The biggest of the guys grabs the badge out of my hand as I flash it forward.

"This is no cop's badge," he snorts and throws it back.

I roll Brian over. The blood pours out of his nose onto his old Dartmouth golf shirt.

"Get me some ice," I yell to the bartender who hasn't changed his expression and is still wiping glasses. He looks at me but doesn't seem to hear.

"Get it yourself."

"Does it hurt?" I whisper.

Brian shakes his head slowly. Even the skin of his arm feels cold and lifeless as if the blood has already stopped flowing.

"Leave me alone," he says, closing his eyes.

"We have to get you to the hospital."

"There's no use. Just leave." He struggles to sit up and, refusing my help, manages to pull himself to his feet by the end of the bar. He sits down on one of the stools.

"We're closed, Brian," the bartender says. He's a friend of Brian's, but he never lifts a finger to help him. Brian doesn't want him to. The bartender doesn't even seem embarrassed or disturbed—he has a few more glasses to clean before he goes home. He sees my brother's type all the time.

"I'll leave when he's gone," Brian says, nodding his head toward me.

I wait outside for him to leave the bar, then follow him home to make sure he gets into the room.

It's just a few hours now from our morning shift, so I lay back in the car outside Brian's apartment and close my eyes. At seven in the morning he's headed down the street toward me. I roll down my window.

"Where were you headed today?" I ask.

"Don't know. Might head down to the noon AA meeting."

"Do you want me to pick you up there?"

"No. I'll have coffee with a bunch of the guys there afterwards."

Plans are being made to be somewhere else. He's tapping his foot against the curb, the toe coming out of the sneaker. The plans are in the foot. They're in the ash dangling like a crooked finger and then floating down to the pavement.

"Let me give you a ride. Anywhere you want to go."

"Let's just ride up to the Eastern Prom and back, to see the ocean."

He seems cheerful this morning—probably doesn't remember a thing from last night. He rolls the window down and flicks the ash out. At the Prom the cool morning wind blows steady in from the south, rolls up the shore under our noses, and passes into the city. Brian walks down ahead of me with his arms outstretched—at first just slightly out to the side but extending up into the air as if reaching. His brown hair floats up and it seems like he could fly. I think of Andrew's friend racing toward the ground without a chute. Brian thinks he will continue up over the giant elm at the edge of the park into the sky. The entire time I have been watching him fall, he has been waiting to rise.

*

Andrew arrives a minute ahead of schedule. He rests his coat on back of the chair, places both hands on the desk, and stares ahead at the wall.

We head out to the car and turn on the scanner. We listen but do not respond. Not until they call specifically for us.

"Forty-five Thorton," the dispatcher says, but she is not speaking to us. An attempted suicide. Andrew reaches for the volume on the radio, but the announcement is over.

"We're only a mile from there," he says.

"They didn't call for us."

"We have to go."

I shake my head.

"I have to go!" he shouts this time, grabs for the door handle, and pushes it open at forty-eight miles an hour. I pull off the road.

"Shut that door!" I yell. He pulls the door closed but doesn't take his hand off the handle. "You are not in love with that woman. You think you are, but you're not." He sets his jaw and grips the door handle until the veins emerge on his forearm. I realize he will go there on foot if he has to. I may as well drive him.

An ambulance and two cruisers are parked outside with their lights spinning in the rain. The four officers stand out front in slickers talking to each other. The first neighbor we spoke to comes to her window, still holding her cat, and slides the curtain to the side. She pushes her glasses further up along her wrinkled bumpy nose and squints at us. The dry lips part around her yellowed teeth. The other neighbor paces back and forth in front of her house carrying one screaming kid in each arm. All three are soaked. The kids cling to their mother's neck with both hands.

"I was going to stop by," the woman calls to us frantically. "I know you told me I should stop by."

"Go back inside," I say to her.

"My kids wouldn't settle down. I was going to stop by when they took a nap." The rain has soaked through her bleached hair and run across her cracked lower lip. Andrew runs ahead to the porch where the medics have just emerged with their equipment. I catch Andrew by the shoulder before he makes it to the steps. I stand behind him, wrap my arms around his body and press him to me as I would the next of kin.

"I want you to look at your watch. Take out your notebook," I whisper into his ear.

He looks up to one of the medics who replaces tubes and wires in a large metal case, closes, then locks the lid. The man rests against the side of the house and lets out a long breath.

"He's giving up," Andrew says. "He's giving up too soon."

"He did all he could do."

The other medic kneeling down over his equipment gives me a nod. The motor on their ambulance is still running. They have another call— I can hear the radio from their cab. They have to move on. They both start walking toward the back of the ambulance where they store the gear. They don't smile or cry but just go about their business.

"Don't go in there unless you understand what we have to do. All right?" I ask. He shakes his head, the hair on the back of his neck brushing against my nose. "The guys from the morgue are going to come," I whisper. "We'll ride in the van with them." I can feel his shoulder blades pinching against my chest.

Inside he lays his hand on her cheek and buries his face in his arm. I rest my hand on his back where the muscles erupt as if sustaining punches from inside. Abandoned by breath and voice and heat—things so invisible we can't believe they ever existed, the body has become a shell of cold skin and eyes—the outline of the person. When this melts away it seems as if the person never existed all. It's hard for him to see how it could be important to protect her now when he could not protect her before. But he should know by now that we are not like everyone else. We protect the dead so that others can believe in life.

His Mother's Voice

Andrej Blatnik

Translated by Tamara Soban

In the theater the kid was watching a horror movie. People were screaming in terror. On the screen, an invisible killer was killing off, one by one, the members of a family living in a lonely spot—a house on the outskirts of town. They had not done anything, or if they had, it was not clear what it was; he was killing them, as it were, because it was their fate. All the murders happened in more or less the same way; each time a member of the family would unsuspectingly enter a room where the killer was waiting in ambush for them, and he would slaughter them. Each time the audience would groan: how could they be so stupid! They should have known there was a killer in the house, and yet they were not at all careful. Not even the soft, harmonious whisper that was heard whenever the killer was close meant anything to them, although it was loaded with significance.

The most horrible scene of all was where the killer called to the little son of the family, who had suspected that something was wrong and was determined to act with utmost caution. He did it by imitating his mother's voice. The little boy naively believed that it really was his mother calling him, while in reality she was lying in a pool of blood on the floor, at the killer's feet. Somebody sitting next to the kid whispered: "Be careful, watch out, it's not your mommy, it's not your mommy." At the peak of suspense a woman cried out: "Run!" The little boy did not hear her and did not run away. He went straight to the killer. Everything was clear.

The kid drew in his lips and stared at the screen. He kept repeating to himself that it was just a movie. The killer cut the child to pieces before the little boy could realize that he had made a wrong move, that it had not been his mother. The people felt somehow relieved that it was all over. They had known all along that the little boy would not make it, he was too gullible, it could not have ended any differently, they told themselves. The kid thought: how could he have been so careless and not have recognized the voice? If he had recognized it, he might have been able to defend himself. If only he hadn't let himself be drawn to that room!

Soon afterward the killer was identified and the movie was over. The lights went on in the theater. People were getting up from their seats and straightening their clothes. Each one somewhat hesitated at the exit, as if unwilling to go out, and then went off into the darkness. The kid was among the last to leave. It was the first time his mother had let him go to the late show, and he was scared. He had a long way to go home, as they lived on the outskirts of town, in a lonely spot, and because of the energy-saving cuts the electricity was turned off at ten, so the streets were not lit. In every bush the kid thought he could see the killer, and while walking he listened intently to every sound, as he could not see anything. Once he suddenly heard something behind him that strongly resembled the whisper that betrayed the killer's presence, but when he turned around it was only a rat running from one sewer to another.

After a few terror-filled minutes he arrived home. At first he was almost relieved, thinking that he was safe now and he could tell his mother about how he had been so afraid; the fear would then disappear and they would laugh at it together, as they had many times before. But the house was dark, no lights anywhere. Something seemed wrong. Cautiously, he opened the door. He entered the hall. He waited. He did not know what to do. The house was quiet, almost too quiet. Something's wrong, thought the kid. Something was in there. Something. . . . What if something happened to mommy? They lived in a lonely part of town, anything was possible. If only he had something that would help if. . . . He groped behind the door. He felt something cold under his fingers. He recognized the thing, it was the ax. Yesterday they were chopping wood for the winter with mommy. Mommy praised how strong he had become, since he could split a log in two by himself.

When he took hold of the ax he overturned something and it made a muffled noise. He heard his heartbeat pounding in his ears. He held his breath and waited. The thing inside, in the house, also waited. Then he heard it call out: "Is that you? Son, is that you?" His first impulse was to drop the ax and enter, then he stopped. It occurred to him that it might not be his mother's voice, although it was similar to it. Very similar. He grasped the handle of the ax firmly. He held it with both hands. Caution. He had to be cautious. Not risk anything. "Son?" Now the voice seemed even stranger. This was supposed to be his mommy? You're not going to get me, he thought. You're not going to get me.

186

"Son, come on in." I'm not going, thought the kid. And I'm not going to run away either. I'll get revenge. You in there, what did you do to her? It's true she let them put me in a special school, so that my schoolmates from the old school don't like me anymore, but all the same, she was my mommy, and tonight she let me go to the late show, although it wasn't a movie for children. I'll get revenge. "Son?" He was perplexed. He did not know what to do. The voice was very similar to his mother's. More than the one in the movie. How childish that boy in the movie was, he thought. No wonder he caught it. He wasn't cautious enough. "Son? Answer me!" Now the voice was closer. He realized it was coming into the hall. He gathered his strength and lifted the ax above his head. "Are you here? What's the matter?"

By now his eyes had adjusted to the dark. He squeezed himself into the corner behind the door and waited. He imagined his mommy lying on the floor in a pool of blood, and tears came to his eyes. The whisper that betrayed the killer droned in his ears. Here it goes, he thought. The killer's outline was already visible at the door. The kid whimpered in fear and the figure on the doorstep slowly turned towards him. Through the tears and the dark he could see that the killer did not only copy her voice, but also his mother's appearance. The resemblance was amazing. For a moment he faltered. At that moment the killer in the disguise of his mother caught sight of the ax in his hands, and in spite of the dark, the kid could see how it made the killer's eyes widen and the whites stand out. The ax in his uplifted hands trembled and his doubt reached its peak. Then the killer in the guise of his mother screamed in a dreadful way. The scream was like nothing the kid had ever heard before, least of all the warm, kind voice of his mommy. He felt relieved. Now he knew.

Night Crossing

Susan Hubbard

They walked along the deck of the ferry, side by side without touching. Galin buttoned her jacket up to her chin. "We'll catch our death," she said.

Will didn't speak. Galin felt his breath on her left ear, and when she turned he was watching her. She'd come to think that his watching her didn't mean anything. It was merely habit. When they first were together, she often awoke to find him watching, his eyes shadowed, fixed on her without seeing her. "What's wrong?" she asked him the first time it happened. He didn't answer. She came to believe that his thoughts at such times had nothing to do with her.

They were running away again. England was behind them. Standing on the ferry's deck, they watched Stranraer recede in fog. The sodium vapor lights along the dock winked and blurred, then disappeared. Next to Galin a woman laughed, and the man who stood by the woman said, "Farewell to Scotland."

Will wrapped his arms around his chest, as if it pained him, and Galin wanted to ask how was his heart. But she knew he would be angry if she mentioned it.

They rounded a corner and came to the ferry's stern. Cold air hit their faces, smelling of sea salt and diesel exhaust. Galin leaned over the rail to watch the wake, a churning grey foam. "You expect trouble tomorrow?" she said.

He ignored that question. She should know better by now than to ask such a thing.

*

"Inside?" Galin said now. Will nodded. They moved through the crowd of travelers. It was a misty autumn night, not yet cold, but before long all of the passengers would move inside for shelter.

The ferry's lower-deck lounge was a series of wide spaces with seats and tables in rows across them and others built against the walls formed by the ship's hull. The walls were a dingy white, marked by the cigarette smoke of countless restless travelers. Will chose a corner table and then went away to get coffee. He came back with two steaming styrofoam cups. "White" coffee it was, what he always ordered—he liked the milk hot and the coffee bitter and strong. It was one of his few weaknesses. She preferred coffee black, but she had taken to drinking it his way. It seemed too much trouble to order two different kinds.

They sipped the coffee and sat in the corner without talking. The couple who had stood near them on the deck came into the lounge, the outer door banging shut behind them. Galin recognized the woman by her laughter. "O foolish love," the man sang, and the woman shook her long brown hair.

Galin felt Will stiffen as the couple approached their table.

"This end taken?" the man asked, and Galin shook her head. "No," she said.

The woman settled into a seat. Galin smelled her perfume, sweet and floral, as she pulled off her jacket. The woman turned to meet her eyes. "We've been traveling all day," she said, as if apologizing. "I'm Maggie. This is Tom."

Galin nodded. She knew what was expected, and she waited for Will to speak. He cleared his throat. "I'm Ian," he said. "My young friend here is Miranda."

Friend, she thought. She said, "Hi."

Tom unfastened a small nylon bag and pulled out a Thermos. "Pleased to meet you."

The voices in the lounge swelled, and Galin was glad for the noise. Will's eyes moved slowly across the crowd, and she leaned back, against the wall. Maggie stretched out her hand for the Thermos, her fingernails long, painted with peach-colored polish. Maggie ran her free hand through her hair and Galin thought, *Mine's lighter,* before she realized that her hair no longer was brown—she had dyed it yesterday.

She glanced at Will and thought how unfamiliar he looked. He had let his hair grow long over the summer. It fell back from his forehead in a wave that made her think of a gypsy man. His eyes were dark and restless always. He had the kind of looks her mother called *Black Irish*— "handsome as the devil, but with a cold heart."

She wondered if her mother would recognize her now.

*

Maggie giggled softly. Tom was whispering in her ear. Then he turned in Will's direction. "We've been to Ibiza," Tom said.

"We had a week of sunshine," Maggie said. "And then a weekend of rain with Tom's brother in Glasgow."

"But it's all over now," Tom added.

"Yeah, back to work tomorrow," Maggie said.

"Real drag," Will said. Galin thought, *Isn't it as obvious to them as it is to me, how he grudges every word?*

"Where are you from?" Maggie asked. Suddenly Galin could stand it not a second more—she didn't want to sit and hear Will lie.

"Off to the loo," she murmured, and left the table. She felt Will's eyes following her, all the way across the lounge.

*

He had lied about his age when she met him two years ago—said he was older than he was. He lied about the car—said it belonged to him, when it was stolen. He lied about his religion—he didn't have one—and about his politics—he was a ruffian more than a patriot.

Those were some of the big lies. She didn't want to think about the others.

There was a crying baby in the loo. Its mother said, "I've tried everything. He has the colic."

Galin nodded. She washed her hands in a rust-stained sink with a balled-up packet of crisps in its drain. Then she splashed tepid water on her face and looked at her reflection in the mirror. Black hair didn't suit her, she decided, and then she thought, *so what.*

"I've had no sleep for days," the baby's mother said. She was a pale, slight girl with shadows under her eyes. The baby in her arms looked pinched and yellowish.

Probably anemic, Galin thought. *Both of them.*

"My husband hates the noise." The girl moved her arms up and down, to lull the baby, but its cries continued. "My husband's back in Inverness," she said. "I'm going home to my brother in Ringsend, he said he'd take us for a while."

Galin nodded. "It must be hard," she said. "It's always hard to go home."

The girl seemed to laugh, but it was impossible to hear her for the baby's crying. "I've got nothing now to look forward to," she said, the words coming out in a rush.

Galin dried her hands, and thought, *I'm glad I'm not you.* "Good luck," she told them. She left the room quickly.

*

They'd got Will talking, she saw from across the lounge. His elbows rested along the top of his seat. Even as his mouth moved, his eyes met hers.

When she reached them he was saying, "And Miranda here—she doesn't do much of anything."

"That's not fair," Maggie said.

"Cruel but true," Galin said, sitting next to Will again.

She thought for a moment of her teachers at school, of the compliments they'd paid her. "You've a good mind, a curious mind," her history teacher said one day after class had ended. "I hope you'll apply your abilities with the seriousness that they deserve." She was the first one in her family to go to grammar school—odds were, the last one. Her four sisters weren't interested in much beyond homemaking and hairdressing. Her three brothers cared only for drinking and rugby and cars. Yes, great things had been expected of her.

"Tom here was on the dole until last spring," Maggie said. "Then a mate of his pulled some strings and got him hired by the gas board."

Tom set down his Thermos cup. "You'll have heard about my mate Sammy. He's the fellow the soldiers set upon last week, on the Shankill. He was walking home when the bastards jumped him. Broke his nose so bad he couldn't breathe. Half killed him." Tom shook his head. "Funny thing. Sammy isn't even Catholic."

"They do it to everyone," Galin said.

Will said, "Yeah," but he might just as well have said, "Shut up."

Maggie laughed nervously. "Come on."

Tom patted her arm. "I'll sing you a song, my Maggie," he said.

Tom sang a song about sailors who found watery graves. *And it's feared she's gone down with all hands,* the chorus ended.

Two old women on a near-by bench clapped their hands when he had finished.

"That's a fine thing to sing when we're at sea," Maggie said.

"I do like the old songs," Tom said.

Will turned to Galin, but spoke so that the others could hear. "Let's get some sleep. We've got a long day tomorrow."

"Right." Galin thought, *Tomorrow we'll make a fresh start.*

*

Will laid his head in her lap. She looked down, astonished that the touch of him had the power still to make her want him. He smiled, as if he knew what she was feeling. Then he closed his eyes.

They rarely made love now. He had a bad heart, and since finding his prescription pills she always held back in bed. Once he sensed her holding back, and he shook her and said, "Come on," his voice rough. But by then it was too late—she had forgotten how to be free with him. Their lovemaking became infrequent, furtive, over in a few minutes. Now they rarely touched each other.

But tonight the feeling unexpectedly came back to her, and she felt fiercely possessive and protective of him—of Will, who had taken away her name, ruined her looks, taught her how to steal and to do worse things.

*

She'd just turned fifteen when they met—in a Belfast pub, amid a bustle of soccer fans. Will had been deep in conversation with two men when her eyes were drawn to him. She put down her glass of cider and went over. "Aren't you Cissy Kelly's cousin?" she had said.

He had watched her coming and he turned away as she spoke to him. "No, kid," he said. "Not even close."

But the next day after school she saw him in the street and he came up to her. "Tell me your name," he said. He brought her back to a friend's flat, got her drunk on cider, took her to bed. It had hurt, and she bled a great deal, but she didn't cry.

He waited for her often after that. Three months later, when he told her he was going abroad and asked didn't she want to come too, she never hesitated.

She had in time become an efficient thief, but she never felt right about it. She was caught once—stealing bread, of all things—in a baker's in Finsbury Park, in London; that was when they were hungry, later that year when the money ran out entirely. She'd got away, shook off the shopgirl's grasp on her arm and ran. When she reached the flat she forgot their signal and came in to find Will crouched on the landing like a jungle cat, a gun in his hand. "It's only me," she'd said, looking up the staircase at him.

He looked down at her, and that gaze of appraisal, that cool approval, was as close to a declaration of love as he would ever come.

She didn't know, then, all that he was mixed up in.

*

Snow had swirled on the streets, when she telephoned home to Belfast. "I won't be there for Christmas," she said.

The streets of Birmingham smelled like burnt chocolate. "Not for Easter either," she said.

Down the street Will's new car waited. Inside it Will was talking to a man. As she watched the tail lights went red. Then the car broke into motion.

"Don't you worry," she said, and hung up the receiver. But the car already was gone.

That night she'd slept in a laundrette. As often as not strangers were kind to her, and that night the attendant, a scrawny old woman with a pink curler hanging over each ear, made her a cup of tea and lent her a blanket. Galin curled across two plastic seats to sleep.

Next morning the car was parked down the street again. She picked her way toward it through the snow. As she came close someone grabbed her from behind. A hand pressed over her mouth. Her first instinct was to bite, then she began to kick.

"Damn you," Will's voice said in her ear.

He pulled her round a corner, into someone's back garden. Then he shook her, hard. "You stay away from that car," he said. "It doesn't belong to us anymore."

She nodded. He let go of her. She breathed deeply and took a step away, but he grabbed her arm and said, "Wait." They stood without speaking, waiting. Snow began to fall again, large flakes that caught in his hair. The flakes, little stars, melted on his forehead.

When her breathing was normal again, he said, "Now we'll walk." They crossed a street and moved down the block. They might have traveled half a mile before she heard the explosion. The sound made her shake; she couldn't tell if the ground was moving or if what she felt was only her own trembling. She thought at once of the old woman in the laundrette.

Will's face had no expression. He was watching the faces of strangers.

They must have walked six miles farther before she spoke to him. "I'll never tell," she said, her voice flat.

He shook his head slowly. "Why are you forever saying the wrong thing?"

*

A month later she had lost so much weight that he laughed at the sight of her legs. Then her periods ceased. Will thought she must be pregnant, and accused her of trying to trap him. She had to have a test at a clinic before he was persuaded. He said, "Trust you to be a medical marvel."

"There's nothing marvelous about it," she said.

She told herself it was a blessing. She would never want to have a child.

"I understand the political reasons for what we are doing," she said one morning. "We are coming to terms with history. We have no choice but to continue."

But she said it to the bathroom mirror. To Will she said only the things that were necessary.

*

She wasn't sad to leave Birmingham. Will had begun to accumulate things: boxes, packages. She collected some of them from the post office. Their postmarks were unfamiliar. Once she carried a suitcase on an airplane to London and then to Glasgow before coming back without it to Birmingham, never knowing why.

Then one evening Will loaded the boxes and packages into the car— another new car, a sedan, the color of cherry brandy. She packed her clothes in a shoulder bag.

"We're running away," she said as she settled in the passenger seat.

He paid her no attention, except to ask questions, all of which began with "Didn't you."

"Didn't you remember the iodine?" and "Didn't you bring the bucket of ice?"

She had remembered the iodine. She had brought along the ice.

It was his notion that the ice would allow them to travel without stopping. They embedded food in it; as it melted, they drank the water.

They arrived early next evening in Stranraer. At the security checkpoint Will was blithe. "Going back to give me mother-in-law her Christmas presents," he told the guard. "Old cow thinks we're made of money now."

The guard snickered, glanced at the backseat, and waved them through. Their car was the first one in line to board the ferry, which approached with alarming speed across the grey water. Small lights shone from its deck, and it looked to Galin like a seaborne village. She felt a slight thrill at the sight of it. It seemed to suggest a forbidden adventure, one for which she was too young.

But no one forbade it. No one had stopped them, and their car rolled across the ramp onto the lower deck.

*

She must have dozed. Next thing she heard was Tom's voice saying "Maggie," and Maggie's voice raised in a whispered quarrel at the other end of the bench.

"—never meant to—"

"—makes me feel like someone's mother—"

On and on they went. Galin tried not to hear. It reminded her of her parents' quarrels—they never reached a point, they never seemed intended to solve anything. They were expressions of easy irritation, people talking instead of thinking.

What first drew her to Will was that he seemed so different. He never said much; she imagined he must think a great deal.

Even now, with his eyes shut, he looked as if he were thinking, as if he were watching her, his dark eyes a thin gleaming line beneath his eyelashes. But she might have been mistaken. He might only have been asleep.

*

She awoke again, this time with a start. Will had half-risen from her lap, his arm flung out on the bench to support his weight. His body was shaking. His head moved from side to side, as if he were frightened. She put her hands to his face. She said, "Will, Will."

His eyes opened and then his head fell back. "I thought I was dying," he said. His voice sounded small and constricted. "The air went right out of my lungs."

"Breathe deeply," she said.

He shook his head again. "The car," he said. "If anything happens to me—"

"*Breathe*," she said. She moved her hands to his shoulders.

"The keys. My left pocket." His face flushed. "Phil knows the numbers,"

195

he said. "But don't tell—" Then his head bucked. She strained to hold him steady. He spat up milk. The warm vomit hit her neck, and she recoiled, but she held his shoulders tightly. "That's all right," she said.

She heard Maggie's voice, and Tom's, and she felt the presence of others all around them—she could sense the buzz of voices but could hear no words. She slid the keys out of his pocket. Will's eyes closed and his mouth worked, as if he were trying to speak. "That's all right," she said.

He fell back, and she struggled to hold him. "Will," she said.

Someone pushed Galin away, against the bench. They lifted him and stretched him out on the floor. Three men bent over him. After a few minutes she could tell there was no use.

Maggie came over to Galin, carrying a blanket. She bent to rest her hand on Galin's shoulder, then lifted her hand and straightened. "Your poor shirt, love," she said. "Don't you want to change?"

Galin said, "No." She must have spoken loudly, because all the faces suddenly turned toward her. Galin stared back. "All right," she said, trying to make her voice quiet. "I'll change. It's all right."

And all the while, as Maggie backed away, Galin watched their faces, calculating the degree to which they trusted her.

*

Back in the loo Galin stuffed the car keys into a pocket of her jeans, stripped off her shirt and splashed cold water across her face. She felt someone's eyes on her and whirled around—but it was only the young girl she'd seen before, with the baby lying across her lap. They were sitting on the floor under the mirror, a large suitcase and a carry-bag beside them.

"Do you never leave this place?" Galin said.

The girl smiled apologetically. "He wanted changing before we get off the boat," she said. "And it's so noisy outside. He's happier in here."

Galin took a pullover from her shoulder bag and stuffed the shirt inside the bag. She slipped the pullover on. Then she unzipped the other side of the bag and got out a denim cap, a lipstick, sunglasses.

"You'll have a miserable time carrying all that lot," she said to the girl. She stuffed her hair inside the cap, made her lips red, and put on the sunglasses. "Lucky I'm here to help you."

*

It was easier than she had expected. She carried the suitcase, chatted with the baby's mother. Other passengers let them go ahead in the line to disembark. The baby was crying as they walked toward the checkpoint; the guard waved them through. Galin carried the suitcase to the bus and rode along with them to the town center. By this time the noise of the baby's crying made her head ache.

The girl had tears in her eyes when she had to bid Galin good-bye.

"You're the only friend I've got," she said, and Galin thought it was probably true. At the bus-stop the girl borrowed a pencil from an old woman and wrote her brother's address on a chocolate-bar wrapper. Galin pushed the wrapper inside her bag. She left them standing on a street corner. Two blocks away she dropped the car keys into a sewer grating and tossed the crumpled wrapper into a rubbish bin.

*

Her mother cried at the sight of Galin, but she asked few questions. Galin said she'd been in love and now she wasn't. She moved back into the bedroom she shared with two sisters. She dyed her hair brown again. She applied for a job selling cosmetics at Boot's.

Every morning she read the newspaper, and a week later she read of a coroner's inquiry into a death on the Larne ferry. The man had died of a heart attack; he was carrying medication for his heart. A sister had claimed the body. There was no mention of a car or of a companion. Everything was all right. Everything was gone, except for the shirt Galin had worn that night.

When she first came home she hid the shirt in an empty suitcase. She noted its sour smell, its odor of milk and vomit. She never washed it; for her the smell would always be the smell of death. A few weeks later, she took the shirt out and folded it into a plastic bag. She slipped the bag back into the suitcase and slid the case under her bed.

The smell faded, over time, but she never forgot that the shirt was there. It was all she had left of Will, of their time together. She imagined it was as close as she would ever come to having what other people called a conscience.

The Bed

Stephen Dixon

His mother died in his arms. "You shouldn't keep telling people that," his wife said. "It sounds as if you're boasting." "But she did die in my arms. At home, in her hospital bed there. I was holding her, had her propped up." "I know; you've said. But from now on with other people, when you're telling them about it—this is only a suggestion—just say she died at home. Peacefully at home, because that's how you said it was except for that last terrible moment which she might not have even been aware of." "I'm sure she was; I saw it when she opened her eyes after they'd been closed so long." "That could have been involuntary; some automatic physical reflex. You raised her up, she started vomiting, her eyes opened." "But it was what I saw in her eyes that made me feel she was suddenly conscious." "All right. I'm not arguing with you, sweetheart. But the thing with your arms—which is true, I'm not disputing that either, if the way you say it happened happened that way." "What other way could it have? It's not something I'd forget or make up. I was there with the woman who takes care of her weekends." "Ebonita. I know all that too. And she seemed as devoted to your mother as the woman who looked after her during the week." "I was sitting beside my mom. Ebonita pointed out this phlegm rising in her mouth. It was white and loose almost like water and a little bubbly. Maybe it wasn't phlegm, I now realize. Some other juices from inside, but we thought it was and a good sign because we'd been trying to get the congestion out of her chest for a day. Raising her, trying to get her to cough up. But there was a lot of this stuff right below the top of her lips, just staying there. She'd been having trouble breathing for a day and I didn't want to take her—send her— have an ambulance bring her, I mean, to the hospital, because even the doctor said—" "And he was right. Of course he should have come over and seen her to say this, but he was still right. All they'd do at the hospital is stick needles in her, try to keep her alive for another day, if they were lucky, and maybe even help get rid of her before she would have normally passed away at home. But we've gone over this. What I'm saying now, though, is that some people might think this is just another terrific story you're telling. Not 'terrific.' That the dramatics of it is of equal importance or even more important to you than what you were feeling at the time and are no doubt feeling something of now." "I feel terrible, as low as I've ever felt. Or did feel that low for a few days and now just feel terrible, almost as low. And just talking to people about it, and right here with you . . . " "I know, dear, I know, I'm sorry. But you still don't want to convey the inaccurate impression that you're focusing on certain aspects of what happened to make it sound more interesting. In your arms. Hugging her and crying out the things you did at the end. Who wouldn't want his loved one to die in his arms like that. Peacefully for the most part. Not in a hospital where they shoo you out of the room at precisely that moment or a little before and then come out later and say she's gone." "That's why I didn't call EMS or that Haztollah or whatever that ambulance service is to take her to a hospital. I knew she was going. The doctor, from everything I told him, said so over the phone, and she'd been declining for a few weeks and it was clear to Ebonita and me that this was it. I wanted her to be comfortable at home. She'd told me long ago that that's what she hoped for also, no tubes and to die in her own bed. Well, it wasn't her own bed—it was this nursing service loan of a bed. And it wasn't even in her bedroom—it was her own dining room converted into a bedroom so she could be taken care of better, but at least it was her own home. And, she said, surrounded by— well, there was just me and Ebonita there and some old ghosts maybe. Dad, my brother who didn't live till what, five? but did live in that apartment his last two years. I'm sure she would have wanted you and the kids there, but that couldn't be and I wouldn't have wanted the kids to see it, and the main person who took care of her, Angela, but she was off for the weekend and we couldn't reach her by phone. And also Ebonita's daughter just sitting there in a chair in the room and not looking scared or saying anything, just curious as if this were an interesting new thing she was seeing, though Ebonita told me her daughter had been in the hospital room the moment her own grandmother died. So maybe that was it, reliving it, but I think more out of not knowing what to do and curiosity, the death and the way I was taking it. I didn't know how to tell her to leave, go to the kitchen, take in a movie, anything, but get out of here please, this was a private moment for me, the worst there was, or for

Ebonita to tell her . . . " "You were right; Ebonita should have if the girl didn't have the sense to leave herself. How old is she?" "Fifteen; seventeen?" "Then old enough to know. And I can see why you'd be unable to say something yourself. Anyway, dear, I overheard you talking to Frederick about your mother and thought I should say something to you." "He asked me how I was. He'd called to make a lunch date. He didn't know she'd died. So I said I was feeling the worst I'd ever been in my life, and then—after he asked—that it was because my mother had died on Sunday." "You said she died in your arms on Sunday." "So that's what I said then." "And that's why I brought it up. But of course do what you want. I just felt I had to point it out." "Okay. I'll remember. You're probably right. Anything else?" "No, nothing. I'm making myself tea. Like some?" and he says "No thanks," and she grabs his hand and squeezes it and looks up at him sympathetically, he fakes a quick smile, she says "I understand," and wheels herself to the stove to get the tea kettle. He should help her but he suddenly feels in his throat and eyes a cry coming on and wants to be alone. He goes into the living room and sits but no tears come and the swelling in his throat and itchy feeling around his eyes go away. What's that mean, he's finally adjusting to his mother's death? No, he's sure he's in for a few more bad days of it. The tall memorial candle's burning on the fireplace mantel. He brought it from New York, something the funeral home gave him along with several cardboard boxes to sit in mourning on but which he left behind, and lit it the day after they drove back from the funeral. So it's been lit for more than two days and seems to have burned less than a third of the way down. His wife wanted him to put a dish under it but he said "Why? That's for regular candles when the wax is dripping. This one's inside a long glass cylinder, and it couldn't be safer, because the lit wick gets lower down the longer the candle burns. She said the glass might break, burning for so many days—"Have you felt how hot it is? I did, just as a test, and wish I hadn't, or had licked my fingers first, for it burned me," and he said he knows it gets hot, he doesn't have to touch it to find out, but he's sure that that glass is the kind that won't break from such a small flame, because when she felt it did she also see how thick it is? He gets up and touches the glass; it's hot but didn't burn his fingers though would have if he'd kept them on longer, and maybe the heat from the bottom of the glass will do something to the mantel wood when the candle burns way down, but he has about three days for that. Where's the camera? and sees it on the piano and using the flash takes a picture of the candle for some future day when he may want to remember exactly what it looked like, Jewish star and funeral home name on it and everything. It could also turn out to be an interesting photo, a few condolence cards and the little *Prayers and Meditations* book, which he took off a side table in the funeral home sitting room her casket was in, lying beside the candle, if maybe come out looking too much like the outside of one of those cards. He opens the book to "Yizkor in Memory of a Mother." What's yizkor mean again? Not "again": he never knew. Certainly not "may," which seems to be the translation in each of the seven yizkors in the book: "for a Wife," "for a Son," et cetera, and one just "Yizkor Meditation." The prayer in the book he likes best, or maybe it's a meditation, is "At a Mother's Grave," but the book stayed in his pocket at the burial—the rabbi did all the reading—and he's only read the prayer to himself in bed a few times before reading a couple of sad poems and shutting the light and going to sleep. He sits on the box with the book, starts reading very low the yizkor for a mother, something he's done when nobody was around at least once a day since she died. But he shouldn't be reading while sitting, should he? even on this mourner's box. And he doesn't want to stand up and read, nor read it any louder—his wife might come in and say something like "You, never a believer or worshipper or even someone who observed a single Jewish holiday or ritual, not even circumcision if we'd had a son, now going on every day like a yeshiva *bucher?*"—and reading it silently standing up or seated doesn't mean anything. Later, when the kids are asleep and his wife is in one of the other rooms, he'll read it or another prayer or meditation while he stands by the candle, as he's done the other times since he's been home. He's cried every time while reading from the book—oh, don't go into it. He moves to the easy chair and opens the *New York Times*, tries reading an Arts article but thinks of her. He's almost always thinking of her, or in ten minutes or so of doing something else he always seems to return to thinking of her, and sometimes of her reading this same paper, but the Late edition, which she loved doing every morning over coffee till she couldn't anymore because of her cataracts. Regrets: why didn't he ever drive her down here to see this house? They bought it more than three years ago and she never saw it once. But he's gone over that. She was frail, couldn't take the train or plane anymore, four-hour car trip would have been too tiring and maybe even painful for her, it would have been too much for him to deal with, taking care of her and also seeing to his wife. Two wheelchairs in one house: in his head he didn't like the way they looked together, especially at the dinner table and on the little patio outside, though he didn't think it would have bothered his wife. But he could have made the car seat comfortable for her, stopped as often as she wanted along the way, driven more slowly than he normally does, taken Angela with her, put them up for a few days, Angela in the basement, his mother on the day bed in his wife's studio, an intercom hooked up between them, or moved his kids to the basement and had Angela and his mother in their adjacent bedrooms, driven them back and then returned the same day. The last two summers when he drove back from Maine he told his wife he was definitely going to have his mother down for a few days this fall and she said it'll be difficult but it was all right with her and that was the last he did of it. She would have loved that he owned this house and lived in such a neighborhood: tall trees, small hills, lots of birds and perfumy air, nursery school playground across the street and all those children's voices, house on one level and with ramps, extra wide doors and a bathroom big enough for a wheelchair to turn around, hospitable supermarket nearby. Regrets: why didn't he call her every day as he'd promised? Remembers his father saying lots of times "When I got married and moved out I called my mother at least once a day till she died and saw her twice a week for dinner or lunch," and his mother saying a number of those times "It's true, your father was an unbelievable son: almost too good, to where he neglected his own family." He remembers thinking this was a nice thing to do and he'd do it too with the phone once he grew up and moved away from home. He called her every other day or every third day and for the last year she frequently didn't know who he was or took him for someone else: one of her dead brothers, his father, a name he didn't recognize and when he asked who's that she said she'd never heard the name before and why'd he bring it up? But in a minute or so, after he kept saying "It's me, Mom, Gould, your son Gould," recognizing him and saying at first she didn't hear him because he was speaking so softly or it was her bad hearing or the girl didn't put her hearing aid in right this morning or the hearing aid must need a new battery or never worked right: "You'll have to take me to the place we got it at. I forget where but you'll know or Angela must have it written down. But you will come around to see me soon, won't you, dearest? I'd really like that," and he'd say she knows he's in Baltimore, right, and not in New York? and weekdays there's his job, not too demanding, but also driving Fanny to and from school and weekends the kids always have so many things going for him to drive them to, and Sally, of course, takes some of his time, but he'll be there in two weeks, he promises, take her to lunch on a Saturday, and she'd say two weeks sounds like such a long time when one has nothing to do, but if it's the best he can do she'll have to live with it. Or sometimes she'd say "That was dumb of me to think you were Dad. Probably because I didn't get enough sleep last night. All I could do was run my life through my mind and not like most of it, so aggravation there too. And also vegetating here watching inconsequential TV shows the girl likes makes me stupid and forget what year it is and where I am. Tell me, is this my home I'm in?" and he'd say "Your old apartment for almost sixty years. It's just it's a different kind of bed than you're used to and it's in the dining room because your bedroom was too far away from the bathroom, so maybe you don't recognize your surroundings because of that," and she'd say "All that's probably true. Though I still have a suspicion this isn't my regular home, but then why would you want to trick me?" Regrets: sometimes he'd call and Ebonita or Angela would answer and say she's resting or on the potty or sitting under the water in the shower and he'd say he'll call back in an hour but usually never did. Why? Because he'd think he already called that day, his duty was done, Angela will tell her he called and she'll be pleased by it though disappointed she missed him and later think something came up at his home where he couldn't call back. When actually talking on the phone to her the last few years was often frustrating, where she couldn't understand what he was saying and he'd have to shout for her to hear him and sometimes she'd give the phone to Angela and say "You talk to him and find out what he wants; he's speaking loud enough but I still can't make out a word." He should have called back each time and if she was still on the toilet or had gone from the toilet to the shower or bed, say he'll call back again in an hour or two or sometime that day and then call back as he said. Regrets: he'd tell her he was coming to New York to see her for the day and half the time he'd call a day or two before to say something had come up at home—Sally, or one of the kids got sick, so he'll have to put off the trip till next week. Usually his Sally or sick-kid excuse was a lie: he didn't want to make the trip, too tired to or thought he'd be, or he had work to do and wanted to do it at home and not on the train, or heavy rain was forecast for New York, so he wouldn't be able to wheel her to a neighborhood restaurant, which made getting her there—which he wanted to because he found having lunch with her at home suffocating—even with Ebonita or Angela helping him, tough because he'd have to get her and the wheelchair in and out of cabs and sometimes she was a dead weight. He also wouldn't be able to take her to the park after lunch, which she liked doing and frequently fell asleep for an hour or two there while he watched people and read. Regrets that he found having lunch with her suffocating. Regrets that she slept so much when he was in the park or even at home with her the last couple of years, but nothing he could have done about that. Regrets that he didn't take her down to the river after lunch, which he thought of doing lots of times on hot days but it was about fifteen minutes away while the park was right up her block. But he shouldn't have disappointed her so much, since that's what she obviously was—her voice, or silence after, or "That's all right, your family comes first, and maybe you have some important outside things to do too," whenever he told her he couldn't come in this weekend as planned. Regrets: why didn't he initiate conversation more and follow up the questions he did ask with more questions about what she was talking about when they went out for lunch or spoke on the phone or sat in her home the last few years? The calls to her were usually over in a couple of minutes, sometimes less; a few perfunctory questions, and mostly the same ones: "How are you? You feeling all right? Eating okay? Anyone drop by lately? Do anything interesting recently?" "Like what?" she'd say. "When you're not here, and I'm not going to a doctor with one of the girls or your lovely cousin, all I do is sleep and eat a little and listen to the radio or TV." A couple of times he said "Then anything interesting on the radio or TV?" and she said "I can barely see or hear them," and then silence on his part and after she asked him a few things about his family—"Your kids all right? Your wife okay? Is that new medicine she's taking, working? Listen," she said maybe twenty times, "I hear they're discovering new things all the time for what she has; is she involved with any of them?"—she'd say "So, I guess that's it; I can't think of anything else worth mentioning. Thanks for calling; you're a doll. I love you," and he'd say "Same here, Mom; Sally and the kids send their love too, and I'll call you tomorrow," and she'd say "I look forward to it; I always do." Face it, he usually wanted to get off the phone with her soon as he could. The same conversations, same difficulty in holding those conversations, and whatever he told her she seemed to instantly forget. But he should have faked it, put more life in his voice, asked friends for jokes and told her them—she liked a good joke—and laughed at the punchlines if she didn't. Thought of lots of different things she might want to talk about, repeated what he had to say over and over till she finally got it. Prepared questions to ask her before he dialed. Stayed on the phone five minutes, ten minutes, even thought of follow-up questions to ask her, written all these questions down, even. She must have thought sometimes "He's got to be bored with me by now; probably thinks I don't understand a word he says and haven't a brain left in my head. That I'm old so I'm demented. He's probably only calling out of a sense of duty. I should ask him more about him and his family, not just general questions but specific ones—'What courses are your girls taking in school? How are they doing in them? Do you have to help them much with their homework? I'm sorry, I know you once told me, but what grades are they in again?'—but I can never think of this when we're on the phone. I should also call him more but so many times I don't think he's glad to hear from me. It mostly seems I'm getting him at a bad time, nothing personal against me." At the end of his calls to her she often said "Tell me, what's the best time to reach you by phone?" and he always said "Anytime after five is good; there you're almost guaranteed I'm home. If I'm not and you speak to Sally or one of the kids, I'll call you soon as I get your message, unless it's way too late." She hadn't called him more than three or four times in the last two years, and one day she called him twice and just an hour apart, not remembering she'd already called him. "Do I have your phone number—I don't think you ever gave it to me," she said several times and he'd tell her "It's in the little phonebook on your night table. It's also taped to the inside of the cabinet door above the kitchen phone, and I know Angela has it written down in a couple of other places in case she suddenly has to get me. But don't bother calling me; I like calling you and I try to every day," and she said things like "I know and it's very sweet of you." Why didn't he ever talk to her about some of these things: "You know me, Mom, I was never much of a talker on the phone and it has nothing to do with you if our talks are short. And if I'm relatively quiet or not too conversational, we'll call it, at the restaurants we go to or when we're sitting around at home, it's only because the long train ride's made me sleepy or I had to get up earlier than usual for a Saturday to catch the train and get here by noon or I did lots of schoolwork or something the previous night and didn't get enough sleep, so there also it was nothing you did." Regrets: when he came to New York the time before the last, almost a month ago, and another regret is why he didn't come a week or two after that or every week, and walked into the dining room where she was sitting in a chair and said "How are you, Mom?" and she looked up, no smile, which she normally gave, that she was glad to see him and said "Who are you?" why didn't he get on his knees and hug her and say "Mom, it's me, Gould, your son; oh my mom, why don't you recognize me?" Instead he stood there saying "What do you mean, who am I? It's me, who else could it be? I've come to see you, all the way from Baltimore, and take you out to lunch and spend the day with you," and she said "We're going out? That's nice. I wasn't expecting it, nobody said anything," and he said "But I called last night to remind you and Angela, and we've been talking about it the last two weeks. And you're dressed for going out, aren't you? so you must have known," and she said "Then I don't remember, but please don't make it an issue. I'll have to go to the bathroom first and then I'll be ready—call the girl," so regrets there for upsetting her. Did he apologize? He's sure he did but forgets. He got her wheelchair, "Want to walk it outside?" she said "Right now I feel too weak to," and got her into the chair, pushed her outside, "The girl; shouldn't we invite Angela? We haven't taken her to lunch in a while," and he said "Not today, I just want to be with you alone and I'm sure she appreciates the break, especially when she's working the weekend this week too," when it was really because Angela picked at her food and took a half-hour longer to eat than his mother, turned around in the areaway and pulled her up the steps to the sidewalk, "Want to try walking the wheelchair now? It's good exercise for you, and only a little way," and she said "I don't feel I can move a step. I'm sorry but I don't know what's wrong with me today," and he said "Mom, come on, you should only do what you're able to," pushed her to the restaurant she liked going to most, table by the patio window which she liked sitting beside so she could watch the people passing, after that to a coffee bar on the same block—he got her a decaffeinated coffee but told her it was regular, that's what Angela said the doctor wants her to have if she does have coffee: he'd prefer her to stick with hot cocoa or a mild tea—another regret? No, and even though she wasn't supposed to have a drink either, and if a drink then just a wine or beer, he got her her favorite: Jack Daniels on the rocks with a little water and twist of lemon, "Because what else are they going to take away from me," she once asked, "food and air too?"—and a flaky Danish-like pastry she loved,with peaches and walnuts in it. She asked that day at both places and while he wheeled her along the street the same kinds of questions she usually did and some of them several times: "You feeling okay? Your wife. Everything considering, she's all right, no change? And your lovely daughters, they okay too? They doing well in school? Of course they are, look who are their parents," and he said "Sally, maybe, but not me, and I mean by that, their brains." "How old are they now? I can't believe it, where'd all the time go? You still teaching? You have enough money? You know, if you ever need a loan . . . I don't have much but you can have it all, because what good is it going to do me? Where do you live these days? Not in New York? How far is Baltimore from here? That much? I didn't realize. How long have you lived so far away? You don't think, if you looked, there'd be something closer that was as good?" Another thing to regret? That he's lived down there the last fourteen years? They kept his wife's old student apartment near Columbia, sublet it more than they used it. Whenever they came up, though, and stayed there he saw her every day for lunch and sometimes dropped by around five for drinks and cheese and crackers. Regrets that they didn't come up more. The drive was long and tedious for him but he should have done it more often. She loved seeing the girls. And before their oldest one started middle school, when absences began counting against her, they stayed at their apartment all of June and three weeks during the Christmas break instead of what they'd done the last four years, ten to eleven days. And when she was still in nursery school and kindergarten, they came up for around five weeks and he maybe skipped seeing his mother one or two days. Then he wheeled her home, didn't ask if she wanted to walk the chair, knew she couldn't, helped her onto the bed—"Suddenly I feel very tired. In the restaurant I was fine. I didn't have anything alcoholic to drink, did I?" and he said "Let's just say I kept diluting your Jack Daniels with water so you wouldn't drink it almost straight and get looped there," and she said "Now that was a mean thing for you to do"—sat beside her a couple of hours while she napped and then got up and leaned over her and said "Mom, Mom, listen, I have to be going and I want to say goodbye," and she opened her eyes and smiled and said "Thank you, my darling," and he said "Thank you, nothing; it's been my pleasure. I love taking you out and seeing you and I just wish I could do it more often—I'll try to," and she said "That'd be nice. You're the only one who'll give me a drink and I get to eat a good lunch and enjoy myself so much with," and he kissed her forehead and cheek and then her forehead again—it was wet, didn't feel warm when he touched it with his fingers. Maybe she was sweating because the room was too warm or it was the drink or it could be one of the medicines she's taking or she had a fever. Can a forehead be cold and the body feverish at the same time? Another regret is that he didn't tell Angela about it. Just knocked on her door and she said through it "Yes, sir?" and he said "I'm going." Maybe the infection was only just setting in and in a few weeks gradually grew into that awful hoarse cough and labored breathing—spread to her lungs, he's saying—and was what finally killed her. "She's been declining for months," her doctor said on the phone the day before she died. "She won't pull through this time, a hospital's not going to improve her chances, so it's mainly a matter of where you think she'll be most comfortable. I always tell the patient's immediate survivors that unless there's physical or emotional suffering involved on either side:

home's the ideal." Then she shut her eyes, smile gone, seemed to fall back to sleep and he got his coat and briefcase, stuck his books and newspaper in it, looked into her room, she seemed to be sleeping peacefully, thought of going over to kiss her, didn't want to disturb her, and left. He'll call her when he gets home, he thought, walking to the subway. She'll most likely be up and will like hearing from him. He didn't. Another regret. Would have been so nice. "Mom, I just got in"—she'd ask where, he'd say "From New York, where I saw you today: I took the train, and first thing I'm doing—I don't even have my coat off—is calling you. No, too obvious. "Mom, I just got back from New York where I saw you and wanted to know how you are and if you had your dinner." Forget the dinner. Just "How are you, what are you doing?" She'd have said "I'm all right, I guess" and "Nothing, as usual." Another regret is that he didn't stay overnight in their apartment, come over in the morning and take her out for breakfast, and if it was raining or too cold, made her breakfast in her apartment with things he brought over and knew she liked: bagels, Canadian bacon, strawberries, Friendship pot cheese, a special fruit juice, and then left for the train. Or just stayed longer by her bed that afternoon. Read, maybe taken a quick walk. Then had a drink with her when she awoke: Jack Daniels on the rocks for him (it was the only hard stuff in the house, though he could have bought a bottle of vodka in his quick walk), a very watered-down one for her, because there wasn't any great need for him to get home before the kids went to sleep, and it was Saturday so they'd still be up at ten or eleven and he could see them if he got on the train by seven or eight. And the kids didn't need to be driven anywhere early the next morning that he remembers. Even if they did, he could have called Sally and asked her to get a friend to drive them or the parent of the kid whose house his daughter was going to; that it was more important he go home later that day than he thought or to stay the night in New York and leave tomorrow around noon because his mother seemed to be getting weaker—she was definitely getting weaker and thinner and less lucid and he wanted to spend as much time with her while he had the chance. Misses her, can't stop thinking of her. Well, it's not as if he tries to stop. He's just always thinking of her or a lot. He can be doing anything, taking a run, a shower, shaving, slapping something on toast, sitting in a chair eating or reading, talking on the phone (he's only been able to talk—won't even pick up the phone when it rings; his kids and wife have to and then tell him who it is—to a few close friends and his mother's accountant and the cousin who looked in on her in New York the past few years and is now going through her own mourning and calls up to talk to him or Sally about it: "How strange. I never knew I'd feel this way once she was gone. I almost thought it'd bring relief, to me and her, though I can't especially say how, since she for the most part was in relatively good health for someone her age and I enjoyed her company, and now I grieve that I won't be catching the one-oh-four bus to see her and stopping in a store along the way to get her a buttered soft roll," and he said "Same here, though not the relief part. But honestly, Lottie, I can't talk about it yet like this"), when suddenly she pops into his head, if he isn't already talking about her, like with Lottie, and he often starts crying. He thinks about writing a poem about her. Anything: her youth, what she meant to him, times with her when he was a boy, her relationship with his dad, one composed of just phrases and things she liked to say. He doesn't write poems. Last was a series of them to Sally a few weeks after he met her and the first time she broke off with him, titling them "2S1," "2S2," till "2S11," and finally "2Sdozen." He threw out his copies of them about a year later but wonders if she kept the originals he sent her one by one after he wrote them, sometimes going outside at two and three in the morning to drop them into a mailbox. He takes out his pen and starts writing, cries during part of it, and finishes it in a few minutes. It all just came. He'd stop about ten seconds between each completed sentence before going to the next. Should he write another? No, this one says what he wants. He reads it and changes only the second "laid" to "lay." How could my mother not be alive?/ My mother has always been alive./ I clutched her around and cried/ 'Mommy, Mommy, it's all right,/ Mommy,' and then she died./ I laid her sideways on the pillow/ and she lay there always./ She has always been there./ When I come to this city I will/ be coming to see her./ Things won't change, will they?/ How could my mother not be alive?/ How could she? Things don't change./ I'll never be the same./ Speak to me, Mommy, speak to me./ It all goes on and I cannot stop." He'd like to be able to— of course he would. But finish the thought. To be able to type it up, change nothing else in it, and stick the original into an envelope and send it to her. He'd like, he'd like. And Express. To go to the post office and get one of those Express envelopes and send it that way so she can get it early the next day. And with a note in it. Now that's enough. But what would he say? "Dear Mom, I'm so glad you can receive this, your loving son, Gould." So what to do with the poem? He tears the page out of the notebook and puts it inside the book he's been reading but hasn't read more than a few pages of since he took it on the train to New York the day she died. Phone rings and he yells out "I don't want to speak to anyone now, no one, not even my cousin," and his wife says from her studio "I understand, but what should I say if it's for you, you're not here?" Phone's still ringing. "Say, if they don't already know, that my mother died and I am here but I don't feel I can talk to anyone now but her and my kids and wife. That I'm low—feeling as low as I've ever felt in my life." "You want me to say that?" "Pick up the phone if you want and say anything, but please stop its ringing; the damn noise is killing me," and she picks it up and he quietly moves to the kitchen by her studio and listens as she says "No, no, it's coming along; he's very upset, of course—" and he says "Upset? What a word for it. I don't know exactly what I am but I'm a helluva lot worse than upset," and she's probably looking his way, shaking her head, doing things like that and the expression to go with it—he can't see her nor she him—and she says "Please, Gould, don't make it any tougher," so her hand's probably on the talking part of the receiver, and he says "Sorry, no harm meant, but what can you expect? Though that's no excuse," and goes back to his chair in the living room. The cat comes in and heads toward him and he says "Listen, I don't want to pet you and you've already been fed plenty, so go away," and the cat gets by his feet and seems ready to jump into his lap. "Did you hear me? I don't want that," wagging his finger. Cat jumps up and he puts him on the floor. Jumps right back up and he says "What is it with you? I know you know something's wrong and you're trying to comfort me, but not . . . right . . . now," and with one hand underneath he holds him over the floor from about three feet up and lets him drop. The cat scoots up onto the chair opposite him, stares at him after he settled himself and then tucks his front paws under his chest and closes his eyes for sleep. "You understand," he says low, "that it's that I don't want to touch or be touched by my wife either for any kind of loving or solace or easement. My kids, yes, to hold them, but right now, and for I don't know how long but I'm sure no more than a couple of weeks, I don't want to be held. Oh, what am I saying," and thinks he's got to do something. Sitting here or lying on his bed or walking around the neighborhood all he can do is think of his mother and what he didn't do for her. He goes into the bathroom and pees, though he had no urge to, just to get up and do something. Move, move, keep busy, that's the ticket. Folds the towels on the rack. Then folds them the more intricate but right way, horizontally in half and then vertically in thirds and then over. Then he sweeps the bathroom floor and washes it with diluted ammonia and rags. On his knees, just as his mother didn't do; she used a mop but he can't stand those things, the stringy ones, which you have to wring out by hand if you don't have a bucket with a wringer, or the sponge mops they have that are too damn slow to use, where you have to squeeze them with that metal piece every two square feet of mopped floor. Rags are the best, rags, rags: rinse them under the kitchen faucet after you're through and then throw them into the washer, though make sure you don't wash any clothes or linens with them; all that lint. Same with the kitchen: sweeps it, then spills diluted ammonia on the floor and gets on his knees with the rags and starts swabbing. "What are you doing?" his wife says; "the smell," and he says "Cleaning. I feel I want—I don't feel, I just want, and I don't mean by that correction anything but that I want everything to be clean, tidy, neat, even sparkling. And it's something to do, I need something physical to do." "If that's the case, after you're done, the shed needs emptying out and tidying up." "Good, will do," and he finishes swabbing and then dries the floor with paper towels. But first finish cleaning the house, he thinks, and vacuums every room, changes the kitty litter boxes, remakes all the beds, scours the kitchen sink, cleans down the refrigerator and stove and countertops, takes the clothes from yesterday out of the dryer and folds them and puts them away in various drawers, cleans the toilets and tub and shower stall and refolds the towels in the other bathroom, goes outside and cleans out the shed, has a whole bunch of things from it and the basement to take to the dump and puts them all in the van, yells out to his wife "I'm off to the dump," and goes. While he's driving he thinks turn the radio on to one of the classical music stations, but there might be voices, news, promos, thank-yous for contributing to a recent fund drive and so on, and he really doesn't want to hear music right now either. He thinks his mother would have liked to come to the dump if she were here. *Knows*, unless she was too weak or tired to. Places like dumps, the kids' music schools, just ordinary chores, driving in neighborhoods she hadn't been to before or not for long, and especially shopping with him, and especially grocery shopping when she stayed a week or two in Maine with them each summer, she liked. A week; his wife felt that was long enough for either of their mothers but he always felt bad sending her back to the hot city and wanted it to be more. She'd be in the front seat. Last time she was in the van was about six weeks ago when he drove her and his family to dinner at his cousin's apartment in New York. No, last time was when he drove her home after dropping off his family at their apartment, since she lived farther downtown. She was in the back seat. There because his wife had been in the front seat and there didn't seem to be any reason for his mother to move up for such a short trip. He said something to her, she didn't answer, he turned around, she sat frozen, it seemed, staring straight ahead past the front passenger seat. "Mom, you okay, what are you looking at so hard?" She continued staring, didn't move. "Mom, anything wrong, you all right, why don't you answer or look at me?" Nothing. He thought: is she dead? Is this it, then? He reached over and touched her shoulder and neck. She seemed to be breathing normally but still stared straight ahead without moving. Should he pull over? he thought. Maybe she needs to be rushed to a hospital or for one of those EMS ambulances to rush to him. But he's near her building and maybe she is asleep and something's wrong with her eyes that's keeping them open and she'll snap out of it before he gets there. He kept looking back at her as he drove, she stayed the same, he parked at the hydrant by her building, put the emergency lights on, ran around the car and slid the side door open and she suddenly stopped staring, turned to him and smiled and said "We're home? So fast? I must have slept," and he said "But your eyes were open. You were staring out the windshield, or seemed to, the whole way after we dropped off Sally and the girls," and she said "I couldn't have. Nobody sleeps with his eyes open; at least I never have." He got her into the chair and wheeled her down the steps and into the building. Regrets that he didn't tell Angela, or whichever woman was working that night; and also called her doctor the next day about it. He still doesn't know why she froze up like that. Next time he sees his doctor or his wife's—not the kids'; she's strictly pediatrics—or meets one before then at a dinner or something, though the way he feels now he doesn't know when that will ever be, he'll mention it. He'd talk to her now if she were in the car. Last time they spoke she was hallucinating. It was the night before she went into a coma; next day—no, the day after that—she died. Ebonita called him; said his mother had been babbling for three hours straight, she'd never seen anything like it. About her children, husband, work, her family when she was a girl, a jump rope she played with for years, mostly though her mother and sister. "I can't get her to stop. Maybe you can." She put his mother on and she said "Party, party, party," and he said "Mom, it's me, what do you mean 'party'? What's doing?" and she said "Let's go to a party. I want to party, party." "Mom, it's Gould; you're saying you want to go to a party? What kind?" and she said "How's business?" and he said "I'm not in business, Mom; I teach, I write," and she said "I'm going to bake a cake. First I should get out of here. I want to bake lots of cakes. I have to get up now and start baking if I'm to have the time to do it." She was speaking away from the phone, maybe to Ebonita, and Ebonita said "Talk into the phone, Mrs. B. It's your son, so say something to him."

"Party, party, party," she said into the phone. "I want to make and bake. Cookies, bread, cake." "You always made great herb breads, Mom, do you remember? And what you called a zucchini bread, though it was more like a cake. Everyone loved it. Is that the kind of cake you mean you want to make?" "My sister's coming today and she likes chicken the way I bake it and she loves my zuccini cake." "Which sister? You come from a large family." "We'll party and party. Lizzie and Ethyl, Harris and Rita. Zippie, though that wasn't her real name." "What was her real name? You and Aunt Zippie and Uncle Pete never wanted to reveal it." "Party and more party. Are any of my family alive? I think they're all gone and deceased, since I haven't seen any of them in years. Could be they don't want to come see me. Who would want to come see an ugly old mess. Is it fair that I'm the only one of my family left? What happened? Where'd my mother go? What I do?" And then more talking to herself it seemed snd where he couldn't cut in, till he yelled out "Ebonita, it's all right, you can take the phone away, I want to speak to you." About two months before that his mother said "Tell me, and I want you to be honest"—he was sitting on her bed, she in her chair, the newspaper she couldn't read anymore because of her cataracts but still had delivered every day, on her lap—"how old am I?" and he said "Ninety-two." "No, am I really that old? How'd I get to live that long? It doesn't run in my family. And I drank and smoked and your father made life hell for me and I lost a child and never ate right because I always wanted to be thin and for the most part neglected myself in all the other things. I don't get it." He told Ebonita on the phone, his mother babbling in the background: "I'm coming tomorrow to see her. I'll get the eight o'clock train and be there around eleven. She doesn't sound well. But you say she has no fever and is eating and urinating okay?" and she said "Everything but the talking's normal. And she's eating and drinking her food like she's enjoying it." His youngest daughter woke him around four the next morning and said she couldn't breathe. "You mean you're having trouble breathing?" and she said "No, I can't get breaths. My throat's stuck." They later found out she had the croup. He gave her medicine that was for his oldest daughter's asthma, called Ebonita around ten and said he had to take his daughter to the doctor now and he'd either see his mother much later in the day than he'd planned or early tomorrow, all depending on how sick his daughter and mother are. "How is she?" and she said "She babbled endlessly till two this morning and is now sleeping like a baby," and he said "She talk about anything different this time? Things or people or events you never heard her speak of before?" and she said "No, it's mostly her mother and sister and some her father and cake and bake and chicken and such. You a lot too, that you're her only person she can really count on," and he said "That's not true at all. There's you and Lottie and Angela and some people from the street. Don't take it personally. In fact, if you want, and you can say this idea came from me, tell her if she can count on me so much, how come I'm almost never there? But it must be very difficult for you, tending to her so many hours straight, and I'm sorry I'm not there to help out. Anyway, she sounds much better already, but I'll call you later to make sure." He called later and his mother was still sleeping peacefully though she had sat up for a few minutes to take some special canned food supplement through a straw. "Good, that means she got some food and you got to rest." He dumps the stuff he had in the van, goes home, parks, then while still in the car he thinks there's a road near here he's for a few years wanted to take to see what's around it and where it goes but he's always given himself excuses not to: has no time, it's a silly or childish impulse to carry out, and so on; but do it now, and he drives to it—it's only a mile away and he passed it on the way to the dump and back and almost every weekday when he drives his oldest daughter to high school—and it winds through an area with homes and woods and hilly lawns like his own and ends up on a familiar road to the main town in this part of the county. He drives home on the familiar road, since it's the shorter route of the two, parks and walks into the house and his wife says "Was that you in the carport before?" and he says "You mean about ten minutes ago in the van? Yes, but I suddenly forgot something," and she says "What?" and he says "I don't know, something. My mother call?" and she says "What are you talking about?" and he says "Just being dopey, that's all, and possibly thinking 'Well, you never know.' Anyway, the last few years she hardly ever called. I called her though, almost every day and sometimes every day for a week. I tried to call more, every single day I was away from her, really I did." "I know, my darling." "It would've been nice if she had called—now, I'm talking; I'm not concerned or ever felt slighted she didn't call me much the last few years." "Of course you weren't." "I'm sure she wanted to but didn't think of it. Or she thought of it and then the thought quickly disappeared. She'd never stand on ceremony with me either—that's a term she liked to use. But you know, that 'He's the son so he should call me,' and it for sure wasn't that she was too cheap to call. That was my father. 'Penurious,' I liked to call him—I mean if I had to put it in words—though some people, including my mother sometimes, called him cheap. Oh, the trouble he gave me as a kid when I wanted to phone a friend. 'Your father got stock in Bell?' and so on. But my mom? Just the opposite. 'Call when you like, but better now than when your father's around. You know how it upsets him,' and of course an upset him would start upsetting her. But do you think she took that tack to sort of get me on her side and a little against him, or just to establish what distinguished them? What am I trying to say here? Help me," and she says "She might have been showing you she approved of a number of things you did that your father disapproved of, and certainly that she didn't think your calling your friends was a big deal." "She was always supporting me and my work. Is that what you meant? Probably not. And I'm not referring to money, though she would've given me some to do what I wanted with it, within reason and her limited budget, and often offered. 'Do you need any extra cash?' Even now—I mean up until maybe two months ago—and I'd say 'No, Mom, I'm working, so I got enough coming in.' But before I met you, to live off of while I did these so-called artistic or creative things, or for grad school or travel, but I never wanted to take it and hardly ever did. I wanted to be Mr. Independent, and I didn't want to be taking money she might have, with a lot of difficulty, extracted from my dad. And after he died, money that'd make her own life a bit more comfortable and secure. He was a good guy, though, and had a kind heart, I wasn't alluding to anything about that. Everybody thought so, except sometimes my mother. A sense of humor too—both of them, though I forget who I was originally talking about there. Though she, for some reason, became even funnier after he died—real witty lines and retorts which I never remember her saying before. Let's see, what would be one? That crack about the Jack Daniels, when I tried diluting it because I thought it was too strong for her and she hadn't had anything to eat yet. I think I told you it. Others. 'If I get any older . . .' Something about if she got any older than she was and Stone Age culture, but I forget. And both were affectionate to me most times, my father, earlier on, more than my mother—'A kiss, before you go to bed every night you must give me a kiss'—and never raised a hand. Well, he raised it to me several times but it never struck. But she? Not a finger, except, and when I probably deserved it, to wag. I really loved them both, though if I had to make a choice . . . this, by the way, was the one impossible question to answer when I was a boy: 'Who do you love more, your mom or dad?'— it'd be she. It's true, I'd have to say it, I never said it before, but it was she. Not because I knew her twenty years longer. She was, all in all, just nicer and more dependable and predictable and with a more even disposition and she made me feel better when I needed to and understood or tried to understand me more. But them both, you know? I've no regrets in what kind of parents I had in them both." "I know. Try not to be so sad," and he says "I can't help it. I feel miserable. This goddamn crying's a pain in the ass sometimes, when it just spurts out in the worst public places and tears my throat, but I suppose it also has its good. I should've got a vaporizer for her room when she started breathing poorly again a few months ago. I didn't want to take her money so she'd be more comfortable and secure in old age? So why, when I had the chance and the income, didn't I give her everything she needed—gone into hock doing it, if I had to? Now I look back and think what the hell was I saving the money for anyway? I'd only have been spending her money, wouldn't I? when you think I'll probably end up with a small bundle from her when the estate's settled. Laziness, that's what it was. That I couldn't pick up the phone and call the drugstore nearest her and say send over a vaporizer, send her everything she needs or the woman taking care of her says she needs." "You did that. The women with her could have ordered anything they wanted, and no doubt did. And it was already costing you and your mother a big bundle keeping those women there and feeding them." "That I just couldn't have picked up the phone every day and even twice a day, morning and night, and not mostly from my office, and spoken to her a few minutes? I had to keep it to once a day and most times not even to that? And laziness that I didn't take the train in to see her more." "You saw her a lot." "Not enough. I was bored with the trip, I also found the car ride in tedious, but I couldn't have made the sacrifice more? What would it have taken? Bought some good stuff to read on the train. Or saved up, let's say, since to me newspapers are much easier to read on trains than books, two to three days of the *Times*. Or the whole Sunday paper, no matter what day I left, or just the arts and magazine and week-in-review sections—the book I would have already read—or made myself tired by not getting much sleep the night before the trip so I'd sleep on the train most of the way." "Now you're carrying out these things you could have done too far, both for her and yourself, and it's not good for you, it's really not." "I should have put her up in a nursing home around here—there are plenty that are good and cheerful, people have said. Closed her apartment first and driven her down, or temporarily closed it, in case she didn't like the home, and seen her twice a day at this place, but she wouldn't have gone in one." "Then don't raise it as a possibility. She was a New Yorker from birth, and even if she didn't have any friends or close relatives there left, except for her niece—" "I should have gone in to see her the day before she died. That kills me the most:

the last thing I could have done and I didn't. But Josephine was very sick and I worried about the kid once she came into our room and said she couldn't breathe. And I sort of made a secret decision with myself that day that I had to see to the sickly living before the dying dying. That's an awful thought; cold, crude, awful, and something I didn't even think then, so why'd I say it? Did I use Josephine as an excuse not to see my mother that day before? Again, laziness? No, I wanted to see her, absolutely, truly, and would have, and I thought my cousin was looking after her well or would, plus Ebonita or whoever was on—" "Ebonita was." "But I—but my mother was ninety-two and I knew she was definitely failing, but I also wanted to make sure Josephine got to the doctor. But she would have seen me before she went into the coma. My mother. But I didn't know she was going into a coma and seeing me wouldn't have stopped her from going into one or dying though it might have made her feel better for a few moments. I could have shown her pictures—longer than a few minutes; hours. But pictures of the kids and you, photos I mean, recent ones she hadn't seen, or just old ones of her and the kids and you and where everyone looks happy and well. Photos of her parents and brothers and sisters. I could have got them out of the breakfront drawers where she always kept them; kept them there when I was a kid. Of herself when she was a beauty. The same drawers. She still was a beauty, a beauty for someone her age and maybe ten years younger; she would have won a contest if there was such a contest for beauty at that age, but not on those final days. I wouldn't have brought out the photos of my brother, no matter how cheerful and healthy-looking he appears in them and beautiful or handsome or whatever a boy is when he's so young. And my father, of course, or maybe not 'of course,' since their marriage wasn't that great. But photos of them together, just dating and in the latest styles; with friends, all of them arm and arm in a park once. One where she's cuddling a dog, though when I was growing up she hated them, and where he has on these long sporty striped socks and what do you call those pants that end just below the knees?" "Knickers? Jodhpurs?" "He was a rider too, in Prospect and Central Parks: rental horses. And at their wedding reception. She looked gorgeous, holding what she said were a couple-dozen long-stemmed roses my father got her, and he so handsome in cutaway and top hat. And one in a bathing suit; she, I'm speaking of—his legs were too thin for him to look good in them—holding an open parasol above her as if imitating a beauty contestant, and with a fashion model-of-today's figure but showgirl's legs. They're all still there. I'm going to get them next time I'm in and maybe

But the EMS guy who came hours later—we didn't notify them sooner because we still thought she might be alive—said she'd been dead from about the time we'd originally said and that what we thought were signs of life was just the dead body beginning to break down and settle—I think those were his words—and the gases, or maybe that's the same thing. I told you what he did, right?" "With his two fingers quickly on her neck and saying she's gone?" "After, while we were waiting for the police, I said can't he, to make sure, use an instrument or something so we know she won't be carted away alive? and he shrugged, as if saying 'All right, to make you happy,' and monitored her heart with a stethoscope and pinpricked her skin and did something else with another gadget and then said 'Nothing, I'm sorry, my condolences.'" "That part I hadn't heard." "I held her up, those moments I thought were her last. That's not what I wanted. I mean I didn't plan it that way—come in for it—have any idea it would happen—some dramatic moment like that—but that's how it probably ended and the EMS guy was right. What do you think her babbling meant? She did it for almost half a day straight. I wish I'd been there to hear it." "I know, you've said." "It was like she was describing her entire life in that relatively short time, different than what you usually hear about it passing through the dying person's mind. I would have learned—but I told you all this. Stuff about her family and my dad and her childhood that she only would have revealed in the unguarded state she was in. It even could have been embarrassing for me to listen to—things about herself and my father and maybe other men before—I doubt there were any after—though Ebonita said in that hour and a half we had together before she died that there was nothing that made her or her daughter blush or anything she hadn't already heard. Well, she probably had told Angela and Ebonita everything, including things about me that weren't so good—I'm saying, in the years they had looked after her. If only Josephine hadn't got sick, but what can you do." "It was a freak coincidence. Of course, you were frightened for her, just as I was." "You don't think Josie's illness was in any way connected to knowing my mother might be dying? I mean, we were all at dinner when I got that first phone call and I talked to Ebonita on your portable phone." "I don't see it. Listen, dearest, try for a while not to think of those last two days. Or think of them all you want; I'm not sure what's right either." "No, you were right the first time. I'm going to rest, I think. Try to nap, anyway." "If you need me," her arms out, "I'm here," and he says "Thanks," and goes into their bedroom, makes sure the phone's off and lies on the bed. "Party, party, party," she kept telling him over the phone. Or at least said it while she held the receiver and he was on the phone. Though maybe Ebonita was holding the receiver for her and his mother didn't even know she was talking to him or even talking on a phone. No, she knew she was talking to him, or part of the time, since she asked "How's business?", something he thinks she said before in relation to his work, the teaching or writing or both. He's sure she said it before, and more than once, and one time as a joke. But what did the "party, party" mean? And she sounded so chipper on the phone, better than she had for months. "My sister's coming and she loves my chicken and I have to bake a cake" and "buy a new dress," Ebonita told him she'd also said that day several times. Did she mean one of her dead sisters was coming to take her away? That she knew she was dying? That the party was some idea she had of joining up with her favorite dead people in heaven or some afterlife place—her beloved mother, whom Ebonita said she went on about most, and of course her first-born son—or some notion she had of freedom and fun once she was released from the physical discomfort and misery she'd been in for years. That the cake was what she wanted to make for the party as an offering of sorts? Or just that when you go to a party you always bring something, which is what she thought. The new dress might have meant to her—or did Ebonita say a "fresh" dress?—but anyway, a shroud or just a nice outfit to look good in her coffin in or something presentable to wear to a party. If that's the case, what's the chicken mean? Nothing right now in his storehouse of symbols, but maybe there was one in hers. Or the chicken was a chicken, something she baked with a coating of corn flakes that her sister did like, and that made her sister coming to her more realistic. But if this is how she approached death, then she went fairly resignedly, right? Or not anxious or frightened and maybe even gladly, and that's a good thought for him to have. But what else did she say? Oh, don't start analyzing every word. "First I have to get out of here," she told him, and she wants to bake "lots" of cakes. Well, the "out of here" is easy enough to explain, not that he'd be right, but "lots of cakes"? Maybe to give everyone she joins up with in this afterlife place. Anything else she say? He wrote most of it down soon after he spoke with her, a little of it even while he was on the phone, but doesn't remember anymore of it now nor where he put those notes: probably in his top night table drawer, but he doesn't want to look: what'd be the purpose? Her arm thrashed a lot that last hour and a half and for a few hours before that, Ebonita said, and always the right. So, she was a righty, and what's it mean anyway?—it's all involuntary. His dad's thrashed for two days when he was in his last coma, and maybe in the coma before that, and both arms, back and forth in front of his face and sometimes crossing but never hitting each other. When he tried to hold them down they'd push up and his face showed pain or intense frustration at that moment, so he let them go, hoping his father wouldn't hurt himself like breaking his nose. He called her doctor the day before he went to New York and the doctor said that from everything Ebonita told him and the visiting nurse said about her, she's failing. "I'm afraid she'll never leave the hospital this time if we send her there." "Alive, you mean," and the doctor said "To be absolutely frank about it, yes. The decision's ultimately yours though. But if I were you I'd get to her side quickly and try to make her as comfortable as you can at home. If you need to reach me, and for any reason, call day or night, even if I don't think you'll have to except, perhaps, for a pep talk. I'm sorry, Gould. Your mother was a brave woman but you have to remember we never thought she'd last this long and from my conversations with her, she didn't think so either." "Why, what'd she say?" and the doctor said "I forget, but something, since she was always a pessimist regarding her longevity and health." After that phone call he remembers thinking What's the guy talking about? She's not dead yet. That whole last-nail-in-the-coffin business, which they also used on his father, is a bunch of hooey. His father pulled through three or four of them after the doctors gave him just a few days. He said to the doctor this time "There is a problem though. My youngest daughter's sick with a bad croup and my wife's unable to drive her to a doctor or hospital if it suddenly becomes a real crisis, so I want to stay till early tomorrow to see how it turns out. You think I have time?" and the doctor said "Never a guarantee. Your mother could be expiring this moment as we speak. You just have to hope she holds out that long. Keep me informed." He wrote down most of what the doctor said, while he was talking to him and what he remembered after when he was sitting by his mother the next day. All those notes—several pages of them—are stapled . . . not stapled; he doesn't have a stapler. His kids do, one between them, but he didn't use it. How come he can't remember that simple word of such a common object, one he's used thousands of times or at least a thousand, both as a word and an object? It binds pages, holds them together. It's the first time he's forgotten it—paperclip, he paperclipped the pages and put them someplace, probably also in the top night table drawer with that other thing he was thinking or talking of before and thinks he put in there and which he also now forgets what it was. Something to do with his mother? He means, did this other thing have something to do with her? Photos?

He doesn't think so. More notes? It's possible but doesn't ring a bell. Since when does memory loss have anything to do with grief? Or the other way around: grief cause memory loss? Maybe he's just tired. But he's slept more the last few days than he has, in so short a time, in years. And he's only sleeping this much to avoid remembering things about her. Should he reach over to the drawer—it'd take just a little turn—and get them out, the notes plus that other thing, if he put either of them there? No, he doesn't think he'll ever want to read those phone conversation notes. Why would he? So why'd he write them down then? When he was on the phone: it seemed important at the time, as if he were being given instructions on how to take care of her at the end. When he was with his mother: just to do something, he supposes, or more than that, but he forgets. He also doodled; he also tried reading; he also cleaned his nails with his thumbnails and bit off most of the torn cuticles; he also just stared at her for minutes, hoping her heavy breathing would suddenly ease up and that she'd open her eyes, blink, give some recognition that she knew where she was, turn her face or just move her eyes to him—he'd be saying softly "Mom? Mom?"—and smile and maybe even say something, his name, how is he? where's her dear friend Ebonita? she's thirsty and would like something to eat, and so on. He also remembers thinking What is she thinking? Is there anything going on in her head? Is it more like dreaming? Then what is she dreaming? Is she in any pain? Is her heavy breathing and chest congestion affecting her thoughts? Is there anything he can do to make things better for her? A different position? Raise or lower the top of the hospital bed? Another pillow? One less pillow? Put a cushion under her feet? Should he be talking to her? Should he read to her from a book or even today's paper so she just hears his voice? Would that bring her out of it? What would help her come out of what more and more seems like a coma? Is she shitting, peeing? She wears paper diapers, but do these have to be changed? He'll know when she starts smelling. Water? Shouldn't she have water or some sugar solution so she doesn't starve? Is she really dying? Can this be it? Will she never recognize him again? Can he really be sitting here the last day or hours of her life and where she'll never wake up? If she hears his voice—he was told when his father was comatose that the last sense to go is hearing—will that help her see him in whatever pictures are in her head? About those notes, does he think—he also thought a few times while he sat there looking at her: Maybe it'd be best if she went now without pain rather than have to go through this another time and then maybe another time before she dies. But does he think that, let's say in a year or two or even six months, when he's going through that top drawer for something else and comes upon the notes, if he put them there—or any place he put them—that he'll read them or leave them in the drawer without reading them or just throw them away soon as he recognizes them? How can he know that now? But what does he think? He thinks How can he know now what he'll do? though he thinks he'll more than likely throw them away unread. But things she said that he took down—in fact, isn't that what that "other thing" is?—he'll keep and read, keep forever, in the drawer or someplace safe, not just what she said on the phone the last time but all the things she's said the past few years that he's taken down, and regret if he couldn't find them and regret more if he thought them lost. After about an hour and a half of sitting near his mother—he got up once to make coffee, another time to get it after it was made and wash the carafe and coffee machine cone—Ebonita, sitting a couple of feet further away from her than he, pointed out phlegm dribbling over her lip and he thought I suppose she wants me to wipe it, she obviously isn't getting up; well, she spent a long night with her, didn't get much sleep, and he got up and wiped his mother's mouth and chin with his handkerchief. "Tissues," Ebonita said. "We have a whole box of them and more boxes in the closet," pointing to what was the broom closet when he was a kid but which now held all kinds of medical supplies and things, and he said "Sorry; it's also not sanitary, using this rag," and stuck the handkerchief back into his pants pocket but first, he remembers, folding the wet part up so it wouldn't soak through to his thigh. Ebonita, he now remembers, had actually said "Look at what's coming out of her mouth; we should fix it." Then more phlegm spilled out and Ebonita stood beside him and kept supplying him tissues to wipe with, and he wiped her mouth and inside her lips and with wads of tissues dabbed her tongue and around it to absorb the constant rise of spit, dropping the tissues and then wads one by one into an old ice bucket that was being used as a trash container by the bed. "How come she doesn't have a real trash can?" he said. "There used to be lots of them in the house. This one fills up so quickly," and she shrugged and said "Up till now this one did all right." Then his mother started coughing while he was wiping her mouth and he put his arms behind her and raised her up and held her there with one arm, thinking this'll help her cough up the mucus better and maybe even help her breathing and where she won't choke on all that stuff, and it'll also be easier to get the phlegm out of her mouth. Then, as long as he had her up and she had stopped coughing and bringing up phlegm, he thought about giving her water. "Don't you think she should have some water? How long has it been?" and Ebonita said

"Hours. I tried to before but none got in. And she hasn't evacuated for a long time neither, which isn't good. But it isn't easy getting liquids down her; she coughs it all up." "We should have an eye dropper to give it. Even drop by drop would do some good. You don't have one around, do you? I thought of bringing one—I sort of knew she'd need it—and found some old one at home but left it." Regrets. He did think of it but never looked for one. His wife had said "If she's unconscious or too weak to drink anything, how do you get medicine and fluids into her? Probably she should be in a hospital and on IV," and he said "Believe me, they'll only make matters worse for her there, forcing things down, sticking a million needles in. Maybe I should bring an eye dropper—I know we have one here—or go out now for one of those dropper-like spoon things we used for the kids when they wouldn't swallow their medicine," and she said "We never had to give them it that way," and he said "Then I've seen them displayed in the pharmacy here," but that's as far as it went. He could have driven that night to a local Giant that has a pharmacy and big drug department or bought one in a drugstore when he walked to her building from the subway or gone into the drugstore at Penn Station, but forgot. He didn't forget; he thought of it when he got out of the subway and passed a drugstore but then thought just get to her building; you could miss seeing her alive by minutes, and started to jog. When the train was pulling in to New York he thought of calling her from Penn Station, but after he got off he ran through the terminal to the subway station with a token in his hand and ran up the stairs to the platform, not wanting to waste a minute calling, but had to wait several minutes for the uptown train. He looked for a phone on the platform but the only one operating was taken and continued to be taken till the train came. Then the person hung up and got in the same car with him. He set his mother down and said to Ebonita "Can you get me . . . no, I'll get it; watch her," and got a tablespoon and cup of water from the kitchen, raised her in his arms again and while Ebonita held the cup he got a spoonful from it and stuck it in his mother's mouth. It seemed to go down. "Good, Mom, good," though she didn't open her eyes or make any response or motion that she knew of anything going on around her or happening to her. He got another spoonful of water and was ready to stick it in her mouth when the other water, or some of it, dribbled out. "Mom, if you're hearing me," he said, wiping her chin and neck, "you have to take some water; you need it." "Maybe you gave her too much, though I didn't see her neck swallowing any of it. Try half," and he spooned half a tablespoon of water into her mouth and looked and it seemed to go down. "It's gone. Did you see her neck moving this time?" and Ebonita said "I think so, but

I can't say for sure." Then some white liquid rose from her throat and he said "Oh my God, what the hell's that?" till her mouth was almost full of it and it was about to spill out and Ebonita threw her hands to her face and said "Oh no, this is the end, I'm sure of it. Delilah," to her daughter, sitting there looking at his mother, "cover your eyes," and he said "What are you talking about? Get me a towel; lay it down here," while he held his mother up with one arm and stuck a bunch of tissues into her mouth to soak up the liquid and when the towel was down he held her face over it and all the liquid seemed to come out. He held her there a few seconds more and then got her in a sitting position to wipe her face and see if anymore liquid was there and some seemed to be coming up, white again, and he held her face over the towel and said "Get it all out, Mom, this is good for you; all the junk in your lungs is coming up," and when no more of it came out he held her in a sitting position and wiped her face and patted her cheeks and head with damp tissues and thought of getting a damp rag to lay across her forehead when she started choking and her eyes were open and he said "Mom?" and she looked blankly ahead while her body started shaking and she was still choking and he said "Mom, what is it, can you hear me, what can I do for you?" and her eyes never moved and she was still shaking and choking but nothing was coming up and he yelled "Mommy, oh no, Mommy, oh Mommy," and held her to him with both arms and put his mouth to her forehead and said "It's all right, Mommy, it's all right, I'm here, Gould's here, I'm here with you, Mommy, I won't leave you, oh no, Mommy, my Mommy, oh Mommy, oh please don't go, Mommy, please please don't go," and Ebonita said "She's stopped, she's quiet, I knew it, close her eyes, close her eyes!" and he held her head up and shut her eyes and let her head down softly till it hung over his shoulder and he kept her that way for around a minute, his eyes closed and head against her neck, hugging her, and then laid her on her back and put his ear to her chest and mouth and chest again and then rested his head on her chest and started to cry. The cat jumps onto the bed, walks around him on both sides and then steps up on his chest and lies on it facing him, and he says "Please get off, you weigh a ton, I can't breathe with you on me," and the cat stays and he picks it up and drops it on the floor. It jumps right back up and lies on his chest the same way and he says "Listen, I told you, I know you mean well and want to help me, but you're just too big a load," and raises his arm to lift it off him again. The cat sits up, resettles itself on his chest till it faces his feet and stretches out more so there's much less weight in one place than before and he says "Okay, all right," and rests his hand on its back, "you don't feel so heavy now, stay."

when it visited. We saw some of the great legends—Callas, Jussi Bjoer-ling. . . .

CARTER: When did you start writing poems? Who could you show them to?

WILLIAMSON: I started writing poems around fifteen, though I'd always thought of doing something in the arts. I wrote an opera when I was twelve. In high school, I don't think I wanted to show my poems to anyone. In college, I had some wonderful teachers, Guy Davenport, and Alfred and Isabel Satterthwaite, and a best friend, Richard Wertime, who's gone on to become a very fine, though not a prolific, fiction writer. In graduate school, there was Lowell, and the brilliant circle around him, Frank Bidart, Richard Tillinghast, Anne Winters.

CARTER: When did you first start reading poetry, and what poets did you read?

WILLIAMSON: I suppose I started reading seriously around the time I started writing seriously. Given my background, I read pretty widely in the English tradition. But my first great loves were Eliot and Dylan Thomas; then Baudelaire and Rimbaud; then Hart Crane; then Lowell, Plath, Berryman. . . .

CARTER: In your essay "My Father's T. S. Eliot and Mine," you describe going home on the IC train, after Eliot's reading at Orchestra Hall in Chicago, and feeling that the urban landscape, which "would not have struck most people as a beautiful, or a safe, place," became "a haunted place," for you, because of Eliot's poetry. Would that one night qualify as a kind of turning point, or breakthrough, in which poetry, Eliot's in particular, spoke to you directly, instead of being filtered first through your father?

WILLIAMSON: It wasn't that unique, but it will do as an emblem. Works of art got past my father's grid, as it were, by speaking to me on the level of sensibility. They expressed, or changed, the feeling-tone of how I saw my world.

CARTER: You once told me that you'd wanted, like the Beat poets, to work any job you could get and write in your spare time. Your father, however, convinced you to go the professorial route. Was critical writing something that came naturally to you? How about teaching?

WILLIAMSON: Well, it wasn't quite that clear-cut. Those were the early years of the Vietnam War, and if one left school, for whatever reason, the draft board tended to take notice. Also, the academic world was what I knew, and I was a little scared of any other world, however much I yearned in that direction. Still, I had a fear of having lived my father's life instead of my own, which only went away when I *did* take off for a couple of years, after I was denied tenure at Virginia, and lived in Europe.

CARTER: Critical writing?

WILLIAMSON: It always came very naturally to me. But I was a little neurotic about the idea that it was too intellectual, too unengaged, and that I'd be known for it rather than my poetry.

CARTER: But the critical writing never interfered *creatively* with the writing of your own poems?

WILLIAMSON: Honest answer would have to be, I don't know. Did it make me a better writer to have thought so much about writing? Or did it make me second-guess myself, perhaps hold back from larger, sloppier projects? Have I given too little time to my art? Or has my other work kept me from worrying at it, given it time to grow naturally in the unconscious? Both/and, both/and.

CARTER: And teaching?

WILLIAMSON: Oddly, teaching has been very much the right career for me, I think. Especially the one-on-one, apprenticeship kind of teaching, which is why I like Warren Wilson so much. My tenderness toward my own uncertain adolescent self carries over very easily onto other people's. But it took me a while to understand this. Of course, the other kind of teaching—large classes, students who take them just to fulfill a requirement—that is the toad work squatting on one's life, there's no getting around it.

CARTER: Have you written poems continuously through the years? Or have you endured periods of dormancy?

WILLIAMSON: I tend to produce about five poems a year, regular as clockwork. Ten, maybe, if I have lots of free time or am obsessed with some subject. I don't think I've ever gone more than half a year totally without writing, though I've certainly had spells of not liking anything I wrote.

CARTER: I've often heard that one's first book of poems consists of the best of one's work up to that point, while one's second and third books grow more out of a vision of the book as a whole. Did you find this to be the case in your experience?

WILLIAMSON: Yes, in my own case. I hope *Presence* has coherence, but it was worked and reworked, mainly to make it more appetizing, over twelve years of collecting rejections. Whereas with *Muse of Distance,* I intended a single style to carry all the way through; with *Love and the Soul,* an obsessive subject-matter.

CARTER: Twelve years of rejections? Was that difficult to endure? Did your faith in your own abilities as a writer ever falter?

WILLIAMSON: Those were hard years, yes. I think my style was to become angry and paranoid, in order not to become self-doubting. But it contributed to some fairly prolonged spells of depression.

CARTER: Do you think, with seemingly more and more people writing poetry, that it's getting even harder to get a first book of poems published?

WILLIAMSON: I'm afraid so. Also, there are all the ideological quarrels surrounding poetry, the uncertainty about standards. But some good writers are also lucky, as in my—or any—generation.

CARTER: On the cover of your second book of poems, *The Muse of Distance,* is the Hopper painting "Summer in the City," painted in 1949. Did you decide on the cover art after the book was finished, or did you have that painting in mind somehow when you were writing, for instance, the title poem?

WILLIAMSON: That painting is described, actually, in a different poem, "The Light's Reading." I've always loved Hopper. His paintings, for me, give a feeling of erotic and even spiritual presence at least as great as the sadness and desolation—exactly balanced with it, in fact.

CARTER: I guess I felt the very scene, in the title poem, of the "girl in a mean, dawn-blue room," was like Hopper's woman sitting on the bed looking out the window, the man behind her sleeping with his face to the pillow, suggesting a certain identification with the female. . . . Do you recall feeling this connection as a child? Or the seed of this connection?

WILLIAMSON: The "girl in a mean, dawn-blue room." Well, it actually did happen, as I say in another poem, that I did have this teacher, a sort of minimally closeted gay man, who played matchmaker with his students, and he did say to me, "You might give it all up, get married, go and work in the steel mills." I think that gave my adolescent fantasies of idyllic union with a woman a kind of proletarian, South Chicago twist. But I'm fascinated that you see female identification there, since that's the subject of the psychoanalytic prose book I'm working on, at the moment.

CARTER: I'm thinking, too, of that lyrical passage in the middle of "The Muse of Distance," in the middle of your childhood reminiscence, "and, as I grew older, imagining / someone waiting—" And then her becoming (I say "her" because of the "scarps toward your breasts") the very embodiment of distance—"the empty watery taste of motel air at day's end / is a scarf / you left behind you." Here the female image, or sensation, is idealized, mythic, the muse of distance, and yet, you know how she feels: "We are lying together so far across the moonlight, / you can feel the weeds start growing through your hair." Is this muse of your own making? Or is she whimsical, with a mind of her own, coming and going as she pleases? Is she always available, to your imagination?

WILLIAMSON: There's a lot to answer, here. To start very concretely: my early erotic fantasies also focussed on the landscapes of those family trips. That is to say, the sense of aesthetic response to a landscape became indistinguishable from the fantasy of a sexual encounter with a girl—glimpsed or imagined, very intuitive and wise—who lived there. Later I've found a very few other male writers who've recorded a similar experience—Pavese, Proust. Proust's landscape-woman is kind, available; Pavese's isn't.

The larger implications of your question leave me speechless. I think I do, in some weird way, embody my imaginative self in the image of a sexual companion. And I agree with Winnicott that all *real* creative work goes straight back to that stage of infantile play that negotiates the space between feeling fused—with the mother, with the world—and feeling separate.

CARTER: To go back, for a moment, to "The Light's Reading". . . I see now that the third section begins by describing that painting exactly: "The man sleeps, his back a shell." But what interests me suddenly is another image, the image that section ends on: "So desire towers, and towering, holds us / over what is beyond any / object: the empty clockface, the rims of time." Isn't this "empty clockface" the circle on the cover of your third book of poems, *Love and the Soul?* Is your attraction to this image rooted, somehow, in your study of Zen?

WILLIAMSON: You know, I'm sure all those choices—those images, my Zen practice—do cohere, on a level so ingrained I don't even notice. Consciously, I just liked that painting, by my friend Elaine Hansen—a sometimes floating, sometimes vertiginous sense of space that's there in all her work. Also, I wanted the cover of *Love and the Soul* to be abstract— somehow to purify those big nouns into Platonic categories. No romantic couples, this time!

CARTER: You've said that translating Pavese helped you change your style, in *Love and the Soul.* How did that work?

WILLIAMSON: My poetry has often been called nostalgic—oriented toward the past. What I loved in Pavese's last poems—written during a tragic love affair, and just before his suicide—was the ability, or the courage, to write in the present tense, in the midst of a volcanic, appalling, ambivalent flux of feelings. When I started translating him, there was nothing like that in my life—it couldn't have been more settled, on the surface. Then it, too, turned melodramatic; and thanks, somehow, to him, my hand was trained . . .

CARTER: I love the movement, in *Love and the Soul,* from its first poems, which deal with the past complexities of a very specific relationship, to the simple, more universal joys expressed in its final poems . . . the timelessness of "Highway Restaurant" ("We all have places we step out of time and are perfectly happy. / This is one of mine"), for instance, and the present moment awareness near the end of the last poem, "Tidepools"

("When I have managed to forget / everything but my breath, the story has touched me / at all points at once, its clangors / and bright screens"). Did the order of the poems become evident after they were all completed, or did you have a sense of the book's structure as you wrote the individual poems?

WILLIAMSON: I knew that this book, unlike any of my others, had to have an argument. I wanted it to answer those big questions, or demands—"Not to have to believe / that what lights up the world from within is always the wrong thing," or "when / does one get to what one holds to, what one doesn't lose?" To say something about "why things darken so quickly, between men and women," not only in my life, but in many people's lives. So I worried endlessly about structure, tried to write poems just to move the argument along. And, of course, I kept hoping that life would hand me a happy solution! When it didn't, I more or less had to end on the poems that express love of the world, rather than love of a particular individual. Which are, of course, the more Buddhist ones . . .

CARTER: What prompted your initial interest in Zen, and when did you start to practice Buddhism seriously?

WILLIAMSON: It was a long, slow approach. In my twenties I read Gary Snyder, and Heinrich Zimmer's *Philosophies of India,* where he says that Western culture is on the edge of a crisis—that of taking religion in a more purely experiential, non-theistic direction which India passed through seven centuries before Christ. Later, my ex-wife was involved in one of the programs in the Boston area using meditation and yoga in the treatment of chronic pain. Then, the first time I was at the MacDowell Colony, in 1987, I actually went out and sat zazen on a rock. And something really did change, in my experience of time, of the closeness of the world around me, even of the idea that life *needed* an explanation. After that, it was only a matter of time till I learned the forms of Zen, and found a congenial group . . .

CARTER: Has your Buddhist practice affected your poetry?

WILLIAMSON: I would hope that any practice of mindfulness—of acute attention, both inward and outward—would have a good effect on writing. Beyond that . . . most American Zen poetry tries to naturalize the calm and clarity we perceive in Far Eastern poetry in an Occidental setting. Snyder is the great master here—there's no going beyond him, in this direction. What I'd like to get in my work, somehow, is the impact of meditative practice on a quirky Western ego, brought up in the anguished and individualistic traditions of Western art.

CARTER: Speaking of the "individualistic traditions of Western art," we've hardly touched on Lowell . . . And then there's Bishop, whom you also knew personally. Do you think that knowing two such major poets (didn't Lowell once say that Elizabeth Bishop was the only woman writing at that time whom he considered a major poet?) made you, somehow, feel you were part of the family of American poets, part of the next generation? Did it give you, do you think, any added sense of courage, or place?

WILLIAMSON: Did Lowell say that? He got some flak, I know, for classifying poets by gender. But he also spoke very highly of Plath, Rich, Eleanor Ross Taylor. I loved Robert Lowell. When I was twenty, he seemed to me the one poet who was utterly contemporary, yet had the kind of grandeur I was looking for. Like my father, he was hard to please. Unlike my father, he was actively leftwing, lived dangerously, was willing to know a lot about the dark side of himself. His very survival was a source of courage.

I didn't know Bishop nearly as well—or understand how great she was, while she was alive. There was one wonderful evening when she came to dinner, and got quite drunk despite Frank Bidart's best precautions, and talked very openly—about how she'd only been prolific during one rather disoriented period as a young woman, the period of *North and South;* how she wished she'd written more. And she told a funny story, about climbing a pyramid in Yucatan, with Neruda waiting at the bottom, and, knowing his reputation, being careful to hold her skirt down . . .

Did they teach me confidence, or over-confidence? A few years ago at Warren Wilson, several of my colleagues were saying how, in their twenties, they realized a great democratization was coming in poetry, and they welcomed it. I didn't—see it, or welcome it. I kept waiting for the mantle to descend on me! But I think that uncompromisingly ambitious attitude of Lowell's and his friends'—"the good is the enemy of the best"—was a great gift to younger writers. You'll never do all you can, if you think "the good" is enough.

CARTER: You have a new book coming out, *Res Publica,* which, as the title indicates, ventures into the public, the political realm. Could you talk a bit about that?

WILLIAMSON: As you know, my first book was about Lowell as a political poet. So that interest has always been there. Maybe I stayed away from it for so long, for fear of merely echoing Lowell's methods and style. But I think there are some important stories that aren't being told, much, in our public poetry. One is the story of what it was like for my generation to outlive the 60's—the diminished expectations, especially of our own moral effectiveness . . . Robert Bly said, in a recent letter to me, that we seemed to "open so far," and then everything shut down. The Res Publica poems are a kind of elegy for that, and for the weirdness of the world we've stumbled on into . . .

CARTER: John Ashbery complained, about political poetry, that "the sentiments reiterated in it are usually the exact ones I already harbor, and I would rather learn something new"—though he made an exception, actually, for one of your earlier public poems. How do you avoid this danger?

WILLIAMSON: I try to have my poems contain all of my mixed feelings. I don't want them just to say easy, likeable liberal things. I'm appalled by the horrendous economic inequalities that have only increased in our society over the last twenty years. But I also harbor, and want to include, concerns maybe more typical of a white male my age— the loss of literacy, the apparent acceptance of casual violence as a norm. And, over all this, the strange unreality created by the omnipresence of the media—how everything becomes "information," "image," "representation" . . .

CARTER: Do you get anything *positive* from popular culture, for your work?

WILLIAMSON: Oh yes! I still love the music of the counterculture, Dylan, Leonard Cohen, Janis Joplin . . . And I love the Indigo Girls, who seem to suffer the 90's with the same trenchant social alertness, the same lyricism. I'm a less critical moviegoer than most of my friends. In fact, many of the *Res Publica* poems are, on the surface level, about representations—movies, TV movies, songs . . . I feel strange and ambivalent here. It delights me to evoke those textures; but I'm also reminding myself, and the reader, that that is how we know, and fail to know, social reality . . .

CARTER: Does this wider, more inclusive scope in your poetry change your view of yourself?

WILLIAMSON: Let me turn the question around. If one thinks one has anything useful to say about big subjects—politics, religion—as one gets older, the urgency increases. There's less time. But also—the Gnostic Gospels promise, "If you bring forth what is within you, it will save you." That doesn't just mean one's neuroses, one's dirty secrets.

CARTER: You mentioned, earlier, that you're working on a psychoanalytic prose book. Is that part of the push toward largeness? What got you interested in it?

WILLIAMSON: When I finished *Love and the Soul*, I felt there were things I knew intuitively, about "why things darken so quickly, between men and women," that weren't quite in the poems. Then someone showed me Jessica Benjamin's *The Bonds of Love*, and it was an illumination—her discussion of separation and merging generally, but particularly of male identity formation, why the feminine is so necessary, but also fearful and even repugnant, to men. And I thought I could write something about (mostly straight) male writers who have partly resisted this conditioning, who have identified with women or regarded their own creative selves as feminine. A book that would partly challenge, but remain in dialogue with, some of the typical feminist representations of men. It also allowed me to write about some people I've always wished I could write about—Lawrence, Rilke, Pavese again, Jarrell.

CARTER: Does the book have a title? How long have you been working on it?

WILLIAMSON: I started it around 1992, and actually I've just finished a complete draft, though it may need some reworking. It's called *Almost a Girl*, from the second of Rilke's Sonnets to Orpheus: "it was almost a girl and came to be / out of this single joy of song and lyre," in Stephen Mitchell's rendering.

CARTER: What effect, if any, is the widespread emphasis on what is "global"—the twenty-first century push to "save the planet"—having on your poetry?

WILLIAMSON: Well, if one writes a book, and the publication date is going to be "1999" or "2000," one doesn't want it to be trivial. More seriously—I've been a closet ecological radical for a long time, partly through Gary Snyder's influence. But I'm not a very optimistic one. I think we're only beginning to sense the effects of world overpopulation on all of our lives. And the more "global" market capitalism becomes, the more short-sighted and harmful its decisions seem to be, for people, cultures, plants, animals, air . . .

CARTER: And your feelings about the electronic age, and the future of books?

WILLIAMSON: Dread, basically—which I'm sure marks me out as a hopeless fossil. What will be, will be. But to try to put my reservations sanely: Yeats wrote, "How can they know / Truth flourishes where the student's lamp has shone, / And there alone, that have no solitude?" With the Web, the Net—everyone constantly sending out their own first thoughts, and receiving hundreds of other people's—I'm afraid that "solitude" will vanish, and a certain seriousness with it.

CARTER: Do you write mostly on the computer, or by hand?

WILLIAMSON: I write almost everything longhand, first. But I couldn't do without the computer for prose, and even for complete drafts of longer poems—the freedom to switch things around . . .

CARTER: Do you find, as your body of work increases, that you approach your current projects with greater confidence?

WILLIAMSON: I do seem to take on more things at once, and to carry them through more quickly, more decisively. But when I look at the lines on the page, and wonder if they're anywhere near as good as the dead poets I love—that never gets easier.

CARTER: If you—who you are now—could visit with yourself as a young poet, before, say, the publication of *Presence*, what would you tell him? Is there anything you'd have him do differently?

236

WILLIAMSON: Hundreds of things! What's particularly sad is coming on an old fragment, and realizing that it's more interesting than a lot of poems I finished, and that I didn't finish it because it didn't fit some image of who I was, or thought I should be, as a poet. Basically, I'd tell him to loosen up. Not to be careless—but be a nicer person, try out more things, don't cling to so many opinions.

Red Cloud

Alan Williamson

                                    The cat
had to come into restaurants. She was too rare,
there were "catnappers." So your parka went down over
the carrying-case, like a parrot's silence-cloth,
and you gripped the handle through it, hoped the waitress
kept her eyes up, on me.
                                    It worked, oddly—she knew
when not to mew—except one off-hour dinner . . .

In between, sharp Abyssinian ears
back and forth in the rear-view mirror.

                            *

Power plant past Reno, with four white blinkers
on the tallest stack to warn low-flying planes;
and then the hills fold down. . . . always the gateway
to the earlier country where slow freights stretch out
a mile or two in the Sinks; where gypsum chutes
rise through openwork toward rust-iron roofs . . .
Rock Springs where you wrote down a conversation
between two bullet-heads, in the Chinese
railroad-car diner, and the cat kept quiet:
"horseflies in Texas—stung the cattle to death—
but you could drown them in oildrums filled with beer—"
"AIDS—should stay in Africa—they started it . . . "

You said, too, one night, "We never talk, just argue"—
my travel nerves, bad as my father's—

*

To Cather, transplanted from Virginia,
an erasure of personality . . . the roads
petering out in bunch grass, land *bare as a piece of sheet iron.*
When a lark flew up, she couldn't stop herself crying.
All her life she feared going back, even drowsing off
in a cornfield, in case she happened to die there.
But when *the country and I had it out,* she was *gripped
with a passion I have never shaken.*

*The writer
fades away into the land and people of his heart.
He dies of love only to be born again.*

*

We're here. Bald brick of the one-crossroads town—
our one pause, in your five-day rush home to school—
with little Romanesque or Arab zigzags
out of the brick itself, or out of red stone,
or white capstones on the windows—Dr. Archie's
second-story office, we've found it, there's a plaque—
and the turreted, townhouse-size bank, the "Cather Museum" . . .
You compose your pictures, your first way of focussing
on anything at all, this summer . . .

The streets themselves cobbled with brick. In the background,
    always,
the flat hot sky... as if it were a law that the soul
has to feed on what is most unlike it; that creation
begins in erasure—not just this place, but all Being
slipping past the horizon a block away.

*

Upstairs was *ours,* the children said. No grown-up
ever came up there—the unplaned beams and rafters,
the siblings' cots, and then the nook she finally
made wholly her own, with the red-and-brown-rose wallpaper...

She dragged her bed to the window, hot summer nights
she'd rather have been out *walking—as if her heart were spreading*
all over the desert . . . vibrating with
excitement, as a machine vibrates with speed.

You especially want to photograph that dimness,
but it's too strong in the end—the roses indistinguishable
from old tears in the paper . . .

                              In reality, life rushes
from within, not without. There is no work so beautiful
it was not once all contained in some youthful body, trembling.

                    *

The soul has to learn about cruelty.
                              Vivisection,
her "favorite amusement"; her high school speech in praise of it
still framed, in the bank, past the old-fashioned teller's
brass bars...
                    The old doctor
took the girl on his rounds in the buggy, let her give
the chloroform once.

After that . . . to be inside
another being's skin, actually *see* the blood flow past . . .

Was it shadow-revenge, outrush of power
in one who'd lost so much? (Biographers tell us
a boy once threatened to cut off her hand.)

Or an indecency native to art?

—A taste, at any rate, she eventually
gave the worst man she ever wrote about,
then gave him her loveliest woman.

                    *

Toward sundown. The trackless "Cather Prairie"
just before the sign on the empty road says "Kansas";

but we don't get far in its messy, spiky tangles . . .
Why still so vivid?

        I was losing the power
to read your face, its doughiness, its charm
more opaque, this puberty summer—fearing each bad moment,
each dinner I was silent through, or snappish,
might become permanent . . .

        And already enough
sense of destiny a kind of iron clenches
in your voice when you say, "It's so hard to be good at anything,
good so it matters . . . "

        But still, this twilight,
by the locked Depot—you wandering, taking pictures
from the weeds, the disused spurs—there's such peace in the air
I might be your age again, or She
still holding it all—the stationmaster's chair
sealed up, fifty years?—in her vast, impersonal eye . . .

Three bows, down to the dirt, palms lifted over
my head
        I won't make here, but two months later,
by her grave in the icicle warps of crisp New England
fall morning light . . .

The world is bare as a piece of sheet iron. And no work
was not once contained in some youthful body, trembling.

Contributors

Erin Belieu is the author of *Infanta* (Copper Canyon Press, 1996), which was selected for the 1995 National Poetry Series. Her work has appeared in the *Atlantic Monthly, Grand Street,* and the *New York Times.* She teaches at Kenyon College. ★★★ **Richard Blanco** was a finalist in the 1996 National Poetry Series and was recipient of the 1997 Agnes Lynch Starrett Award from the University of Pittsburgh Press. "Mango, Number 61" is from his book, *City of a Hundred Fires,* which will be published in the fall of 1998 by the University of Pittsburgh Press as part of the Pitt Poetry Series. ★★★ **Andrej Blatnik** is from Ljubljana, Slovenia. His stories have been published in fifteen languages. "His Mother's Voice" is from his collection, *Skinswaps,* forthcoming from Northwestern University Press. ★★★ **Bruce Bond**'s most recent collections of poetry are *Radiography* (BOA Editions, 1997) and *The Anteroom of Paradise* (Quarterly Review of Literature, 1991). He is the Director of Creative Writing at the University of North Texas and poetry editor for the *American Literary Review.* ★★★ **Jason Brown** is a Stegner Fellow at Stanford University. His collection, *Driving the Heart and Other Stories,* will be published by W.W. Norton in April of 1999. ★★★ **Michaela Carter**'s poems have appeared in the *Antioch Review* and the *Blue Penny Quarterly.* She lives in San Clemente. ★★★ **Michael Chitwood** has published three books of poetry, *Salt Works* (Ohio Review Books, 1992), *Whet* (Ohio Review Books, 1995) and *The Weave Room* (University of Chicago, 1998). ★★★ **Stephen Dixon**'s story "The Bed" is one of three stories from his upcoming collection, *Thirty* (due out from Henry Holt in the spring of 1999) to have appeared in *TriQuarterly.* In 1999, Coffee House Press will publish *Two Collections.* ★★★ **Stuart Dybek**'s poems have appeared recently in *Poetry, Boulevard,* and the *Ontario Review.* He is teaching this fall at the University of Iowa. ★★★ **Jeanne Foster**'s collection, *A Blessing of Safe Travel* (1980), won the Quarterly Review of Literature Poetry Award. She teaches at St. Mary's College of California. ★★★ **Bruce Jay Friedman** is the author of the classic modern novels *A Mother's Kisses* and *Stern*. His plays include *Scuba Duba* and *Steambath*. ★★★ **Judith Grossman** writes fiction, essays, and criticism. Her novel, *Her Own Terms*, was published by Soho Press in 1988. "Sayings of Ernesto B." is from *Hetero World and Other Stories*, due out from Johns Hopkins Press in the spring of 1999. ★★★ **Rachel Hadas,** Professor of English at the Newark Campus of Rutgers University, is the author of eleven books of poetry, essays, and translations. Her new and selected poems, *Halfway Down the Hall*, will be published in 1998 by Wesleyan University Press. ★★★ **Forrest Hamer**'s first book of poems, *Call and Response* (Alice James, 1995), won the Beatrice Howley Award. ★★★ **Ray Hartl** lives and works in Salem, Wisconsin. His photographs have been exhibited at museums and galleries throughout the United States and are represented in many public, private and corporate collections. ★★★ **Susan Hubbard**'s second collection of short fiction, *Conversations With Men*, will be published by the University of Missouri Press in 1998. Her first collection, *Walking On Ice*, won the Associated Writing Programs' Short Fiction Prize in 1990. She teaches creative writing at the University of Central Florida. ★★★ **Joshilyn Jackson** is the managing editor of the online magazine *Playground*. Her plays have been produced in Atlanta and Chicago, and her fiction has appeared in magazines and anthologies, including *Calyx* and *Chick Lit*. ★★★ **Ruth Prawer Jhabvala** is the author of twelve novels. She has won the Booker Prize for her novel *Heat and Dust*, as well as two Academy Awards for her screenplays "Howards End" and "A Room with a View." She recently completed a screen adaptation of Henry James's *The Golden Bowl*. A new collection of her stories, *East Into Upper East: Plain Tales from New York and New Delhi*, will be published later this year by Counterpoint Press. ★★★ **Lee Roloff** is Professor Emeritus in the Department of Performance Studies at Northwestern University. He is the author of *The Perception and Evocation of Literature*, as well as articles on literature therapy and the psychology of performance. ★★★ **Alan Shefsky** is the author of a book of poetry, *Amelia Absent Amelia Present* (Clay Springs Press, 1995), which was adapted for the stage as *Amelia: Inside/Outside*. He is administrative coordinator for the Department of Performance Studies, the Integrated Arts Program, and the Center for Interdisciplinary Research in the Arts at Northwestern University. ★★★ **Neil Shepard**'s book, *Scavenging the Country for a Heartbeat*, won the Mid-List Press First Book of Poetry

Contributors include:

Wendell Berry

Olga Broumas

Jorge Luis Borges

Mark Doty

Jan Freeman

Suzanne Gardinier

Jane Gentry

Jane Kenyon

Barbara Kingsolver

Yusef Komunyakaa

Ursula LeGuin

George Ella Lyon

Jim Wayne Miller

Marge Piercy

Reynolds Price

Robyn Selman

James Still

May Swenson

Reetika Vazirani

Marie Sheppard
  Williams

and many more

THE AMERICAN VOICE
ANTHOLOGY OF POETRY

Frederick Smock, Editor

The American Voice looks to find the vital edge of modern American writing. The journal, whose contributors come from the U.S., Canada, and Latin America, often publishes work by writers denied access to mainstream journals.

Writings from the pages of *The American Voice* have been regularly reprinted in prize annuals such as *The Pushcart Prize*, *Best American Poetry*, and *Best American Essays*. This fifteenth anniversary anthology collects eighty poems from some of the most original and daring writers of our time.

This volume brings together some of the best selections from an award-winning journal, making clear why *Small Press* dubbed *The American Voice* one of the "most impressive journals in the country."

"To write or publish poems is to hold out some hope for the world, to contend mightily with the brutal politics of the marketplace, advertising, and the cheapening of the word. It is one interpretation, or application, of Dostoyevsky's belief that we will be 'saved' by beauty."
—*from the Preface*

$24.00 hardback, $14.95 paperback

THE UNIVERSITY PRESS OF — AT BOOKSTORES • OR CALL 800/839-6855

KENTUCKY

Psycho-Marxism: Marxism and Psychoanalysis
Late in the Twentieth Century
A Special Issue of _SAQ_
Robert Miklitsch, special issue editor

Psycho-Marxism: Marxism and Psychoanalysis Late in the Twentieth Century
(SAQ Volume 97, Number 2) is available for $12. In the U.S. please add $3 for the
first copy and $1 for each additional copy to cover postage and handling.
Outside the U.S. please add $3 for each copy to cover postage and handling.

Send orders to Duke University Press, Journals Fulfillment, Box 90660,
Durham, NC 27708-0660. Fax: 919.688.3524, http://www.duke.edu/web/dupress/

 To place your journal order using a credit card, call toll-free,
within the U.S., 888.DUP.JRNL (888.387.5765).

Black Warrior Review

University of Alabama

Sample copy $8; one year subscription $14
P.O. Box 862936 Tuscaloosa, AL 35486-0027
http:www.sa.ua.edu/osm/bwr

Barry Hannah
C.D. Wright
Max Steele
Tony Hoagland
Yusef Komunyakaa
Janet Burroway
Billy Collins
James Tate
David Wojahn
Lucia Perillo
Bob Hicok
Nicole Cooley
D.C. Berry
Pamela Ryder
Deborah Luster
and more...

Fiction

Poetry

Essays

Interviews

Reviews

Photography

MICHIGAN QUARTERLY REVIEW

ANNOUNCES A SPECIAL ISSUE FOR THE FALL OF 1998 ON THE OCCASION OF THE 50TH ANNIVERSARY OF *DEATH OF A SALESMAN*

ARTHUR MILLER

Symposium: 21 eminent playwrights comment on their experience of *Death of a Salesman* and Miller's life and work. *Plus* a new interview with **Arthur Miller** about the play

Plays: Two previously untranslated theatrical sketches by **Anton Chekhov**; scenes from a play by **Robert Hayden** about Harriet Tubman; a new one-act play by **Arthur Miller**

Essays: **John Barth**, "Further Questions?" (The Hopwood Lecture, 1998); **Christopher Bigsby**, "Arthur Miller: Poet"; **Enoch Brater**, "Arthur Miller: The British and American Perspectives"; **Laurence Goldstein**, "The Fiction of Arthur Miller"; **Brenda Murphy**, "Willy Loman: Icon of Business Culture"; **Gerald Weales**, "Arthur Miller in the 1950s"

Fiction and Poetry: Short stories by **Linda Bamber** and **Nina Kossman** on themes of theatricality; new poems on subjects pertinent to Miller's life and work by **Michael Blumenthal, Jennifer Compton, Philip C. Kolin, David Lehman, Eugenio Montale, Nicolette Nicola, Larissa Szporluk, Baron Wormser, Jody A. Zorgdrager**

Graphics: A 16-page portfolio of photographs, many of Arthur Miller, with an artist's preface, by **Inge Morath**

Reviews: **Michael Szalay** on new books about salesmanship, the consumer culture, and Cultural Studies; **Richard Tillinghast** on the poetry of Hopwood Award winners Anne Stevenson and Nancy Willard; **Robert Vorlicky** on the contemporary American stage

---

For a copy of the Fall issue. send a check for
seven dollars (includes postage and handling) to:
Michigan Quarterly Review, University of Michigan
3032 Rackham Bldg., Ann Arbor, MI 48109-1070

http://www.umich.edu/~mqr

Treat yourself. Treat a friend.

NEW LETTERS

"One of the best literary journals in this country."
Charles Simic, Pulitzer Prize for Poetry

New Letters quarterly has, for more than 60 years, published fiction,
art, poetry and essays by the world's finest new and established writers,
including Pulitzer Prize winners, National Book Award winners and
Nobel Laureates.

"*New Letters* is one of the very few indispensable
literary magazines."
— Susan Fromberg Schaeffer, novelist

Often selected for *The Best American Poetry, The Best American Essays,
Prize Stories: The O. Henry Awards, The Pushcart Prize Anthology* and
many other honors. Join our family of subscribers.

Magazine subscription rates

Individuals: $17 one year   Libraries: $20 one year
                $28 two years $34 two years
                $55 five years $65 five years

New Letters, University of Missouri-Kansas City, Kansas City, MO 64110

Where

you can

still

hear

people

thinking

for

them-

selves

Personal Voices on Cultural Issues

Edward W. Said, "From Silence to Sound"

Richard Rorty, "Marx, Strauss, Dewey"

Jacqueline Rose on Virginia Woolf

Frank Kermode, "Explorations in Shakespeare"

Elaine Showalter, "Young Girls, Popular Culture"

Adam Phillips on the life of the earthworm

Annie Dillard, "Sand and Clouds"

Arts • Literature • Philosophy • Politics

RARITAN
Edited by Richard Poirier

$20/one year $36/two years
Make check payable to RARITAN, 31 Mine St., New Brunswick NJ 08903

THE PROSE POEM:

AN INTERNATIONAL JOURNAL

Volume 7

David Ignatow

WITHOUT RECRIMINATION

It is wonderful to die amidst the pleasures I have known and so to die without recrimination towards myself and others, free of guilt at my shortcomings, happy to have lived and happy to know death, the last of living, my spirit free to sing as when I felt it born in my youth. The youth of it returns in dying, moving off from anger that racked its throat.

With death before me, I look back at my pleasures and they were you whom I held close in loving, and in the poems I've written for this truth, which is their beauty and lets me die in pleasure with myself. I did not fail my life.

A magazine exclusively devoted to "that which is neither poetry nor prose, but both," THE PROSE POEM offers a lively annual forum for new work by contemporary writers from home and abroad, reviews of recent books of exceptional interest and significance, and occasional theoretical commentaries on the form. Some recent contributors include:

Robert Bly
Russell Edson
David Ignatow
Naomi Shihab Nye
Yannis Ritsos
Charles Simic
Rosmarie Waldrop

The Prose Poem:
An International Journal
is at

http://www.webdelsol.com/tpp

Volume 7 includes an
interview with Robert Bly

All correspondence and subscriptions should be directed to Peter Johnson, *The Prose Poem: An International Journal,* English Department, Providence College, Providence, RI 02918. **Manuscripts will be considered only between December 1 and March 1 of each reading period.** Unsolicited work submitted before **December 1** will be returned unread. Please include an SASE and a two-sentence biographical note. Please send no more than 3 to 5 poems.

☐ Please send me _____ copy/copies of *The Prose Poem: An International Journal,* Volume 7, at $8 each.
☐ Please enter my subscription for 2 years at $12 and begin it with Volume 7.
☐ Please send me a sample copy at $4.

• Make checks payable to: Providence College.

Name: _____

Address: _____

TriQuarterly thanks the following past donors and life subscribers:

Mr. and Mrs. Walter L. Adams
Amin Alimard
Lois Ames
Richard H. Anderson
Roger K. Anderson
Sandy Anderson
I. N. C. Aniebo
Anonymous
Gayle Arnzen
Michael Attas
Asa Baber
Hadassah Baskin
Sandra Berris
Simon J. Blattner, Jr.
Louise Blosten
Carol Bly
Susan DeWitt Bodemer
Kay Bonetti
Robert Boruch
Mr. and Mrs. Richard S. Brennan
Van K. Brock
Gwendolyn Brooks
Timothy Browne
Paul Bundy
Eric O. Cahn
David Cassak
Stephen Chapman
Anthony Chase
Michael Chwe
Willard Cook
Mr. and Mrs. William Cottle
Robert A. Creamer
Andrew Cyr
Kenneth Day
Mark W. DeBree
Elizabeth Des Pres
Anstiss Drake
J. A. Dufresne
John B. Elliott
Christopher English
Carol Erickson
Steven Finch
Mr. and Mrs. H. Bernard Firestone
Melvin P. Firestone, M.D.
Mr. and Mrs. Solway Firestone
Paul Fjelstad
Torrence Fossland
C. Dwight Foster

Jeffrey Franklin
Peter S. Fritz
Mrs. Angela M. Gannon
Kathy M. Garness
Lawrence J. Gorman
Maxine Groffsky
Jack Hagstrom
Mrs. Donald Haider
Mrs. Heidi Hall-Jones
Mrs. James E. Hayes
Ross B. Heath
Charles Hedde
Gene Helton
Donald Hey
Donald A. Hillel
Mr. and Mrs. David C. Hilliard
Craig V. Hodson
Irwin L. Hoffman
Irwin T. Holtzman
P. Hosier
Mary Gray Hughes
Charles Huss
Curtis Imrie
Helen Jacob
Del Ivan Janik
Fran Katz
Gary Michael Katz
Dr. Alfred D. Klinger
Loy E. Knapp
Sydney Knowlton
Mr. and Mrs. Martin Koldyke
Greg Kunz
Judy Kunz
Conrad A. Langenberg
John Larroquette
Isaac Lassiter
Dorothy Latiak
Elizabeth Leibik
Patrick A. Lezark
Patricia W. Linton
Philip Lister
Mr. and Mrs. W. J. Lorentz de
Haas
Kubet Luchterhand
Ellen L. Marks
Richard Marmulstein
James Marquardt
Charles T. Martin, Jr.